THE OTHER SHORE

ORDINARY PEOPLE GRAPPLING WITH EXTRAORDINARY CHALLENGES

MADHU BAZAZ WANGU

AUTHOR OF *CHANCE MEETINGS*

ADVANCE PRAISE

"In this collection, Madhu brings us heartwarming and beautiful tales to enrich our lives and bring a soft glow to our souls. Thank you for these gifts."

—LISA DIANE KASTNER
Author/Founder of Running Wild Press and RIZE

"*The Other Shore* showers you with aesthetic pleasures ... Wangu's tales are filled with physically vigorous and mentally vital moments that exist in the now."

—VINCENT DUBLADO
Readers' Favorite (Five-Star Review)

"Madhu Wangu is part gentle guru, part teasing sprite, and part firm realist in this wide-ranging collection of lovely stories. Rich with surprise turns and unexpected outcomes, and convincingly presented by a gifted and skilled teller of tales, this volume will definitely be worth your time."

—TIMONS ESAIAS
Author, Poet

"Dr. Wangu takes us to lands both exotic and familiar, to real-life locals as well as places where magic rules. [*The Other Shore*] guides us on the greatest journey of all—the journey inward. It is a potent reminder of the power of fiction to restore and transform."

—MEREDITH MILETI
Author of *Aftertaste: A Novel in Five Courses*

"Each story resembles a precious jewel, unique in its beautiful appearance while reflecting underlying nuances upon close perusal ... An uplifting and enriching read."

—SHRABASTEE CHAKRABORTY
Readers' Favorite (Five-Star Review)

"*The Other Shore* ... has something for readers of all genres. From magical realism to women's fiction to romance, and with multicultural and inspirational stories as well, Dr. Wangu concludes this lovely assortment with tales about fear of death, an ending that is both fitting and poignant."

—ABIGAIL DRAKE
Award-Winning Author

"Characters that capture the attention ... Each story features strong and well-developed themes, from death to spiritual awakening, from protecting nature to falling in love. The writing is crisp and descriptive ... employing a storytelling skill that keeps the reader ... experiencing *Wow* moments. Cleverly plotted."

—JOSE CORNELIO
Readers' Favorite (Five-Star Review)

"*The Other Shore* is exquisite and immersive. Each section of tales is fresh and nuanced. Wangu teases out the gorgeousness of all facets of life. A must read."

—KATHLEEN SHOOP
Award-Winning, Bestselling Author

"Each story is unique, told in a style that is engaging and in a captivating voice, brimming with insights about life ... A gorgeous offering for short-story fans, written in beautiful language and exploring topics that are thought-provoking."

—CHRISTIAN SIA
Readers' Favorite (Five-Star Review)

"The narration and the language are exquisite and transport readers into another realm."

—MAMTA MADHAVAN
Readers' Favorite (Five-Star Review)

To all who fear
Who have not found purpose
Who see no meaning in life

May this book alleviate those fears!
May these stories help you find purpose!
May lessons herein give some meaning to your life!

Contents

Fear of Death

FOREWORD

The Other Shore: Ordinary People Grappling with Extraordinary Challenges continues some of the themes from my first collection of stories, *Chance Meetings* (2015). In the interim years I wrote two novels, *The Immigrant Wife* (2016) and *The Last Suttee* (2017). Their themes were focused on lives of independent women woven with outdated rituals and gender injustice but ultimately love and creativity.

One significant thought that my previous books left me with was the emotion of fear and death. I pondered over themes such as searching for an elixir for eternal life, the ways we experience death, imagining other people's lives, unfulfilled ambitions, our relationship with nature, and spirituality. I also focused on how the death of a loved one affects those who are left behind. Why do some good-hearted people die young, but other miserable heartless people live long lives? The stories come alive with characters living in India, in America, their American friends and people from around the world.

Many of these stories fuse art and spirituality. Fiction allows me to enter an imaginary space in the psyche that I may never enter. I want you, my reader, to enter that same fictional world. I want you to grow intellectually and be emotionally touched by each. I hope the pleasurable feeling a story leaves behind lingers for days. Trust that these stories will not only lead you to yourself but also stimulate passion for your own calling and life's purpose.

These stories bridge two realities: outer and inner. Material and essence. One is a human language, the other a language of feelings, thoughts and sensations. When words and feelings become one, when our hearts and minds unite, we are transported to the creative/spiritual realm where there is nothing but pure joy. That's the aesthetic pleasure I want my stories to shower upon you.

As a Mindful Writer I constantly train myself to live in the present. In living here-now I neither think of my personal history nor the mystery of my future. I believe life can be lived only in this moment. And what is life if not a seemingly endless river of physically vigorous and mentally vital moments?

Real power in any writing is felt when the voice of the writer's innermost Self connects with the heart and mind of the reader through the page. Readers find such books either by word of mouth or accidently. I'm delighted you discovered *The Other Shore*. As you read it, let your own light reflect upon it. Experience how life can be lived joyfully in the present moment. Expose your heart and mind to the varied experiences of the people you meet in it and embrace them wholeheartedly.

—Madhu Bazaz Wangu, April 2021

Magical Realism

THE OTHER SHORE

Ten-year-old Mohini breathed in the first autumn air and recalled the scent of June when Grandma and Grandpa had arrived. She had been examining a twitching worm in a muddy bald spot on the lawn with a dried tree branch. Above, her grandmother stood on the edge of the porch next to a weathered column gazing at the grassy expanse below. And against the broad blue sky the yellowing maple and oak leaves glistened. The shadows of the autumn trees had elongated. Summer had flown by.

At that moment, Grandpa came out the back door and joined them. He patted Grandma's back and then leaned on the porch railing.

"It seems like just yesterday yellow dandelions were in full bloom," she said. "They disappeared and gave way to ferns. Now even those have turned bronze and yellow. Soon they will wilt."

"That's the cycle of life for you," Grandpa replied matter-of-factly.

"What did you say?" Mohini looked up. Seeing them watching her from above made her feel fuzzy all over—the way she felt when Grandma read stories to her, when Grandpa played badminton with her, or when the three of them played Monopoly or Chinese checkers.

"I said it's time for me and your Grandma to go back home."

"And time for our favorite girl to go back to school," Grandma added.

"When will you stay with me next?" Mohini held up the worm she had caught on the branch. "Look, Grandma!"

Grandma flashed a sad smile. "Throw it back to wherever you found him. Let it live its life!"

"Okay." Mohini did as she was told, then walked up the steps. On the porch, she stood beside her grandmother. She copied the older woman's posture and tried to look at what Grandma was looking at, beyond the grass, beyond the trees, beyond the hills.

Looking far into the distance, Grandma said, "Do you know what today feels like?"

"Sad," Mohini said.

"Yes, sad. Do you know why?"

"No."

"I feel as if summer wants to stay longer but it's being forced to leave," Grandma said.

"Can't do anything about it," Grandpa chuckled.

"It is kind of gloomy when something you want to stay as is, changes, isn't it?" Grandma said.

"That's how I feel," Grandpa agreed.

I wish they weren't sad, Mohini thought. She put her arms around Grandma and tilted her head onto the woman's waist. The smell of sandalwood enveloped her. It made her feel closer. A drop of warm saltwater from her eyes reached Mohini's upper lip. She tried to wipe it on Grandma's pants lest seeing it would make her sadder.

Grandpa turned to go in. "Time for me to take a nap."

"Grandma, can you roll a paratha bread with brown sugar for me after we wake up?"

"Again?" Grandma smiled. "You had one for breakfast."

"What about almond coconut ice cream?" Grandpa asked.

Mohini took a couple of steps to follow him, then turned. "Grandma, you come, too!" She pulled the older woman's hand. She felt Grandma's other hand on her head and felt warm all over. Her eyes dried. She wanted their walk from the porch to the guestroom to last forever.

Once there, Mohini lay down between Grandpa and Grandma for an hour's siesta. She didn't think she was sleepy but underneath the cozy blanket perched the dream fairy. Then something entirely different.

Mohini tried to turn her body. Soon, she twitched her hands and fingers but couldn't. What was happening? Finally, she jolted herself out of the nightmare. Sweating but relieved, she felt her body then the bed and touched her face. Grandpa and Grandma were no longer beside her. She sniffed and wiped her nose, pushing herself to sit up.

As she stepped down the stairs, she heard familiar sounds from the kitchen. Grandma was frying parathas while Grandpa marinated chicken pieces.

"Grandpa, you're here!"

"Why sure, Mohini. Where would I be? Were you crying?"

"And Grandma, you're here, too," she said with her voice breaking. "Why didn't you wake me? Mommy and Daddy are here. My home is here, and our porch, trees and hills are here." She was simply happy to be home surrounded by family.

"You are here, too!" Her mother gave her a hug.

"Oh yeah, I'm here," Mohini whispered.

Grandma smiled at Grandpa. Daddy nodded to Mommy. Mohini cried, "Don't!"

"Don't what, dear?" Grandma asked.

"Don't go on that boat, don't leave me alone!" Mohini hugged her Grandma from behind. Then she walked to her grandfather. "Don't you go anywhere," she said and closed her burning eyes.

"Had a bad dream, sweetie? Sit here," Grandma said. "Look what I made for you." She placed a glistening sweet paratha on a plate next to a glass of milk.

Without words, Mohini ate. When she finished, she sat quietly watching Grandma clean the stove and Granddad pierce chicken pieces with grilling skewers. Then suddenly she asked, "Is death like being alone on a boat that sails off?"

"Something like that," Grandpa said, meeting his wife's gaze.

"And all of us left back on the shore?"

"Something like that. Well..."

"Why do you ask?" Grandma said.

"I dreamt about it."

"Oh!" Grandpa said. "We all must sail alone for our final journey."

"Final journey!" whispered Mohini. "What does it mean?" She leaned against the old man. She held his hand hard against her cheek then placed it on top of her head like a crown.

"You will understand when the time comes," Grandpa said.

The seasons turned ten times. Ten summer vacations with Grandma, Grandpa and her parents. The more time she spent with them the more their love gelled in her heart like sweet pudding.

So many recollections, some more vivid than others. When Mohini was in sixth grade she had forgotten her lunch and was so worried about not having anything to eat she had been unable to focus on her work. Just before recess she was called to the principal's office. Was not bringing lunch to school her fault, a slip? Would she be punished? As she walked from the classroom her heart beat faster. When she arrived at the office door she was surprised to see her grandpa.

"Come in, Mohini," the principal said.

Grandpa turned with his arms open. "Dear Mohini! Hungry?" He held her lunch in his hand.

She giggled and gave him a hug. The lunch had tasted so much better that day.

And then there was that dress she wanted to wear to her high school graduation party. Her mother had refused to buy an expensive outfit. Each time Mohini passed the neighborhood store window she covetously gazed at it. She would forget where she was or with whom. For a whole month she gazed at the dress whether with friends, parents or grandparents.

The day before her graduation party, the dress disappeared and was replaced by a new one that did not interest her. Mohini gave up hope.

She loved the way her mother made her favorite hairstyle with French braids and decorated it with tiny silver snowdrops. She wore matching earrings and a pendant on a thin silver chain. Her mother kissed the top of her head and asked if she was ready to get dressed.

The doorbell rang. It was her grandparents arriving for dinner. Mohini smiled. Their presence would erase the bad feelings.

It sounded as if they were walking toward her room. *But why?*

"Look what we have for our favorite grandbaby!" On a satin hanger, Grandpa held the dress from the shop window.

The first day at college, Mohini unpacked her belongings in her dorm room. She placed a framed poem on her study table, written by her grandma and gifted on her sixteenth birthday.

The day you were born
I held you close to my heart.
Our heartbeats vibrated in unison.
My fingers spread over your silky black hair.
My hand cupped your tiny feet
as your warmth infused my bosom.

First blessed when I cuddled your mother,
snuggling you blessed me again.
I feel centuries of maternal love
gushing through us three.
The essence of invisible yarn,
like space in a clay jar,
giving meaning to my life.

Our ancestral mothers must have felt the same.
Grandmothers before me and the
granddaughters yet-to-be-born.
Centuries of wisdom to guide you.
Blossom my heart but stay grounded.
And watch the miracle of life unfurl.

Now in her junior year, majoring in Gerontology, it was past midnight when Mohini focused on her term paper, "Death Rituals in Wisdom Traditions." Her whole body ached from mental exhaustion. The next morning was Sunday. She decided to sleep in late and then visit her parents. No sooner had her head touched the pillow than she fell fast asleep.

She heard the beat of drums as a crescent moon rose in the sky. An orchestra of flutes and cymbals led a procession toward her home. Behind them were dancing men and women, then more people carrying bamboo baskets loaded with mangoes, pomegranates and star fruit. Their hair was matted.

"A procession!" ten-year-old Mohini whispered. "What day is it? Not Ganesh puja? Not Krishna's birthday? Not Rama and Sita returning from their exile? No! Then what are they celebrating?"

The tune became sad and slow. It was like cold winter, dark as night, thunder and lightning. It was like a cloud of black birds soaring above the ripened orchards.

She shivered.

The procession stopped outside her house. Mohini blinked. On the front lawn were seated Grandma, Grandpa, Mommy, Daddy, her classmates and neighbors. There was no sound. Suddenly the sky lit with sunlight.

The lawn was full of people. When she walked to the front everyone whooped.

"Why was I not told about this?" Only an instant before, Grandma had been kneading dough in the kitchen. Grandpa was reading the daily paper. Her friend, Neelima, was going to have dinner with them. Instead they were seated in the lawn watching musicians, dancers and fruit carriers doing their acts.

They stopped yelling and started to laugh.

"What are you celebrating?" Mohini asked at last.

"Why," Grandma said, "your day, darling."

"My day?"

"Yes, your special day, better than a birthday, greater than a wedding, grander than Diwali, more amazing than having a baby. It's your day, sweetie. Just yours!"

"But..."

"My darling..." Grandma nudged her arm with the rim of a plate. "Have a sweet. Coconut burfi, your favorite."

It seemed everyone's attention was on her.

"You never did anything like this for me before. How come you are doing it now?"

"Because it's Mohini's day! Don't just stand there!" Grandpa said. "Hurry on. Lead the parade! The boat is waiting."

"What boat? Are we going on a picnic?"

"On a journey!" Grandpa said. "Listen, you can hear the wailing of the boat at the lake."

"Yes, but..."

All those gathered faced the lake and listened with their hands cupped on their ears. They began to walk toward the lake. Mohini accompanied them out of town and down to the shore.

By the time they reached the lake, the sun had clouded over and fog engulfed the autumn sky. At the embankment, the procession and dancers came to a standstill. The musician stopped playing. The fruit carriers unburdened their baskets on the earth.

Mohini heard the mourning sound of a foghorn. Beyond the embankment a ship approached.

"Go on, child, out on the pier," Grandpa coaxed.

"Go, my heart!" Grandma sobbed.

Mohini did not move.

The boat nosed out of the fog, porthole by porthole. At the end of the pier it stopped and let down its gangplank.

"How come this boat has no name?" Mohini asked.

"Well, you see..." Grandma began.

"You board first!" Grandpa pushed her gently.

"It's time! Play some music to march her aboard!" someone yelled from the back.

The cymbals, flutes and drums banged out marching music. Mohini found herself up on the deck.

The gangplank fell. The ship's whistle shrieked. She cried out, "Hey, why isn't anyone else on board?" Mohini realized she was trapped on the boat. "Hold on!"

The boat shrieked and edged away from the dock.

"Hold on now, damn it!" Mohini shouted.

"So long, my baby!"

"Wait!" she wailed.

"Goodbye, Mohini. Goodbye!" her teachers cried.

"So long!" whispered everyone on the dock.

"Wait!" Mohini called toward the captain's cabin. "Go back and bring Grandma and Grandpa! Bring them all! They can come on the excursion, too! All of you can come along," she cried to the hands waving at her.

The baskets of fruit and food had been transferred onto the deck. Mohini turned and yelled, but it was as if they could not hear her. The women wiped their eyes with the end of their saris and the men waved their handkerchiefs.

The boat pulled out into the vast water while fog wrapped around it. She could hardly see the people on the dock.

Mohini now knew the ship was indeed empty. If she looked in the cabin, she would not find a single crewmember. She moved to the prow. Why had the season changed? Why had the cold weather come back? Then she noticed the boat did have a name.

It was The Last Journey. *And it had come just for her.*

Was she dying?

"Grandma, Grandpa, save me! No, no, no, no, oh save me! Please somebody, save me!"

But the shore was empty. They had all left. Grandma, Grandpa, all had gone home. It broke her heart. The fear, the sorrow, the pain of separation, tears of all sorts fell. She gave one uncontrollable shout.

Mohini sat up. It was seven o'clock. The telephone jolted her out of the nightmare. Her mother wanted her to drive home right away. "Is everything okay? Why do you sound so upset?"

"It's about your grandparents. Come home, sweetheart."

"What happened? Is Grandma okay? Is Grandpa sick?"

"No. I'm so sorry. So sorry."

"What? Have they died? I mean..." Mohini's hand shook.

"Yes."

Mohini's brain disconnected from her body. She felt like an ice statue.

"Come now!" her mother said and hung up.

Mohini put down the receiver and went to the bathroom. Gloom looked back at her in the mirror. Her face felt like an icicle.

On her way home, snippets of life with her beloved Grandma and Grandpa reeled through Mohini's mind.

When she arrived, she discovered Grandma had passed away in her sleep. Grandpa had been shocked to find her dead. While arrangements were being made for the cremation, he had a heart attack and he too passed away. Mohini's grief and despair became so intense that her tears dried. Her shoulders sank low and her chest caved in.

At the funeral home the next morning, family and friends gathered in a large room adorned with fresh flowers. Grandma and Grandpa's bodies lay on simple wooden planks. Only their faces, crossed arms and overlapping hands were visible. Their bodies were covered with marigold garlands and rose petals.

Each person paid homage by lighting a candle and placing it and a stemmed rose in the sand-filled containers on the side of each litter. Mohini wanted to go last. After her parents were done, she gazed at the peaceful faces of Grandma and Grandpa, waiting for them to say something. She then forced herself to place a candle and a rose by their sides. Only one thought brought solace. Perhaps dying on the same day was God's mercy for a couple who had lived side by side in love for sixty years—two bodies, one soul.

Grandpa's cremation in the electric crematorium was followed by Grandma's. It reminded Mohini how she and Grandma had followed him at a slower pace, holding hands, during their long walks in the wilderness. Tears streamed as she recalled their many talks about the cycle of life.

Grandma would bring her attention to the lush green foliage of the healthy trees sprouting from the dark branches against the blue sky. Grandpa would draw her attention to new life growing around the vertical trunk of the trees: wildflowers, ferns, fungi and fallen trees dissolving back into the earth. They would kindly and patiently explain how saplings sprouted from the earth where the old tree had lain prostrate, without mentioning death or dying. It all made sense.

Was today Grandma and Grandpa's special day? Better than their birthday, greater than their wedding day, grander than Diwali, more amazing than any other day? Was this their day, just theirs?

A slight smile played on Mohini's lips as her mind overflowed with their memories, their faces, their voices, their adoring appellations for her, the books Grandpa gave her to read, the dishes Grandma taught her to cook.

Mohini's father brought two brass urns for the remains. Her mother placed them in front of the living room fireplace. The scent of fresh marigold garlands panged at Mohini's heart. People came to pay their condolences and left, but she did not move from where she could view her grandparents in their new manifestations.

Grandma and Grandpa had desired to immerse their ashes in the lake near Mohini's home. Her parents had already made arrangements with a boatman. Mohini's father drove as she sat at the back of the car with her arms around the urns in her lap. Her mother sat quietly up front holding a basket of rose petals. They left home and the town behind, drove downhill and uphill until they reached the shore of the lake.

The morning was crystal clear with the sun shining bright. No fog engulfed the spring sky, no procession, no musicians, no dancers, no fruit or food carriers. Mohini walked to the shore and stood at the embankment waiting for the boat to arrive. She felt like a life-size icicle standing under the sun but not melting. *Grandma, Grandpa, are we going on a picnic?* She thought she heard the faint mourning sound of the foghorn. The boat floated closer then stopped. Sounds of cymbals, flutes and drums from her dream echoed in her ears.

Mohini and her parents boarded the boat and sat on benches in front. Slowly, the boat edged away from the dock. At the middle of the lake they asked the boatman to stop. Mohini stood and reverently kissed the urns one by one. Then she emptied their contents.

"...transformed by the fire element, merging with the rest of the elements—with wind, with water, with ether, with earth," as Grandpa once said.

Mohini got a handful of scented rose petals and strewed them over the ashes that were floating away. Her parents helped her sprinkle petals until the basket was empty. Only flower petals remained floating on the water's surface. The act broke her heart.

"So long, on your Final Journey!" Mohini whispered. *I wish I could bring you back. But like old trunks falling, sprouts will soon shoot up.* With eyes blurry she waved one final goodbye.

MAGIC BOX

At the beginning of time, speech was quiescent in the darkness of silence. Bored, the five high deities desired to play. Standing in a circle, from Brahma emanated golden rays, from Shiva silver, Vishnu blue, Devi blood red and Kali black. Their individual energies materialized into a sparkling sphere of immense power. It contained answers to basic human predicaments. No single deity could hold this sphere, so they summoned Vastudeva, the god of visual arts, who conjured up a red box of exquisite beauty.

When the sparks subsided, the deities carefully opened the box and slid the luminous sphere inside. It was sealed for eternity and buried in the bowels of a seven-story mansion at a location impossible to discover. Rings of cinnamon and cardamom trees were planted around the mansion. Encircling the spice trees was a range of low hills with a dense growth of thorny trees. The Snake River wound around these hills then meandered peacefully through the wilderness, small towns and cities.

The sphere enclosed answers to the three fundamental human questions. Why are we born?

What is our life's purpose? Why do we die? And perhaps a potion to defeat death.

But if the deities wanted to keep the answers such a secret, why did they materialize them in the first place? Was it just a game?

Kali, the four-armed goddess of death and dissolution manifested herself on earth to see if the deities would succeed.

Man heard this fantastic legend when he was young, as timeless as the River Ganges, as ancient as the Himalayas, as primordial as Mother Earth. While growing up he queried about it from holy men and saints, philosophers and thinkers, dreamers and down-to-earth folks.

After five family deaths within two years, he became determined to explore and unravel the truth from the legend. Man kept mulling over the question: "Why do we die?" The sediments of his query finally settled at the bottom of his muddy mind. His attention was diverted toward teenage interests.

At fifteen he was allowed to stay out with friends until ten o'clock on the weekends. One Saturday evening he invited them over while his parents were at a restaurant. Afterward when he was cleaning up, the doorbell rang. *Who could that be at this time of night?* His parents would have entered from the garage. At the door, two policemen solemnly greeted him. His parents had been involved in a terrible car crash.

Their death made Man independently rich. The thought of discovering the red box plagued him through his late teens and 20s. The legend ceased to be mere fantasy. He had no doubt that the red box enclosed answers to human questions, his questions.

Ten years later Man's mind asked not only, "Why do we die?" but also, "How can we defeat death?" The only solution he could think of was finding the red box. Man drove from one town to the next and the next. He crossed state lines, bridges and tunnels, took flights, rode trains and buses, and he met and talked to all who would share their knowledge, wisdom and expertise about the red box. He was determined to locate the seven-storied mansion where it was hidden.

That was all he did the whole of his adult life. Nothing else. Until he could find the red box, he was convinced that unease and disquiet would be his only companions.

While eating lunch at a tavern he unrolled his maps on a table. Some contained mythic locations and images and others were drawn by well-trained cartographers.

"Where are you going?" someone asked.

Jolted out of his imagination, Man looked up. Standing in front of him was one of the most charming young women he had ever met.

She cleared her throat and asked sweetly, "Where to?"

"Why would that interest you?"

"I have a degree in cartography." She tapped at a fully spread mythological map. "It looks intriguing, beautifully drawn. Which place is this?"

"If you're genuinely interested, take a seat."

"I'm Woman. Nice to meet you."

She sat next to him with her eyes on the map ready to listen.

Man explained his obsession. She listened attentively. Until then, when he told people what he was doing with his life they would either laugh or believe he had lost his mind. He had given up hope of meeting anyone who would understand. So now when he least expected it, destiny delivered a charming woman. He could not believe his luck.

She neither scoffed nor rolled her eyes. Not even once did she look away as he explained his plans in detail. When he stopped, he felt unburdened. He had poured his heart out to her.

She said she did not wholeheartedly believe the legend was based on facts. But she respected his truthfulness, dedication and utter determination.

Their love of ancient and modern maps, her understanding and his dedication developed into a good friendship. Her keen interest in travel and her equal participation turned that friendship into something more.

Man's parents' death had left a hole in his heart that pained constantly. He believed it would remain with him until the end of his life. But to his surprise and gratefulness the hole began to heal. Woman's care and concern worked as a salve to his emotional wound.

The questions Man asked were not new. Every human consciously or unconsciously had tried to tackle them since primordial times.

Woman may not have been as desperate to find the red box but she loved Man and his quest. Most of all she loved the adventure of searching for something magical and mysterious. His obsession became her passion; his calling became her quest. Together they ascended and descended mountain peaks, crossed rivers, and traversed wilderness and deserts.

Once, having crossed a river, they faced a dense growth of thorny trees. They bruised their arms clearing their way through what Man hoped were the spice trees described in the legend. The image of the mansion danced in front of their eyes. To his utter disappointment Man recognized the trees as thorny acacias.

The search continued.

At one ephemeral sunrise, years of wanderlust finally brought them to the Snake River. The scent of cinnamon and cardamom led Man and Woman near the mansion hidden behind the trees. They breathed the perfumed air. The closer they reached, the farther it seemed to move, like the horizon. For hours they kept walking but didn't find themselves any closer to the mansion.

At mid-morning insects buzzed at their ears as the temperature rose continuously. They came to a place where everything was covered with a thin layer of red powder. When the movement of their feet displaced the fine powder to reveal decorative tiles beneath, and colors and shapes appeared and disappeared, they knew they were getting close. Man wiped the powder from a small area with his foot to expose a colorful mosaic of flowers, birds and beasts.

They looked up. Lo and behold, there it was, the mansion! Red sandstone sparkled under the sunrays. Thousands of years of weathering had not diminished the beauty of its ten exquisitely carved columns. Five on the left depicted subjects of daily life—men ploughing fields, women balancing clay pots over their heads, children jumping rope and herding cows. The five on the right showed images of warring kingdoms—warriors on elephants with spears, on horses with swords and on foot with bows and arrows. The sculptural reliefs were animated with life. Years of sunlight and monsoon rain had failed to diminish their glory.

In the uncanny silence of the noon rays, Man and Woman kept walking against the hot breeze. Under the blazing sun the red sandstone façade shimmered. What should have looked like ruins of a seven-story mansion glittered right in front of them. Its massive front gate stood open, wide like their eyes. They entered and found themselves in a viewing gallery from where a central tower was visible.

"Should we go in?" Woman asked. She seemed afraid.

Man too hesitated. "Let's wait for someone to appear." They waited. When no one did, he shouted, "Hellooooo!"

Flocks of yellow and green birds surged from their hiding in the scented trees.

"Anyone in there?" Woman called.

No one responded.

"I don't see why we can't go in. No guard, no owners," he said.

"Do you think this is the mansion?"

He nodded. "I think so."

"Aren't you sure?"

"I feel a presence. Do you?" He looked at her. She shook her head.

He walked closer to the main entrance, and she followed. "What if the box is actually somewhere here?" she said excitedly, her face flushed.

"Haven't found it yet. Let's get excited when we find it."

"Are you sure you haven't conjured all this up from your imagination?" She wiped her sweaty face with the long end of her sari.

"Pinch yourself and find out... We're here, aren't we? At times what I imagine, or dream, is more real than reality itself."

He looked so energized, so ready to discover whatever he was looking for that she encouraged him. "I truly hope we find what you are searching for."

"If not today, some other day. I will never give up!" He was like the man listening for the winning numbers of a lottery. All but one number matched, and Man was waiting for that last number to be called. "The question is when found, will I be able to open the box and see what is inside?"

"Why do you say that? If we find the box you will be able to open it."

"Those who know say no one has even been able to open it. Ever. *Never.*"

"Perhaps they did not have as much dedication as you." She sat on the edge of a bench in the corridor close to the entrance.

"As I said, those who know say…"

The wall behind Woman was hot. She looked faintly amused, squinting into the sun's rays. "If you do discover the answers to the primordial questions, human life as we know it will cease to exist."

He sat close to her, wrapped his hand around her shoulders and asked, "Do you sometimes feel that you're a fool to follow me?"

"I love the thrill. I love your company. But I am not sure about your quest. I fear you are seeking answers to questions that have no answers."

He ignored what she said. "Anyway, I'm glad you are with me on this journey. I think today we'll find it. One last time, okay?" He kissed her on her cheek and stood up.

They passed through a dark tunnel. Instead of a square or rectangular room they found themselves in a circular corridor facing a ring of connected rooms. They stepped into one. It had two doors— one on the wall facing them and a second cut through the opposite wall leading to a central courtyard.

They exited and circumambulated the corridor. When they returned to where they had started, they entered the first room. Its walls were made of translucent mica.

Man held Woman's hand in a tight grip as they walked up several steps and reached a pitch-dark room. They waited for their eyes to adjust. A cold breeze steered them toward yet another interior space, a little brighter than the grey mica room. Here, they beheld self-luminous red lacquer walls.

A shelf protruded from the longest one. Underneath it was what looked like a coffin.

They shuffled closer so as not to disturb a thing. With some force, Man removed the coffin's stone lid. What they found were mere remains of what once must have been a human body. Man turned to Woman. She pulled out a flashlight from her shoulder bag and focused its beam inside the coffin. The bone fragments made her shudder. Man closed the lid and said, "Nothing here."

"You once told me only the person who had complete faith in themselves could see the red box."

"I did. But now I've started to wonder if I have either faith or determination."

"If you don't have determination and faith in yourself, then I don't know who has," she said.

Something else had absorbed his attention. He yelled, "I feel it! I strongly feel it." With his hand on the lacquer wall behind the casket he said, "Here!"

"Then let's remove the coffin."

"Would that be the right thing to do?"

"At this point there is no right or wrong. We have reached some kind of neutral space. We have come a long way. Why hesitate now?" she said.

They shoved the coffin farther from where it had been located. Behind it a door became visible. Man pushed but the door didn't budge. Woman joined him and they both pushed. The door opened with a creak. It led to a spiral staircase that directed them to the bowels of the building.

Only a flicker of light penetrated the stairwell through the windows, shaped as an eye. They kept stepping down staircase after staircase, a fifth, a sixth. Each eye-window watched them.

At the end of the seventh staircase a dim red light spread from a slightly ajar door. The two found themselves in a space encircled by seven rooms. One by one they peeked into each and discovered them filled with unique artifacts: bronze urns, ceramic vases and crocks, casks of terracotta, clay statues, red sandstone statuettes, gold jewelry and red and black glass beads.

They would have to carefully search each room and each artifact to find the red box. Woman hesitated, but knowing how powerful Man's intuitive sense was she followed him. They searched the overflowing shelves. They examined from top to bottom but found nothing that even remotely resembled the object of their quest.

As Woman entered the next room, she heard a muffled sound coming from the last eye-shaped window. She peeked through. How could she see the courtyard? Weren't they deep underground? Outside, a female stood staring at the mansion. Another searcher?

Woman smelled something but couldn't figure out what it was. She turned to find Man standing behind her. He showed her a bottle. It was red. "I found this on the shelf stacked with bottles. There was some liquid in it. I smelled it. It urged me to drink, so I took a couple of sips."

Woman stared at him. "That must be a thousand years old! Damn it! It urged you to drink?" She trembled. "Let me see!" She felt cold.

"It was in the corner, on top of this box."

"What? The red box! *The red box!*" She picked up the container and placed it on the wide ledge of the eye-window.

"What do you see?"

"The red box!"

A ray of setting sun seared through the glass. It reflected the fire and lightning like the blood diamond.

"This is it!" she said quietly. "I know it is. You found the red box, my love!"

He looked skeptical. "How can you be sure?"

She bent close and peered into the red glow around the container. "Don't you feel it?"

"Maybe if I open the lid and let it out... whatever it is, I'll know," Man said.

"It's locked. Let me try," Woman suggested and took the box from him.

Suddenly, a voice descended from the last staircase. "If you two will excuse me..."

The strange female's gaze was glued to the red box. "I hate to hold knives without handles." This woman had four arms dripping with blood. They gaped at her bloody hands. "But I have no knife with handles," she added. "I suggest you give that to me without creating any trouble. I have been searching for that box all my life."

"After going through all that trouble? No way!" Man said feeling wobbly. The red liquid had put him into some sort of trance.

"Come along now!" the stranger said to Woman. "Give it up!" She pointed the knife without the handle that she was holding in her bleeding hand. Each of her four hands was wielding an emblem.

Her long black hair was loose and disheveled. "The gods did a lousy job. Can't believe it was as simple as this." She picked up the red box with her bleeding hands and left.

Aghast, Woman watched the stranger escape as Man collapsed to the floor.

It was a moonless night. The red box was gone. Man felt better. With him on the passenger side, Woman started to drive back toward the city. The car bumped and rattled. Wind blew in through the front open windows. Their car swerved abruptly over the sand slipping beneath its tires.

"Stop!" Man said. "I saw something. Someone."

"Where?"

"Drive slowly... there... see?"

They got out of the car and walked to the ditch. Behind a row of dense shrubs, the stranger with four arms lay folded over, unmoving. Her eyes were wide open. Woman turned her flashlight on the stranger's body and saw two flames burning in place of her eyes.

"Where is the box?" Man asked.

"I don't see it."

He jumped into the ditch and rolled the body over. She now had only two arms. The knives were gone.

"How do you think she died?" Woman asked.

"Can't tell, no wounds."

"Couldn't have just stopped breathing? Where is the box?"

"I'm looking," he said.

After a few silent moments she asked, "Did you find it?"

"No. It's not here."

"Perhaps someone was following her!"

They scanned the darkness around them. Far off, in the starred blackness, they saw what looked like shimmering fireflies.

"Look!" she said.

They turned back. The body in the ditch had disappeared.

"Where did she go?" Woman cried, backing up.

"I heard once if someone finds the box, and opens it, they will disappear."

Woman looked exasperated.

"But I need to follow the fireflies. You don't have to come if you don't want to."

"Are you serious? I don't want to end up vanishing, as I'm certain you would if you don't give up this madness."

They got back into the car. She drove toward the fireflies as he directed.

She steered hard over roads and between stone cliffs. On one cliff were carved exquisite faces of the high divinities. She had noticed them that morning from afar but something felt different now. The gaping mouths of the faces caused her to tremble. A shiver started at the end of her spine and rushed to her head. A downpour of pebbles fell from the top of the cliff and disappeared into the valley below. Her pulse raced. Her lips trembled. At the top of the cliff, which looked like the end of the road, she stopped.

Man got out and flashed his light all around. The red box glittered next to a body. This new stranger's extremities were aflame as firecrackers sputtered and disappeared in a blaze of glass shards. The shards melted into liquid. Liquid became mist and mist turned into night breeze that was carried toward the sky.

Woman moved the car closer but remained inside. She hugged herself, feeling the goosebumps over her arms. From the open window snowflakes flicked onto her nose, lips, cheeks and fingertips. She felt cold and closed the window.

Woman watched Man pick up the red box. He held it away from him, gazing at it for a long moment. His hands trembled as he opened it. A red flash reflected on his face. He pulled out the sparkling sphere of immense power that the Gods had materialized with their powerful energies. This was followed by a few long still moments. Were his doubts ending? Were his questions answered? Would his fears, guilt, shame and suffering dissolve?

Woman didn't want him to die. Their love had flowered even while their perspectives clashed. She wheeled the car closer and opened the window. It was icy cold and deadly quiet. She heard him say, "Is this what I always wanted? Is this what I was afraid of? I longed for everything else but this." He breathed in the air. "I will cease to be. A drop merging in the ocean, an immense sea of nothingness but..." Once again he inhaled the draft of air coming from the red box. "... I feel wonderful, wonderful. I am floating." He giggled. He laughed.

And the red box dropped from his hands onto Mother Earth. Fireflies swirled all around Man.

Woman waited, forestalled by the fireworks, the melted glass, the mist, the night breeze. Nothing. She walked to where he was dancing. There was no body. But the box was there for the taking.

The pain in her heart was like a deep slash. She sighed but felt fortunate to have accompanied Man on his wanderlust and wonderment. She kissed the air where he had fallen, then turned purposefully toward the car.

She sat in the driver's seat and rolled down the window... and smiled faintly at the rising sun.

Seated in a semi-circle, five deities watched Man and Woman. Kali gaped at them and said, "Human beings are capable of overcoming amazing feats. Conquering death is not one of them."

"That is our domain," Shiva said, momentarily satisfied. The deities smirked and lazily moved their gaze on to someone else.

TREE TALK

I had toiled for months over med-school applications and essays. I dreamed of becoming a doctor to ease people's pain and to soothe their physical burdens, instead inviting pain and suffering of my own. My body hung like a carcass from a butcher's hook. The doctor diagnosed mononucleosis and prescribed complete respite. "Somewhere in nature," he recommended.

I now gaze upon a century-old cottage in the mountains of West Virginia where I will convalesce under my mother's care. Nestled amidst unfamiliar trees and bushes, I scan its green environs before entering our temporary home. A cool breeze passes through those trees that wafts an otherworldly fragrance. I am awed with comfort from an unfamiliar wilderness. I turn to take another look at the expanse of greenery.

For the first week of our stay, Mother helps me take one short walk in the morning and one in the evening. We circumambulate a chapel with stained-glass that is actually a library. As I gain more strength and can walk a mile, Mother plucks a leaf and asks me to memorize its shape and tree name—sycamore, elm, oak, maple, Japanese maple.

The following week she suggests we try other trails, especially the one that continues behind the chapel library. Its colorful windows shimmer in the sun. On the right is a six-foot oak stump. A green placard with a brass engraving is nailed to it.

> *I am a very important and most honored tree. Roger Green, the builder of this chapel, was struggling with the decision of where to locate it. As God saw fit for my 400 years of life to expire, I, through God, gave Mr. Green his answer.*

On the left stands another giant oak, living and thriving and exuberant. My mother and I discover we can borrow books from the chapel library, so I select volumes about local trees, plants and foliage, and about National Forests and Parks. From their back covers, I read that trees can live 500 or even 1,000 years, and have their own intelligence. Such facts impress me.

I learn that trees within forests are connected. The roots of one find roots of another, and produce more young trees. Beards of lichen hanging from their branches inject essential nitrogen back into the living system. Trunks, roots, fungi, lichen, soil, and rot form a partnership. Forest life grows above and below, spreading in all directions. The knowledge boggles my mind. My heart beats faster. If I am lying down, I have to sit up to slow my breath.

I continue to read. I learn that it takes centuries to grow vast natural forests but only days to pulverize them. The federal government, private companies and individuals plant hundreds of thousands of saplings, but they remain mere fragments. True forests must propagate naturally. They must rot, turn into soil and sprout fresh growth. Their value lays in the reciprocity of tiny segments. Although all this is new to me, I feel its truth at a subliminal level.

After every walk, every meal, every siesta hour, I look forward to immersing mind and body in the borrowed books I have yet to read. Outdoors the sun's warmth and perfumed breeze relax and invigorate me. Indoors the reading opens the windows of my mind.

Around the trunks of aspens, 50,000 baby trees sprout and grow from a rhizome mass too old to date. They don't grow from seed. Across the aspens, tiny buds of maples shower light rain. Tree squirrels gnaw at the massed buds and flowers, sucking out their sap. In those lush trees dwell animals that consume nuts and nibble at the sprouts. Life flourishes above and below ground, between earth and sky.

I read evidence that walking 30-40 minutes in a forest positively affects our health, lowering levels of cortisol, the stress hormone. Plants emit aromatic compounds called *phytoncides* that strengthen immunity and lower blood pressure. Another study concludes that surgery patients in a hospital room looking onto a forest heal faster than those kept in rooms facing a brick wall.

"Wow!" I say aloud. *But in return, what are we doing for the trees?* From another tome I learn that severe deforestation by logging companies is bringing an excruciating death to forests.

As the human population grows, we need more forests to produce vital oxygen. Trees are as much a part of Mother Earth as humankind. Nothing is separate. "Birds and branches are as connected as flowers and bees."

A month passes swiftly. I begin to notice the "presence" of trees. I inhale their scent, relax in their shade, and lean against their trunks watching the sun rise and set.

What could I do to help the forests? I was only getting acquainted.

Then it is time to leave. Mild pangs of separation surprise me. I bid a sad farewell to the green surroundings before sitting in my mother's car. Soft music plays as we pass by—oaks, pines, sycamores, maples, glorious in their beauty. They now feel human to me. Had we developed some sort of kinship? They had healed me during my convalescence. I literally depended on them for my health, for my breath, for my life.

"Why don't these truckers keep their distance?" Mother's words interrupt my musings.

She wants to yield right but the driver speeds up and passes us. I look at the loaded trailer and freeze—freshly chopped massive tree trunks. A knife slashes my heart—rage, regret, helplessness. I imagine a pile of dead bodies in a trench, their lifeless trunks dumped at some logging company.

I stifle a scream. I wish I could stop the driver. But what would I say? Besides, he was just doing his job.

Our home overlooks an expanse of rolling forested hills. I had seen it every day without taking note. When we arrive home, I now race to my room on the second floor and gaze admiringly out the window.

The following morning after breakfast I go for a walk. I cross our wooden deck with its timber-railing. I imagine the boards in their former life as trees. Inside and outside our house is so much wood—furniture, floor, walls, railing. I had never before paid heed. Now I feel concern. *What can I do to change all this?*

I descend a quarter of a mile, noticing a pleasant grove. I spend time amongst these trees before returning home. How could we be so ignorant of our environment to sever our connection with trees?

At home, I moan, "Why do we ignore issues of such importance?"

"Forget about trees!" Mother says, and hands me an envelope from one of the medical schools to which I had applied. She massages her palms and restlessly waits.

I open it. I have been accepted. But why don't I feel any exhilaration?

My mother is over the moon. She shouts, "Our daughter got in!" to my father in the next room and gives me a big tight hug. "Aren't you excited, honey? You worked hard for this!"

"Yes, Mom. But... it's the trees."

"Oh, the trees! I felt the same way when I read *Unbendable*. Did I mention that book to you? I suggest you read it."

She does not understand how agitated I have felt since we left that cottage in the wilderness.

"It's about trees and deforestation. A fascinating journey of a woman, whose name I can't recall," she tells me, "about her childhood in rural India and her outstanding work with trees and their effect on humans. She is a leading environmentalist and an ardent advocate for the rights of trees."

That very day I purchase the book and carry it to my favorite place to read—the grove of trees on the low hill behind my home. I read that its author, Uma Devi, was sixteen when she participated in *Chipko Andolan*, the conservation movement that started in India in 1963. Its supporters were mainly womenfolk, affected by the rampant felling of trees that led not only to a lack of firewood for cooking and fodder for animals, but also to a lack of drinking water and irrigation.

For her dedication to the ecologically-sound use of natural resources, Devi was awarded Padma Bhushan, India's prestigious national award. Her life's work had inspired other women, and similar eco-groups, to help slow deforestation and to increase social awareness of trees. At one point she asks, *"When will humankind stop the short-term greed? Deforestation? Climate change? Why are we bent upon turning the luxuriant Earth Mother into a bald-headed widow?"*

Was it a case of serendipity that Uma Devi was currently teaching at the department of Forest and Natural Resources Management at SUNY? A feeling of elation shoots through my body as I lie splayed on the durrie. I gaze at the majestic green canopies and marvel at their root systems mirroring their crowns underground until my eyelids grow heavy. I drift into sleep and am transported to the land of make-believe.

Multifarious trees stand rooted, staid, expansive, lush, blossoming, fruiting, elegant, gnarly, tall. They are in touch, attentive and communicating their messages. I comprehend what they share. I feel jubilant yet afraid to disclose this ability. I refrain from speaking. A serious oration is in progress.

> *We give flowers and fruit and sugar and*
> *wood, and receive sun and rain and air in*
> *return. We make soil. Everything. Nothing.*
> *The scents and aromas, some pungent,*
> *some sublime—a sensuous orchestra of*
> *cinnamon, pineapple, vanilla, jasmine.*

"Miraculous, marvelous nature!" I murmur. I breathe in orange, coffee, chocolate, amazed that I am able to recognize each one. Then I hear the tree chorus:

We are trees.
Fig. Chestnut. Aspen. Olive.
We are never just me.
We are a forest connected.

By means of roots, fungi and truffles,
High in the air lichen hang from our branches,
Adventitious roots grow from them to penetrate the earth.
We in the forest are like leaves on the branches
Sharing the same sap.
We are the Bodhi, the Peepul, the Ashwattha
Indestructible Tree of Life with roots above and
branches below
My trunk connecting heaven and earth.
I the Tree.

In the quiet that follows I see myself bowing in front of a thousand-year-old oak. "Dahlia," it says, "you and I have a common ancestor. A billion and a half years ago we parted ways. Did you know that I was on this earth long before humans? I propagate the whole world. I sustain an ecosystem on and around me. The sap that runs through my body is similar to the blood that runs through yours. You are my sibling, young woman, closer to me than you think. I too germinate from a seed, also root. I too am nourished by water and sun and air. I too become what I become then merge back into the soil like a river into the ocean."

"Why do we look so different?" I ask.

"We have traveled an immense distance in separate directions. Search in your heart, find me there. My lineage germinates, grows, flourishes like you. I feel like you. I sense danger like you. I sense when other trees are attacked by insects or afflicted by disease. And I also sense leisure. When the sun shines on me I make chlorophyll. You and I are like yin and yang. What you inhale, I exhale. What I exhale is your life. What you exhale is my sustenance."

When I wake, the first image that reels through my mind is the truck hauling tree carcasses. The vivacity and eloquence of the trees in my dream makes that image barbaric, brutish. I lay looking at the dense leaves above, the flowers that have turned into fruit. The truth is self-evident. Trees provide the view, the aromas, the fruit and vegetables, the medicines from roots and barks essential for human health and healing, humbly and unnoticeably. It is in the nature of the arboreal world to give.

They seem aware, watching, listening. They may not point a finger, but they produce chlorophyll, pump sap, spurt oxygen. What language do leaves unfurling, buds sprouting, fruit ripening speak? Can we hear the grass grow, the lotus bloom?

As I fold my durrie, I have an epiphany. *I will apply for admission to SUNY to the department of Forest and Natural Resources Management!* A thrill of excitement passes through my body that was missing when I received the med-school acceptance letter. I float all the way back home.

My parents do not appreciate my decision. But my enthusiasm keeps them quiet. I search for other colleges that best suit my newly found passion. I want direct experience in silviculture, environmental science and forestry. After graduation I hope to monitor forest ecosystems, protect centuries-old trees from logging companies and also from invasive insects, diseases and other destructive agents. Two places match perfectly: SUNY as I'd previously noted, and the University of Massachusetts at Amherst. I apply to both.

The next morning after breakfast, I consult with our local librarian about books on trees and related subjects. She leads me to the stacks and points out a few volumes. I browse and finally pull out four: *Audubon Society Field Guide to Trees*, both eastern and western editions, *The Hidden Life of Trees* and *The Architecture of Trees*. I carry these hefty tomes to a quiet carrel and eagerly page their treasures.

The two Audubon volumes are regarded as classics. Each contains 700 species of trees in full-color photographs of leaf, bark, flowers and fruit. The text is meticulous, detailed and informative. But not what I had in mind.

The Architecture of Trees has exquisite quill pen drawings, and 550 illustrations. *"The Bible for tree lovers,"* its back cover declares. This too is not what I was looking for.

Disheartened, I move on to the fourth book, *The Hidden Life of Trees*. It says the forest is a social network and trees are like human families. The processes of life, death and regeneration in the wilderness are as vibrant as in human social groups.

I flip through the pages and read, *"Ancient civilizations admired and revered trees, even plants as the focal point of prayer. Before there were temples and churches, synagogues or mosques, it was the tree that people worshipped. Each religion designated one tree as sacred. In India it was the Fig, in Africa Baobab. Rooted in the earth, still and silent, tree trunks must have looked sagacious, sentient, alive."*

Once again, an image of the truck hauling lifeless trunks flashes through my mind. "Sheer barbarism!" I utter. I borrow this book.

As I walk home, the touch of a gentle breeze makes petals fall here and there—white, pink, mauve—like the pitter-patter of rain. From that day on, I spend my mornings in the dense grove on the hill. I walk on the compact walkway that turns into pebbles, dirt and dry leaves. I ascend to the grove and enter through two majestic trunks, choose a place where sunlight nuzzles my back as I lay on the durrie near the trunk of an old oak. I declare it to be my sacred spot for reading, writing and thinking.

There I carefully and critically ponder the acceptance to the medical school that I am about to refuse. Am I sure a career in medicine is not right for me? *Yes*, I say to myself. The unease that has stirred within settles down. The more I ponder my decision, the more right it feels. The air blowing through the spirited trees feels softer, fresher, friendlier.

Then a nastier thought creeps in. *What if I do not get admission to the new colleges of my choice?* A different unease stirs in my belly. But I push it aside.

Alone with the trees, I sense their intelligence. Their branches reach out to find a place in the sun, their blossoms fade in the shade, their leaves glisten with dew drops. But their intelligence is not like mine. It is the wisdom of old souls: wise, patient, content. A quiet understanding develops between the trees and me.

Another morning I wake, stretch and exhale. I hear noise from afar. I open the window to let in the fresh breeze. Machines buzz in the distance. I focus on the distant sounds. Gas chainsaws and bulldozers are working at full speed. *Are trees being cut?* My anxiety turns to panic. I race downstairs past my mother, relaying my fears.

From the top of the low hill, a felled tree comes into view. *How many centuries old?* All its rings would have records of hard years and good years, all it had endured and withstood. *Why were the loggers mutilating the land? Another luxury hotel? A multistory apartment-building? A factory?*

By the time I arrive, they are cutting yet another oak. The gentle giant is slaughtered and bucketed in an hour and then hauled away. Other workers grind the base and roots, leaving the Earth Mother with a quivering bald spot.

According to what I have read, an oak can live for hundreds of years and nourish plants, insects and critters under its speckled shade. I bow my head and pay homage. *How do you say a final goodbye to murdered trees that were still and strong until this morning?*

I fear they will cut down more and more trees. A current of pain passes through my body. It seems unbearable. When the pain subsides, I wonder how I can help protect the trees and miniature ecosystems.

While I await new college decisions I dive deeper in research—reading, attending lectures, meeting specialists or professors. In a few months I accumulate more knowledge about arboreal and vegetable kingdoms than anything I knew before.

On a hot and humid early August day, I receive a letter from SUNY. I am admitted on a provisional basis. An essay must be submitted, explaining what made me apply for that particular major. The chance to breathe the same air as Professor Uma Devi thrills me. At once I sit down to write the required essay.

I type frantically. Then I read, revise and retype, read, revise and retype for the rest of the day. When my mind is exhausted I stop. The next morning, I reread a portion:

> I was born and grew up in a house that overlooks vast wilderness. But I never paid much attention to it. Six months ago, I fell ill and was advised to rest some-where in nature. In a cottage nestled in the woods where I convalesced, I befriended trees who have now become my beloved companions. It pains me to notice the speedy destruction of these trees that helped me heal.

I mail my lengthy essay, and walk to my sacred spot to share the news with my tree friends. Before I reach the grove, from a distance I notice a house I have not seen before. *Where did that come from? When was it built?* High in the heart of the forest, it was certainly not there before. Then I realize the trees in front of that house have been cut down—

the reason it is now visible. The thought makes me shudder.

I make a detour down the hill and walk in that direction. The house I had seen from a distance is not a regular house, but one constructed on a tree. This "tree house" has been built on the chopped trunk of a Douglas fir. The roots of the sturdy tree are still alive. The base of the house is supported by its twenty-foot trunk and attached with three-inch-diameter threaded bars. Like Atlas with the world on his back, the fir holds the weight of the house—perhaps the pressure of ten thousand pounds!

I marvel at what human beings are capable of creating but at the same time ache for that majestic enduring Douglas. Its trunk has continued to sprout shoots as it has done over hundreds of years. It continues to make chlorophyll and exhale oxygen.

I call out, hoping someone will show up at the window above. When there is no response, I call again.

A woman comes to the window. "Can I help you?"

"How does it feel to live on the top of a chopped down tree?" I ask sarcastically.

"We love it!" She and her husband are ecstatic that the tree has responded to the new and refined bolts. "They not only hold the foundation of the house, but the Douglas has slowly absorbed the wood construction. The tree has grown its rings around the house, letting the bolt and platform stay at their original position," she says enthusiastically. With a laugh she adds, "For our Douglas, the bolt is like a gnat on an elephant. It keeps growing."

"Growing!" is the only word that comes out of my lips. I turn to leave.

"Are you looking into a tree house?" the woman asks. "There are other choices besides fir. Ancient oaks, pines, maples and elms are equally strong. And available. We chose this one because it grows straight up, almost fifty feet before the first branch."

I can't hear any more. I want to scream. *What about the pain, a life cut short? Why on earth would you turn the majestic tree lame? Do you know that Douglas firs are an ecosystem unto themselves? Arrow straight, sometimes they even soar a hundred feet before branching out. Underground, their roots fuse into the tree next to them to join their vascular systems. Did you know they feed and heal each other, keep their young and sick alive, pooling their resources?*

I look up and just scream, "What is wrong with you people? Why did you cut down this beautiful tree?"

She steps back and closes the window.

"Trees *know*. Trees remember what humans forget," I yell.

Dejected, I walk back home. It seems to me that no one cares that deforestation is bringing a slow death to our way of life. Without forests we won't have oxygen to breathe. *Is human life more precious than trees?* Mother Earth is a whole organism of which humankind is just one functional part. There are no individuals, nothing is separate. *"Bird and branch are as connected as flower and bee,"* I recall.

Two weeks later I receive the acceptance letter I was longing for. I once went to the wilderness and was healed by the trees. Now it is time for me to heal them.

I walk to my sacred spot to deliver the good news. Against a brilliant blue sky, satiny pink-white blossoms float toward the earth, some falling on my head. I admire the abundant beauty of my surroundings. Low-hanging branches quiver with heartfelt thanks for my future contributions. The fragrance of surrounding trees connects me to the grove, to the forest, to all the forests... and to the Earth Mother.

Cadmium and Crimson

Valakya dreamed vividly the night of his twenty-fifth birthday.

An ebony casket he had carved was on display. From afar, he watched as Mahadevi, the Great Goddess, appraised, admired, scrutinized. Valakya moved a few steps closer. Cupped in her hands, she held a blue sphere the size of a peach. He noticed a white crane painted on its surface. She extended her arms toward the sky. It rained, first a pitter-patter, then it poured. The crane slowly spread its wings and soared upward. The blue of the sphere ran in the downpour. Underneath, the shimmering glass ball reflected rainbow colors while in the distance, a gong thundered.

Valakya looked down to see his feet turn blue. The land split, he on one side and Mahadevi on the other. Amazed, he watched as an ivory cradle materialized from the depth of the earth—a smaller version of the ebony casket. Lying comfortably in it was a newborn. Valakya felt his heart pulse in unison with the cradled babe. From nowhere, crimson and cadmium butterflies appeared and then disappeared into the ebony casket.

Valakya startled awake. Straight backed and cross-legged, he sat on his wooden bed and tied his long, thick braids behind his head. He breathed deeply and focused on his belly, rising and falling, rising and falling. He breathed until the inhalations and exhalations calmed him. For a moment he felt inner peace.

Now in his seventies, Valakya found solace in the thought that the way one lives is the way one dies. It had taken him many decades to understand; in that long ago dream, he was graced with the rapture of being alive and the cycles of birth and death.

Valakya lived at the edge of town in a mud hut roofed with cornhusk thatch. People knew him simply as the "sage." Each morning, he strolled to his workplace on an unpaved path flanked by mango trees. Sounds of a waterfall and the rustling of leaves, sap green on one side and copper on the other, greeted him as he entered a clearing sheltered by woven palm leaves supported on four banana trunks. Here, he had arranged his workbench, a storage trunk, and an earthenware vessel with a few cups on the floor. Two wooden stools flanked the trunk.

A piece of mahogany awaited the sage on this summer morning. He closed his eyes, praying to Mahadevi, the source of vigor and vitality. He thanked her for his intuitive abilities and prayed for her guidance in making the image that he had yet to begin.

An impression of a figure emerged. With his chisel and hammer he cut, carved, and shaped. His hands and arms, still strong and one with his mind and heart, worked until the sun was at its zenith. When he was thirsty, he drank cool water from the earthenware vessel and returned to his work. As he examined what he had completed so far, he sensed someone nearby. He turned his head and saw Shankara standing several feet away, waiting for his attention.

"Ah, dear Shankara, what a surprise to see you here! Have you been waiting long?" Valakya placed his tools to the side of the roughly shaped mahogany.

The visitor's crisp cotton kurta was stained with sweat at the armpits. "No, sir. Not long." Shankara wiped his forehead and stood with his hands folded. "If you could please spare a few moments, I would like to talk to you."

Valakya poured water for his guest and pointed to the stool. "Come, sit here. Tell me, what's on your mind?"

"I'm very sick. I don't know if you are aware." Shankara walked closer and sat down.

Valakya put the cup in front of his guest before sitting himself on a bench close by. Shankara drank the water at once and thanked him.

The sage's face dissolved into the sweetest, most loving smile. "Yes, I know, son," he said, his heart filled with compassion. "I was sad when I heard."

"Sir, I have started to make preparations for my final farewell."

"That is a wise thing to do, but have you consulted with the medicine man yet?"

"Yes, I have."

"What does he say?"

"He is not sure, one year or five. 'Only God knows,' he says."

"May your body remain free of pain!" Valakya tenderly patted Shankara's head.

The gesture of blessing emboldened Shankara. "Sir, I have come to ask you for something."

"What is that?"

"I wish to be cremated in a casket."

"Why do you wish this rather than to be wrapped in a plain shroud?"

"I want to leave with pomp and show." Shankara grinned sheepishly. "Would you carve a casket for me?" He looked expectantly at the old sculptor.

Valakya closed his eyes. The image of the ebony casket from his dream flashed to mind.

When he opened his eyes, Shankara repeated, "Would you?"

"Yes, son, I will carve a casket for you."

Shankara's perfect row of teeth gleamed against his dark complexion. "Thank you, venerable sir! And there is something else I want to tell you."

"What?"

"I have also asked Bhushan to build me a casket. You know how famous he is and how fond the townspeople are of him. I want to get two caskets made so I can choose one." He waited for Valakya to object, but the sage did not. "Will you still make one for me?" Shankara asked anxiously.

"What has my carving a casket for you to do with whether Bhushan makes one or not? Besides, I admire your honesty."

Valakya had not seen Bhushan's work in years. He mused over his own carved images, comparing his new carvings with the old, considering how his style had changed and ripened, and how his work, in turn, had shaped him.

Shankara took a long breath and reverently looked up at the sage. He saw his own reflection in Valakya's tender eyes. His heart seemed to open up.

"I'm afraid, sir. I am very afraid."

"What of?"

"Of dying." Tears welled in the younger man's eyes.

"You are human, Shankara. Fear of dying is human, more so in your case."

"Why? Because I am sick?"

"No, because you are young. Most people are afraid to die, afraid of becoming nothing, afraid of the unknown. But an old person who has been awake in life is better prepared to die than a young person."

"Are you not afraid to die?"

"I don't know how I will feel when my time comes. Until then, I try to hone the practice of dying through the little deaths so that I am graceful and openhearted in the face of my own—the Big Death." Valakya put his arm around Shankara's shoulders and gently rubbed his back.

"Little deaths?"

"Yes, the little deaths—children leaving home, separating from people and places we love... letting go of unfulfilled desires... and the hardest of them all, the death of a loved one—all of these are transitions. We must learn to befriend them. They are the stepping-stones; they are our teachers."

"Teaching us what?"

"That nothing remains the same. Change, loss, transitions are little deaths between our coming into and our leaving this world. We must learn to let go, Shankara. Everything is in flux, including our physical selves. The only thing eternal is the spark of wisdom and love in the depths of our being."

"Why don't I feel it?" Shankara asked.

"Most people don't. We arrive empty-handed and leave barefooted. As we grow, we get so busy searching outside ourselves that we forget to look within."

Shankara was listening carefully. He gazed at his feet, mulling over what the sage had said.

After a few minutes of silence, Shankara turned to Valakya and said, "Venerable sage, I don't have time to experience little deaths and nurture the glow in my heart. What should I do?"

For a while, Valakya let the silence surround them. He took in a long breath, exhaled, and felt at ease. His repose also relaxed Shankara.

"I know you do not have much time. But I strongly suggest you set some aside for meditation. Constantly focus on a sacred name, an image or the power within as you breathe in and breathe out. If you learn to control the breath, that will alleviate your fears."

"I will do anything you suggest to help reduce my anxiety."

"Find time to sit still in silence every day, preferably first thing in the morning. Do you think you can do that?"

"I will do everything you tell me to do."

"Listen! Every day for some time, sit in solitude and focus on your breath. Watch your belly expand as you inhale, and subside as you exhale. In time, you will learn to go within. It will be some time before you feel a difference, son. Have patience. Pay heed. Listen to what it has to say, and you will begin to understand that fear and courage, good and bad, happiness and sadness originate from the same space. When that happens, your own death will not feel as fearful as it does to you right now. You will feel safe in this space. May you rest in the comfort of that safety!"

"I will follow your instructions. I will take time daily to sit in silence."

"Promise?"

"Yes, I promise, venerable sir!" Shankara thanked the teacher with folded palms and bent head.

Then they just sat for a time. Valakya watched the late afternoon sun sieving through the waving palms and the edges of the mango trees. The birds slept. The waterfall gurgled. The sleeve of his robe rustled in the wind. He seemed to have all the time in the world. Nowhere to go. Nothing to do.

"I hesitate to ask you... but may I?" Shankara broke the silence.

"Go ahead!"

"Have you experienced *moksha*, the inner bliss?"

Valakya had lived a contemplative life for years. Under the tutelage of masters, he had diligently practiced the discipline of meditation. He lived in the light of inner silence, the source of all existence.

With a twinkle in his clear eyes he asked, "What do you think?"

"I believe you have," Shankara said, head bowed and hands folded. "I must leave now. Thank you so much for being generous with your time."

Valakya took out a miniature ivory crane from his storage trunk and handed it to Shankara. "Focus on this when you sit still in silence and solitude."

Shankara placed the gift in his pocket, thanked the sage again, and Valakya blessed him. They bid farewell, and the sage went back to his carving.

Bhushan, Valakya's younger competitor, worked in a lavish atelier adjacent to his palatial manor. Townspeople brought their guests to visit the grounds around his workplace. Here, Bhushan displayed a few of his latest works, changing the exhibits frequently. People not only enjoyed his larger-than-life-size works but also admired his muscular physique and handsome face. He charmed them with almond-shaped eyes and glossy black hair. Underneath his chin, and invisible to most, was a black mole, a blemish in Bhushan's own mind. He habitually scratched it, making it worse.

Bhushan could not understand why the towns-people believed the work of his senior contemporary embodied spirit. Wasn't his own work spirited? When Shankara came to his atelier and asked to sculpt a casket for him, Bhushan was pleased.

"It will be my pleasure to carve a casket for you, Shankara," he said. "You are my friend and patron. Why wouldn't I?" He wanted to make sure that Shankara had not asked Valakya as well. When Shankara said he had, Bhushan snapped, "Why did you ask him?"

"It would not have been prudent of me to ignore him for a commission such as this. Besides, the townspeople respect him, Bhushan."

"You know I will carve such a magnificent casket for you that it will glorify you after death—my work will keep your name alive. I see no reason why you needed to ask Valakya."

Shankara cleared his throat. "I asked him, Bhushan... I asked him because he is wise and compassionate, and I respect the sage."

Shankara's answer quieted Bhushan.

As soon as Shankara left, ideas began to flood Bhushan's mind. Day in and day out, he sketched different kinds of caskets from different angles. The more he drew, the more he wanted to draw. He grew ravenous. Some nights, his ideas would awaken him; they demanded to be expressed. One night, he ran a low fever. He got out of his bed, went to his studio, and frantically drew the creatures swarming in his head. The following day, making sketches and then creating three-dimensional models in clay and wood made him feel better. Finally, he selected five designs that could be constructed into magnificent burial boxes. Choosing just one was unimaginable.

Bhushan could not decide by himself. He summoned his craftsmen and explained his indecision. "Why not make all five?" the chief craftsman suggested. "Who knows? Shankara might set a trend in the city that could develop into a lucrative business." Bhushan was thrilled with the idea.

The construction began. Each burial box took the shape of a mythological animal: the cosmic guardian's hunting dog, the ether god's bull, the storm god's horse, the wind god's deer, and the fire god's ram. The heavenly animals were to be made in the form of winged creatures, ready to soar toward the blue sky.

Bhushan ordered a variety of woods, ivory, marble, schist, gems, and gold and silver pieces. Based on his drawings, craftsmen began to construct, carve, and stud. Bhushan's other patrons were restless. He had previous commissions to attend to, but checked in daily to supervise his best craftsmen working on the five caskets.

Valakya pondered. What sort of earthly vessel would Shankara want to take his final journey? Which casket shape would comfort him, put his mind to rest? Sickness had made Shankara fearful. He had become tender to life. What would a person in such an emotional condition like to be cradled in? By whom?

Valakya tried to imagine an appropriate design. He could no longer work on his mahogany piece. He put that aside for later and contemplated a befitting composition for Shankara's casket. One day in meditation, an image of the cosmic egg emerged, golden in color, followed by the idea of a maternal womb. These were good designs but not entirely satisfactory.

The sage remained focused, imagining, picturing, remembering from the storehouse of his memories. A form suggesting Mahadevi's womb emerged. It was a casket with curved corners and concave walls and lid. Valakya's decision was made. In his imagination, he let its lines refine, its shape define, and its form develop. He was to carve a casket in the form of Mahadevi's womb, a womb chamber.

He began carving the exterior from a beautiful piece of six-foot ebony until he could hear nothing but the sound of cutting and carving. One by one, his senses drew inward. His hands worked in unison with his heart-mind. As the womb casket began to emerge from the block of wood, Valakya's face was flushed and his ears pink.

He worked for months on this one piece. As days dissolved into nights and nights reemerged as days, animal and vegetable motifs appeared on the exterior. On the outer walls, lions and elephants roamed a jungle—animal power. On the interior of the lid, visible only to the one lying in the casket, was a white crane, the bird that swims as efficiently as it flies, the celestial bird that links terrestrial and celestial realms.

While the two artists sculpted caskets in distinctive styles and materials, Shankara made an announcement to the townspeople. He said he desired to be cremated in a casket carved either by Bhushan or Valakya. He wanted the public to choose their favorite when the completed caskets would be displayed on his residential grounds. The cremation ceremony itself, however, would be a family affair. The announcement fanned a wave of excitement throughout the town.

The sun shone brightly on the morning of the show and selection. Champak, mango and pipal trees adorned the vast grounds surrounding Shankara's mansion. The scents of bougainvillea vines, roses, and chrysanthemums in the gardens wafted on the breeze.

Valakya wheeled his casket onto the mansion's back lawn, preferring it to the front. Two young men helped him place the womb chamber on the display platform. Then Valakya strolled toward the freshly mowed and manicured front lawn. He was surprised to see not one but five ostentatious caskets by Bhushan already in place. Shimmering in the morning sun and painted in rainbow colors, the caskets had eyes and wings studded with jewels and gold and silver pieces.

At around ten, the front gate was opened. A river of red, yellow, blue, orange, purple, and white flooded in. Conversing excitedly, the tide of men and women flowed toward the five different displays and surrounded the winged animals, their gaze lost in the blazing colors and structured intricacies. The longer the crowd looked at the winged animals, the louder and more excited they became.

"So many... Bhushan has made... one... two... five caskets!" a plump wife in a sari printed with sunflowers said to her lean husband in a white kurta-pajama.

"He needs only one! Is this the time to show off wealth?" the husband whispered. "Look at this red one; it looks like your bridal palanquin!"

"Yes, yes! And look at that one!" The wife pointed at another box and pulled her husband to the next display. "It's mustard yellow! Doesn't it resemble the lacquer cradle we got for our Munna?"

"Yes, it does!" the husband said and turned his head as if searching for something.

"What are you looking for?"

"Something authentic. Where is Valakya's casket?"

"Someone said his was at the back of the mansion."

"Let's go look at his—the one that expresses a sage's wisdom, not just opulence!" the husband exclaimed.

The couple followed a group of people walking to the back of the house. A crowd surrounded Valakya's womb-coffin. The couple pushed through to take a look. People were whispering. Silently, the couple contemplated the display. A lull had overcome the group. No one spoke. But they all looked intently. Some appeared somber, others a bit disappointed.

"This one gives me the creeps!" the wife whispered in her husband's ear. She said she wanted to leave. The couple turned and walked away. Many more followed to return once again to enjoy Bhushan's boxes on the front lawn.

Bhushan's phantasmagorical burial boxes mesmerized the crowd. The townspeople walked around the exhibits for an hour and then settled on chairs facing a makeshift stage where Shankara, his family, and close friends sat.

Shankara's assistant stood and greeted the guests. Some people, still standing, hurried to the remaining chairs. On Shankara's behalf, his assistant thanked the crowd for coming and repeated what they already knew: their vote, although informal, was important to Shankara. Their choice would be his choice. People cheered. It was pertinent that they let their vote be heard. Then he said, "Okay, good people, cheer if you liked Bhushan's caskets!" There was thunderous applause.

Then, one by one, he asked the audience to cheer for Bhushan's five caskets so that he would know which one to pick. When he mentioned the ram, the fire god's casket, people showed their preference with the loudest clapping.

Once the applause subsided, the assistant cleared his throat and said, "Now it is time to applaud for Valakya's casket. Cheer if you liked his work." This time, the applause was feeble, hesitant. People exchanged glances. A few continued to cheer, hoping more would join in. But they hoped in vain.

Shankara's assistant announced the ram casket as the winner. Bhushan's team of workers shouted and jumped up and down. The crowd stood and clapped louder than before. Relieved and satisfied that a decision had been reached, the assistant sat down.

Bhushan stood and said, "Attention! Attention, please! I would like to heartily thank the venerable Valakya for his creation and also for his personal guidance. Where is he?"

People shouted, "Valakya! Valakya!" but the sculptor was nowhere to be seen. He was seated on a rock nestled in a wooded area, watching the spectacle from a distance.

Between the cheering and applause, the assistant invited Bhushan onto the stage. People stopped shouting as Shankara bowed in appreciation. Bhushan hugged his patron. Once again, people cheered.

Within a few months of that memorable day, Bhushan was inundated with work. People from his and neighboring towns not only commissioned caskets but also floats, chests and display pieces. Money poured in.

The next day of festivities was to be on New Year's Day. A wealthy patron from a neighboring town commissioned Bhushan to make him a float using the same material used for Shankara's winning casket. He wanted Bhushan to construct the biggest New Year's float anyone had ever seen. Bhushan was no longer young, and the work was challenging.

But it gladdened him to know that Valakya had not been asked.

Though he had to temporarily move his studio to his patron's town, Bhushan accepted the commission. The work was elaborate and intricate. Bhushan worked nonstop. It took him and his team a month to complete the project. On the last day of work, as Bhushan was standing on the highest platform examining the float and the land around it from a bird's-eye view, he fell to the ground and fractured his pelvic bone. He remained in bed under the care of the medicine man for months but did not fully recuperate. He no longer created sculptures. People were sorry to see him disabled at the peak of his creativity.

A year after Bhushan's tragic accident, Shankara was cremated in the ram casket. At the time of his death, he was at peace.

Almost two decades passed. The lush green and copper leaves of the mango trees danced under the setting orange sun that shimmered on the thatched roof of Valakya's mud hut. The "sage-sculptor" had gained people's reverence, but he could no longer hear the waterfall or the birds' chirp or the rustle of leaves.

Valakya bent his head and stepped out the door. His silver braids and the collar of his long white robe flanked his bearded face. He walked out to fetch flowers for his daily offerings to Mahadevi. When he extended his arm to pluck blossoms from the jasmine tree, a few white butterflies fluttered. He gathered the flowers in a small bamboo basket and returned to his hut.

Once inside, he noticed that the white silk covering of the womb-casket he had carved years ago had slipped to the floor. He placed the flower basket on a stool and tried to cover the casket with the fabric, now yellowed. Suddenly, he felt an urge to sit at the edge of the casket. With his wrinkled fingers he touched its textured surface, felt its chiseled grooves and crevices, and remembered the dream of decades ago that had inspired him to carve the casket at Shankara's request. The expression of his dream in ebony and ivory had eased the dread of his own death.

Valakya was physically tired, yet he felt an ecstasy within. A feeling of joy infused his whole being so much so that he had to sit still. He had a glimpse of himself prostrate in the casket, the crane waiting, welcoming, wooing. Slowly, he opened the lid and stepped into it. He lay down and made himself comfortable. He closed the lid on himself and crossed his arms over his chest. The celestial bird gently unfolded his wings and rose toward paradise. Valakya's eyes were closed as it soared beyond the blue sky.

Bhushan, helped by his wife, walked to Valakya's hut with the townspeople. They came in the evening, with fruit and flowers, to pay their daily respects. But the hut was empty. They searched for the sage in and around the hut and in the grove, but he was nowhere to be found.

Bhushan and his wife returned to the hut. They noticed the yellowed covering of the womb casket lying on the floor. Bhushan picked it up, and as he was about to spread it back over the casket, a pull at his heart prompted him to open the box. At first, he hesitated, but he paid heed to the nudge and slightly raised the lid. From the narrow opening, crimson and cadmium butterflies fluttered out and through the windows and the door toward the spacious blue sky. When he opened it completely, he found the chest empty.

WOMEN'S FICTION

The Dowry Brides

At midnight, I dragged my feet from the bus stop to my two-story building. Walking was my thing but who enjoys a walk after a tiring day? My work as the assistant-manager of a busy restaurant was exhausting. My head throbbed.

I staggered my feet up the staircase and toward the door to my barsati. I had rented this rooftop studio with a large open terrace, a compact apartment at the end of an open space. Such barsatis were rented by young men starting their lives—writers, artists and such. At age twenty-five I should have felt more energetic, but Saturday evenings and Sundays, while relaxing and fun times for others, were exhausting for me.

Holding my bulging briefcase, I fumbled with my keys, found the right one and opened the door. The telephone rang. It was my mother worried about her first-born son, asking why I wasn't at home at midnight. I said she should be happy that a small-town boy like me had a job at a five-star restaurant in the city. One of the reasons they hired me was because I offered to work on the weekends until midnight.

The best time of my week began Monday morning as I read the daily paper while eating buttered toast and sipping hot cardamom tea. I read it from the first to the last page—political news, local news, entertainment and the feature stories. The rooftop living was open and unencumbered. I enjoyed the sights and sounds of rain, from the pitter-patter of raindrops to the streaming sheets of torrential pours. During the monsoon season I stayed indoors to watch the heavy rain veil everything except hazy shapes. For the rest of the months, I literally lived on the open terrace as I was doing now.

My favorite piece to read was a weekly feature from the Sunday paper: a heart-wrenching or an uplifting story with photos. One morning the feature story deeply touched me. It was about a woman who had refused to go through the wedding rites and rituals because of the exorbitant dowry demand from her future husband's family.

During the months when the temperature was pleasant, I ate, read, napped, and then read some more under the shade of an umbrella permanently fixed over the table and recliner. The view of other rooftops stretching out on both sides of my terrace gave an impression of being connected with the neighborhood, but it was an independent living. I cherished my time in the open air. I read, drank, ate and napped.

The yowling of vegetable and fruit hawkers on the street below was the first thing that I heard in the morning. On weekend and holiday mornings while having breakfast on the terrace, I watched men on their own terraces practicing standing yoga starting with sun-salutations. After the yogis left, I read. In between my reading I was distracted by women appearing with plastic buckets filled to the rim with freshly washed garments of all colors and sizes. They shook out the wrung items, hung them on the clothesline, and fastened each with clothespins lest the hot wind would carry the smaller, sometimes even heavier items with them. The women who came to hang clothes also swirled the oil of the pickling vegetables marinating under the summer heat. Terrace living had a personality of its own.

Depending on the season, I lounged on my reclining chair with a glass of lemonade or a pot of hot tea. The open space, the vast sky and cool breeze washed away my daily exhaustion and petty anxieties.

The feature story about the dowry demand made me angry, but by the end the young woman's courage warmed my heart. It reminded me of my older sister. On the day of her marriage her groom's parents had also demanded a dowry. When her husband-to-be stood mute, she refused to marry him. Our parents were shocked, but I felt such pride and admiration for her as I had never felt before. That deplorable man eventually married one of my sister's classmates. A year later we discovered she died of poisoning. In time I forgot about it, until today.

My attention was diverted by a woman with her back toward me, one terrace away. With the pallu of her sari tucked away she took out garments from a green plastic bucket, shook them out and hung them on a clothesline. As she pinned the clothes, I had a glance of her profile. She seemed around twenty, newlywed as her right arm was adorned with dozens of ivory and red bangles. When the bucket was empty, she happened to turn in my direction. No sooner had she seen me than she tucked her head like a shy duck. The parting of her hair was filled with vermillion powder and her forehead adorned with a red dot. She had all the signs of being newly married. I went back to reading the paper.

I glanced at the photos that accompanied the story and wondered if this newlywed had brought enough dowry with her. Or if her husband had demanded dowry or if he even loved her. Was she happy?

The woman in the feature story had met the man at her first job. He had not mentioned a dowry while he was wooing her and going steady.

On the wedding day when she found out about her would-be in-laws' demands and her fiancé agreeing with them, she was infuriated. In the presence of family and friends, his father put her parents under immense pressure. Furthermore, there was a question of *izzat,* shaming the family. If the dowry demand was not met, the groom and his family were going to depart at once and put the bride's family to shame for life. No one would marry a girl rejected by a man she was to marry despite her education and earning capability.

At first the girl's parents pleaded but when the boy and his parents refused to compromise, helpless, they bent their heads and sealed their lips. The bride could not tolerate the way her parents were being treated. She removed her veil and tucked her sari around her waist. She stood with her back in front of her parents. Facing the groom and his parents she said, "If you love me, tell your parents to stop their demands and insist that you want to marry me. If you don't love me and don't show courage, you are not worth marrying."

"There was utter silence in the arena. The boy didn't utter a word," the feature writer noted.

The bride turned to her parents and said, "Don't worry, Ma and Papa. I love you. You love me, you have educated me, even helped me find my job. Now, I must not hesitate to do what you deserve. I will take care of you rather than spend my life with this spineless man."

Her parents, confused and saddened and insulted, were visibly moved.

The guests looked aghast. Some started whispering about her shamelessness. Some criticized her for being such a loudmouth. Others thought she was crossing her limit as a female. Still others from the groom's side openly and loudly snickered at the situation. Only a select few cheered her decision. They whispered to her that she had made them proud. She didn't seem to care either way.

The groom and his party left. The girl asked her relatives and friends to forget what happened and enjoy the wedding feast.

"What a self-respecting, emotionally balanced young woman! We need more women like her and less men like this scoundrel groom," the journalist had commented.

How courageous and confident for that young woman to order the groom and the wedding party to leave. She brought back some peace and dignity to her parents. "I would like to marry a woman with that confidence and self-respect!" I muttered to myself. I turned to look at the adjoining terrace the newlywed woman had left.

The following Sunday I expectantly waited for her to appear on the terrace. She saw me sitting on my reclining chair. I waved at her in friendship. She turned away to pick up the empty bucket, quickened her pace and disappeared. After watching her hang a load of laundry every Sunday for several consecutive weeks I was getting used to this routine.

She must have guessed that I was being friendly and harmless, so one day she finally responded to my wave with a faint smile. Following that exchange the greeting became a habit. She would hang the wet laundry, swirl the oil of the pickle jar, then turn toward me. I would wave, she would smile and leave the terrace.

The letters to the editor the following weekend were a picture in contrasts. On the one side the bride was criticized as shaming her family and the Hindu Dharma. *"No one is going to marry her now! They deserve it. Why did they educate their daughter? Modern universities and colleges turn our daughters' heads. They are damaged for life!"* On the other side, the letters admired the bride-to-be's courage, integrity and balance of mind. *"Our society needs such confident young women. Only education can infuse young minds with such courage and reasoning,"* a university professor had written. *"They don't merely write papers on the necessity of education and equal rights for women but also act upon them."* The young woman had become a worthy exemplar overnight. *"Women arise! Men wake up! This is the twenty-first century, have some guts,"* and it went on and on.

I mulled over the letters thinking how I could, as a man, make a worthwhile contribution to the society that would uplift women's cause. My sister had inculcated in me the sense of fearlessness, fairness and justice. My chain of thought continued as I went for my evening walk. I just couldn't get the story out of my mind. The courage the young woman had exhibited made me feel good and I cringed at the letters that criticized her behavior, condemning educating girls and their commendable bold actions.

One evening I was walking in the neighborhood. I was still thinking of the letters to the editor when, some hundred feet away, I saw a woman slowly walking toward me. Her head down, she looked like the newlywed from the adjacent terrace. I slowed. When she was about ten feet away, I stopped. She looked up and was caught by surprise. She too stopped, smiling faintly. She came a couple of paces closer when I saw sadness in her eyes.

I waved to prolong our chance meeting and waited for her to say something. Her lips moved but she was unable to utter words. She lowered her head and continued to walk in the opposite direction.

From that day on, whenever I spotted her on the terrace hanging clothes, she would wave with a faint smile even before I had waved at her. During our neighborhood walks when our paths crossed, she would wave and smile without exchanging a word. We had developed a quiet rapport. Some evenings when I did not feel like walking, I walked anyway just to see her smile. Why were her beautiful black eyes sad and, sometimes, red and unslept?

A month passed. Our paths did not cross anymore. One evening as I was walking through the neighborhood, I noticed the main door of the house where she lived was wide open. I walked past it. I heard loud angry voices coming from inside. Yelling. Screaming. Crying. I could smell smoke. *What is the hullabaloo about?*

An ambulance arrived and stopped in the front of the house. Two paramedics jumped out and went inside. Something terrible had happened. I stared blankly at the empty space through the door. The paramedics returned with a woman on the stretcher with her head and face covered by a scarf. I was pretty sure it was her. She was wheeled to the ambulance, hauled in, the door was shut. A young man rode with the paramedics and they drove away.

An older woman anxiously watched the young man. As she was turning to go back in, I said, "Is everything all right? What happened?"

"What business do you have with the private affairs of a married woman?" She glared at me. "Did you call the ambulance?"

"Just wanted to know if she was all right," I said nervously.

"How dare you! What business do you have with her!" She turned abruptly and closed the door with a bang.

The next couple of days I was occupied with my work but could not let go of that incident from my mind. I was certain it was the newlywed woman whom they had carried to the ambulance. What had happened to her? What had they done to her? I enquired from neighbors and found out that she had been cooking on the stove with an open flame. The pallu of her sari caught fire and she got burnt.

"Was she badly burnt?" I asked but couldn't get any answer.

On another of my evening walks I noticed a group of friendly neighborhood women talking. I stopped to join them. After a short chitchat I asked, "I heard the young woman from that house had an accident. Do you know anything about it? How is she feeling?" I saw them exchange glances.

"You mean, Kavita. Oh, poor unfortunate Kavita! They are saying she was careless, she burnt herself," an older woman remarked.

"I heard otherwise," a young woman interjected. "This is a case of bride burning. She has third-degree burns."

"It is a common occurrence. Her sari caught fire," the older woman said.

"Or..." Another young woman locked her eyes with the first young woman.

"Something vile and cruel may have occurred in that house. The police are involved in the case. If something like that had happened, they'd have found out. We'd have read it in the papers," the older woman added.

My heart sank. I managed to say, "Registering with the police doesn't mean much. They register such cases then shelve them. They don't follow up." I bid goodbye.

As I walked toward home, a feeling of loss surfaced in my heart, an old memory perhaps. But I could not remember what it was. I quickened my pace.

So, her name was Kavita—a poem. A sad poem. Why didn't I talk to her? Why didn't I ask the reasons for her sad-red-unslept eyes? What were the unutterable words that refused to leave her lips? Had they already silenced her? I needed to know. I needed to help. But I was neither a friend nor a relative. Would they let me see her? Would she see me?

I decided to visit her anyway.

At the hospital, I was told Kavita Bansali was in the Intensive Care Unit and was in no condition to receive visitors. When she was moved to a regular unit, I would be allowed to see her at the visiting hour. I called every day. After a week she was transferred to the regular ward.

I passed the burn unit. It was much bigger than I had expected. The glow of the fluorescent lights was dull. Things were not clearly visible, but I could see many patients wrapped in bandages, some lying naked under what looked like an inverted metal cradle. None of the patients were covered with sheets.

The regular ward had forty beds. Kavita was on bed #22. With my heart beating fast I paced toward her. When I reached her bedside, a nurse seated next to her remarked, "Glad to see a visitor."

"Has no one come to see her?"

"Her husband admitted her but has not been back since that day. Today for the first time we were able to cover her. She is more comfortable now." She pointed to a thin white cotton sheet. "How are you related to her? Brother?"

"A friend."

"Her face and neck will take several weeks to heal. It could have been worse," the nurse said. "She'd be happy to see a familiar face." She bent down and whispered to Kavita, "Look who came to see you."

Kavita's head and forehead were severely distorted, almost beyond recognition. She opened her eyes and squinted at me standing at her bedside. I smiled and waved. She squinted harder.

Then a trace of surprise covered her face. She turned away from me.

"You want me to leave?" I asked.

She shook her head. The nurse asked me to sit and left the room.

I sat trying to tell her today's news. And some stupid anecdotes from the hotel. After a while she turned her head back and tried to smile through her disfigured face. Her forehead, ears and neck were burned. Her sad eyes looked sadder.

A nurse came to take her pulse.

"Is it all right to make her talk?"

"I don't see any reason why she can't talk if she wants to," the nurse said before leaving.

I pulled the chair closer to the bed and sat quietly.

Kavita pulled out her left hand from under the white sheet and extended it to me. Hesitantly I held it. She gave out a sigh. I held her hand between my palms. The left arm had also been burnt but not that critically. It was not difficult for me to imagine what might have happened. Then she withdrew her hand. She turned her head left and right. She tried to turn her torso but couldn't. She seemed spiritless.

"Where are you from?" I asked to temporarily divert her attention from the pain she was feeling despite the pain-relieving medication they might have given.

"Calcutta."

"Where in Calcutta?"

"A small town you wouldn't know... Are you trying to get in touch with my parents? Please don't. The news would kill them."

"No, no! That is not my intention. I don't even know what happened."

"The night before the accident I had a heated argument with my husband. He accused me of not being a good wife. He said I was unable to give him a son and I did not bring them a decent dowry. When I said my parents gave as much dowry as they could in cash and kind, and that he was being impatient about having a child, he called me names. He called me a barren witch and started to hit me." Her lips were dry. I fed her water from a glass with a dropper.

After a few minutes she continued. "The next morning in the kitchen as I was frying pooris for breakfast, I don't know what happened. I felt a burning sensation from behind, around the small of my back. The part of my nylon sari that was draped over my head was in flame. It melted and was stuck to my head and forehead. When I tried to muffle the flames my right hand and arm got burned. I screamed and ran out of the kitchen. I don't know how it happened," she said as the tears flowed from her eyes.

"I'm so sorry, Kavita," I tried to calm her down. "You're in good hands now. You will get better."

"I'll never go back to that house," she said.

"Where will you go? How will you survive?" I thought of women who were totally dependent on their husband and his family.

"When I get better, I'll find a job. I have a degree in teaching high school, although now it will be harder." She pointed to her head. She got emotional and began to sob. Again I tried to calm her.

"Get better. You'll find a job. Now you rest. Sleep for a while." I called the nurse who gave her a tranquilizer.

Her breath turned shallow. But she closed her eyes and after a while fell asleep.

I gently placed her hand at her side and tiptoed out of the ward.

That night I slept fitfully. How could I go through the day as if nothing had happened? I called in sick. I didn't know what to do, how to help. Visit her? Then what? I decided to walk through the neighborhood. I went to the library and read about the history and incidents of bride burning. I learned that the number of registered deaths of new brides due to fire was growing. A couple of years ago there were 999 dowry deaths per year. That number had increased to 1,786 the previous year. Only this year had police started to register dowry death as a crime. Until now people did not report it and the police did not even take it seriously.

For several evenings I made it my job to walk in my neighborhood, knocking from door to door trying to collect funds to help Kavita.

Many people didn't know who Kavita Bansali was. I explained that she was newly married and had lived in our neighborhood a little over a year.

"Why do you care for a woman unrelated to you?" one woman asked deprecatingly.

"I care because a woman was burnt. She is suffering and no one seems to give a damn. You and I know dowry is evil and greed has no limit."

"How do you know this incident has anything to do with her dowry?"

"She told me and don't be naïve!" I cried.

At a different house a man remarked, "Why do you want to interfere in the family's domestic matter? Don't you have a job or something?" He stared at me suspiciously.

"I do have a job. But I am collecting funds for that helpless woman. Her parents live in Calcutta. Don't you want to contribute for the charity? It will make you feel good about yourself." Then I gave her the statistics that I had repeated to many other neighbors.

"Huh!" he said. "We already do lots of things that make us feel good about ourselves. Don't worry about us. Have a good day." Then he shut the door.

Some neighbors did donate, more than I had expected. They also appreciated my volunteering to help Kavita. But they were few.

A neighbor invited me into her home and offered me tea. I accepted. She was a college professor. Her husband joined us. She asked me why I felt such sympathy for this woman.

I was touched by this rare kindness. I poured my heart out. I said, "Tell me, where does a woman go in a society where a girl's parental home is considered a temporary home for her, not for her brothers? Isn't this a norm that as soon as a female child is born, parents start worrying for her dowry?"

"Yes, for the majority of families that is true," the professor interjected. "Parents take a deep sigh of relief only when she is married off to a stranger and bears his son."

I felt encouraged to go on. "Where does a woman go when the police don't take the cases of domestic abuse and bride burning seriously? Where do the abused women go when neither the police nor her maiden family help her?"

"Or when her husband beats her?" she said. "She can't leave the husband because she is financially dependent. Where does she take her children? The society treats a woman without a man like a leper or worse, a whore, for leaving him."

"Yes, professor, you understand. Where does she go? What does she do?" My lips trembled. They gave me enough money to buy Kavita a train ticket to Calcutta. I thanked them profusely for the donation and the tea.

The next time I visited Kavita she was seated on the bed against a pillow. As soon as she saw me, she started to sob. Quietly I sat at my usual place and waited for her to stop crying.

"Does it hurt? How can I help?" I did not know what else to ask.

"It would have been better if I had died in the fire."

"Don't say that. We need more women like you." I held her hand and patted it.

When she calmed down, I asked her who had selected the boy she was married to. He was her uncle's friend's son. Her parents thought that the uncle had found a good match. Within a week they were betrothed and married. Within the first month of their marriage her husband's family had begun complaining about the scant dowry she had brought. She said that her parents didn't have money even to pay for the wedding celebration. Her father worked in an Income Tax office. Her parents somehow saved as much as they could and managed the wedding feast and the dowry that included a television, refrigerator, gold jewelry and cash. As a schoolteacher she was able to contribute to offset some of the expenses and would continue to earn.

"'We have a noble lineage, we don't let our women work outside the home,' my husband declared. 'No women from this family will blemish our respectability by doing menial work'."

Kavita said she wanted to pitch in to her husband's family finances. But the freedom to work and the pleasure she derived from teaching children were denied to her.

"Teaching is not a menial job," I said, still possessing the confidence of my unmarried self.

"Why do you insist on putting our family to shame?" her mother-in-law had rebuked. *"Married women don't show themselves in public. Aren't you a virtuous woman?"*

"Was I not a virtuous woman? Wasn't my maiden family respectable?" she mumbled to herself. "On the day of the accident I overheard my mother-in-law tell my husband about this affluent family they knew. Their newly married daughter-in-law had brought a car as the dowry and they were already expecting their first grandchild. 'Your wife has neither brought a dowry worth mentioning nor is she with a child as yet,' she taunted.

"As I was frying pooris I smelled kerosene and felt him standing behind me. Suddenly my sari was aflame. I turned around as I cried for his help, but no one was there. I screamed and ran out of the kitchen then the front door crying for help. Someone must have called the ambulance because the next thing I remembered was waking up under a wire cradle."

I was sad and I was angry, more saddened than I had ever been before. My anger about the dowry tradition, the exploitation of women by the society and about the silence against this crime enraged me.

She asked, "Hasn't dowry been outlawed?"

"Yes, it is. It was outlawed in 1961. But laws do not change people's deep-set beliefs. Such laws always fail in traditional societies. Women must revolt; change has to come from the women themselves. Laws don't eradicate evil customs, people eradicate them," I said. "You get better. I'll help you find a teaching job."

She nodded and smiled for the first time.

After a few days when I returned, a smile of hope had settled on her face. Her eyes were no longer sad. Her breathing had slowed. "Once I leave here, I don't know if I will be able to walk again, literally or emotionally."

"Of course, you will! You will retrain your body. You'll reimagine yourself as the schoolteacher you were."

She nodded optimistically.

"Would you like to hear an uplifting story?"

"Yes, please."

I narrated the story I had read several months ago. The story about the young woman who on the day of her wedding refused to go through the marriage ceremony because her fiancé's family had demanded an exorbitant dowry.

Kavita listened attentively. She held my hands between hers and said, "My wholehearted thanks to you for your care, concern and encouragement. You have given me courage to go back to my parents and see if I can teach at the school I used to attend." She kissed me on my forehead and cheeks.

I promised I would visit her one last time and help her travel back to Calcutta. I had collected enough money for the ticket and some pocket money. I bid her goodbye and left with my heart singing. I couldn't return to the hospital for a few days, but she was not to be discharged until the end of that week anyway.

When I returned for one last visit, Kavita's bed was empty.

"Did the woman on bed #22 go home?" I asked a nurse I had not seen before.

"No, I'm sorry to be the one to inform you that she passed away."

"Passed away? How? She was on the way to recovery!" I said panting. "She was going to be discharged on Friday." I began to howl.

The nurse helped me sit. When I controlled myself and wiped my eyes with the handkerchief, she said, "I'm so sorry for your loss." Then lowering her voice, she added, "Sir, please don't tell anyone. I'm not sure, but we believe she was poisoned. The biopsy report will come out today."

"Poisoned!" I screamed. "How?"

The nurse put her arm around my shoulder. "We don't know."

I returned to my barsati, my haven. But the space I had loved so much felt unappealing. I had lost interest in the people who came up to their terraces for various activities. I decided to move out of the studio apartment. The place had lost its charm. When I had first arrived, it felt markedly friendlier and more open. But only now I noticed that the neighborhood was a gated community. The enclave did not only wall the streets and the homes, but it had imprisoned the minds and hearts of the orthodox and conservative people. It was overcrowded by stifling traditions and suffocating actions.

PEOPLE WE DON'T KNOW

"Jyoti, do me a favor! Save my neighbor," Mary said to her friend sitting next to her at the Thursday library knitting group.

"Why me? Why don't you save her?"

"Because you're the social worker."

"Have you known her long?" Jyoti asked.

"Not really. The couple moved into our building about a year back. She was a quiet type. But I've watched her deteriorate. Come to think of it, at first, I noticed her disheveled hair, then her mismatched clothing, then the unseasonal footwear. I didn't think too much about it until her behavior turned rash, at least behind closed doors. Now when we cross paths her head is bent. I find her absorbed in her own thoughts. I remember you once telling us about a similar case," Mary added.

"It's the husband who needs saving!" the grocer's wife chimed in. "I live next door and I hear constant yelling and pots banging. I've seen him in the corridor. He looks mild and friendly."

"Some quiet and controlled individuals can still be vicious," Jyoti said. "Have you tried to talk to her about it?"

"Not yet. When they arrived, I thought she'd be a good neighbor. You can never tell," said the butcher's wife. "You know, she's not only angry with her husband but with the whole world. I've heard her scream even at my husband's store."

The group of women huddled in around the table. At various skill levels, they used wool and cotton yarns to make sweaters, mittens, scarves, shawls and clothes in various sizes. They were retired, still energetic, healthy and generous. Everything they knitted was donated to those less fortunate. But more than knitting together each week, it was two hours to tittle-tattle.

"I guess the woman is home all day. What's her name?" Jyoti enquired.

"Dolores."

"What does her husband do?"

"I think he's some sort of salesman. He travels often."

"She's going to get hurt one day," Mary said.

"Why does she scream at your husband's shop?" Jyoti asked the butcher's wife. "He has to sell the meat, doesn't he?" Her hands rested on the table holding knitting needles.

The other women continued to knit but listened attentively.

"One day I was helping at the store when Dolores walked in," the butcher's wife said. "'*Don't hide the best meat from me! I want a good cut,*' she yelled. Everyone heard her. Now why would my husband hide meat from her? '*Those pork chops look grey,*' she complained in the same breath. '*How much for brain? Give me a pound.*' As he weighed what she wanted she changed her mind. *'No, cancel that, give me a half-pound of liver and two steaks.'* My husband rolled his eyes but got busy. *'Could you move a little faster?'* she said glaring at him. What nerve. He didn't say anything, being polite and all, you know. But she's rude and loud. She must drive her husband nuts." She yanked a length of yarn from a skein in her knitting bag as if she were pulling Dolores's hair.

"You don't really know her. Besides, she could just be a loud talker. She may be rude but keep in mind that you have no way of knowing what really goes on behind those walls."

"If she's impossible to live with, why doesn't he leave her?"

Jyoti and Anna were the only ones who had not seen the woman. They lived in a different part of town, more than an hour's drive away.

"In any case, decades of experience as a social worker doesn't give me the right to knock at someone's door and start moralizing. Does it?"

"Well, we have to do something! My husband also says she's offensive and frustrates the hell out of him," the grocer's wife said.

"Does he know them?" Jyoti asked.

"She shops at his store every week," she said, "She picks and squeezes each fruit and vegetable before bagging it and whines constantly about their color and smell. As you ladies know, my husband sells quality produce. That's why our store is popular. But each time she visits, she upsets him. He's twice her size but, like the butcher, he keeps his mouth shut since she's a regular customer."

Then she looked at Jyoti and added, "One time my husband turned to answer a quick question from another customer, and she squawked, '*Hey, you were helping me!*'"

"Maybe she has some mental issue or fierce anger. Once I read about a woman whose husband shot her because she had enraged him. They'd been married for eight years but something she said triggered him. Bang!" Mary made a gesture like a gun. "Dolores doesn't realize that one day she may lead her husband to a bang. Goodbye forever."

"My husband would shut me up if I was like her," the butcher's wife said. "Why doesn't he divorce her?"

"Someone needs to talk to her," Anna said. "Jyoti, you have to help her, not only because you're the social worker but also because you've known someone with a similar problem."

"What do you mean?" Jyoti shifted in her chair uneasily.

"Didn't you tell us once about another person like her?"

"That was my stepsister." Dolly's pretty face reeled in front of Jyoti's eyes. She hadn't seen her for years. "I'd rather not talk about her. That happened a long time ago."

"I respect that. What about that teenage girl you helped through her rough parental crisis? She seemed to be beholden to you for life. We have to help Dolores. Do something," Mary pleaded.

Jyoti was surprised by the tinge of pain Dolly's face incited in her. She had a strong urge to knock at Dolores's door and get to know her circumstances.

Yet, her experience as a social worker for forty years had taught her that no one wants to discuss their behavior with a stranger. *Someone Dolores knows, loves and trusts needs to sit with her to unravel the knots in her heart.*

As a domestic violence social worker Jyoti had helped hundreds of people—spouses, children and other emotionally troubled individuals—to change their behavior. But she was retired now. She resumed her knitting. Yet she couldn't stop thinking about Dolly.

Jyoti looked up and noticed a lull in the conversation.

She had an insight. "The banging pots and pans against the walls, how do you know it's her and not him? How do you know she's not screaming because he makes her angry?"

"He cowers out from the apartment. At times I've seen him rushing down the steps without noticing me or anyone else," Mary said. "They don't seem to have any friends. I've never seen anyone visit."

"Maybe we can invite her to join this group," Mary suggested. "What do you say, Jyoti?"

Jyoti folded her knitting, put it in her bag and thought for a few moments. "If you want me to, I'll try... but by myself, alone."

On Monday the morning temperature registered 90 degrees. The blue sky was blazing with unforgiving sunlight. Jyoti felt self-conscious standing in front of the bleached walls across the street. There was no sign of Dolores.

The edges of Jyoti's salt and pepper hair dripped sweat. Perspiration ran down her legs. Her sandaled feet felt like a pair of baking bread loaves. She mopped her brow with her scarf and slowly turned her head, first left then right. The air smelled humid.

What if Dolores accused her of being a meddling fool?

Mary's teenage daughter came out of the front door. She noticed Jyoti and walked over to her. "Hi Auntie, why are you standing here?"

"I'm waiting for Dolores." Jyoti's voice felt muffled.

"It's Monday. She'll be out of the building for her weekly shopping, eleven o'clock sharp, as usual. Nice seeing you!" She smiled and left.

Exactly at eleven a heavy-set woman walked out of the apartment building, dressed in a wrinkled pink outfit with big dark glasses and carrying a large black purse. Jyoti could see her intense red lipstick from across the street. Standing at the top step of the porch glancing this way and that, Dolores jammed a plump hand in her purse and fished out a crumpled piece of paper. Grocery list, perhaps? Dolores walked across the street and passed by Jyoti.

Jyoti was thunderstruck. No! No! It couldn't be her. Dolores was actually Dolly? Jyoti stood for a while and then turned to follow.

Dolores set off toward the marketplace. She walked to the main street and abruptly crossed in front of cars, taxis and buses, making them stop with a great squeal of brakes, horn-blowing and cursing.

As a social worker Jyoti had seen worse. She had helped broken families and traumatized individuals change and grow to be emotionally healthier. She had succeeded in helping many bitter individuals to serenity. There were moments when she felt pity for her clients. They didn't even know how actively they were destroying their own lives and aggravating everyone else around them.

Jyoti followed Dolores through the market, to the butcher's and the grocer's and to a drug store. She managed to keep her presence hidden. At one time Dolores turned around and looked at Jyoti but did not seem to recognize her.

The following day, Jyoti gathered her nerves and tapped at Dolores's door. The blaring radio inside made the door vibrate. Jyoti knocked again. Dolores was screaming at someone on the telephone. Her shrieking cut through the door.

How was the woman to hear through the blast of the radio? Jyoti knocked again with some force. No answer. She tested the knob. The door pushed open, leaving her face to face with her long-lost stepsister.

Dolores had the phone to her ear. "Where were you trained? You bum!" she yelled into the phone and slammed down the receiver. When she looked up and saw Jyoti in the doorway her eyes opened wide, her mouth aghast. She fixed an icy stare on her visitor.

"Who are you?" Dolores cried, showing her yellowed teeth. "What are you doing in my house?"

"Do you mind turning the radio down?" Jyoti asked.

Dolores slapped the device and silenced it.

She had not recognized Jyoti because she sucked greedily and jetted the smoke out through her nostrils. Aghast, Jyoti's lips moved soundlessly.

"What-do-you-want?" Dolores asked, snapping a cigarette at her lips and lighting it. "I got work to do."

Magazines were scattered on the dirty blue rug. The glass windowpanes were smudged.

"I'm Jyoti, Jyoti Tagore. Don't you remember me? I was wondering if..." A strong feeling of sadness and pity rose in Jyoti's heart.

"Oh you! The sister-I-didn't-want. No, the sister who didn't want me. How did you find me?"

"By chance, or should I say through your neighbors. But I'm so glad I found you. How are you, Dolly?" Jyoti walked closer. "Are you all right?"

"I'm fine... Go away." Dolores cocked her head through the smoke.

"Could we please just talk?"

"What is there to talk about?"

"I don't know how to begin." She remained standing. "After you left home, I discovered a framed picture of the two of us missing from my room. I didn't tell anyone. My heart hurt wondering what if I would never see you again. I was too young to help then, but I can help you now." Jyoti looked around the room. Unwashed coffee cups stood on a side table next to the recliner along with a lamp marked by dirty fingerprints. The smell of life lived in misery hovered in the room.

"I'm fine the way I am. What do you want?"

"I want to help! You don't have to live a miserable life like this. You've become a poor version of your original self, Dolly," Jyoti blurted, putting her finger to her mouth in surprise.

"Don't tell me what I am! Get out!" she shouted.

"Please! Please give me five minutes of your time to explain, my sister."

When Dolores didn't say anything Jyoti continued, "I don't know how you got this way, how you made yourself sick. Perhaps an event or someone affected you negatively, snowballing gloomy and defeatist emotions, but they seem to have succeeded in bringing you down."

Dolores kept silent.

"I can feel misery churning inside you. You must act out this misery with people you love. Do you?"

"Don't preach. Leave me alone!"

"I'm not preaching, Dolly. You may not be aware of it, but you're drowning yourself in the muddy whirlpool of your own making."

"Are you done, Jyotseena?"

"You need help. You need love. I don't know how your life turned out when you left home, but I can see your experiences have given you burns and cuts."

Dolores remained quiet and it looked like she was bursting with wrath and resentment. Before she could suddenly throw something, Jyoti began to edge toward the door.

"Bullshit! You haven't told me a damn thing!"

The sun was mercilessly burning through the dusty windowpane. Perspiration ran on the soft lines of Jyoti's face. She was surprised to remember the feeling of loneliness and boredom she had felt after Dolly left home in anger. She wanted to leave but something in her kept speaking. "We all take wrong turns at some point in our lives. And if we don't take a U-Turn or a detour, we make it worse and take our frustrations out on others."

Dolores looked at Jyoti as if she were speaking a foreign language. She squinted, tilted her head with her cigarette still smoldering in one hand.

"Without even realizing it, we make enemies." Jyoti swallowed and glanced away from her. "I don't want people to talk about you, see you gone or sick."

Dolores slowly mashed her cigarette in a dirty saucer. "Oh, you've come to save me! Where were you up until now? You meddling fool! I don't need pity. Get out!" Dolores shouted as Jyoti stumbled from the apartment.

At the next knitting group Jyoti looked distraught. Naturally, her friends were inquisitive. "You gals are not going to believe it! Dolores is indeed my long-lost stepsister. Dolly has changed beyond recognition. I don't know what to do! I tried to convince her to get out of that misery but she refused. I have no idea what else to say to her!"

Her declaration shocked the group. "Are you pulling our leg? Give us the details!" Mary said.

"Are you joking? Tell us what happened. Details, please!" Anna was too excited to knit.

"Yes, the details!" both the butcher's and grocer's wives clamored.

She gave them the details of her conversation with Dolores, and at the end added, "If only I knew what to do, how to make her talk to me."

"You'll know. You just can't give up now," someone said.

"No, you really can't!" Mary coaxed.

"I didn't realize how much I missed her when she left home. Even though she refuses any help I feel it must become my priority."

"Especially if you want her back," Anna agreed.

"If something ominous happens, you don't want it on your conscience," the butcher's wife agreed.

"My conscience is already poking at me with questions. I think I'll try again tomorrow," Jyoti said half to herself.

"You want one of us to come with you?"

"No, absolutely not."

The following day, Jyoti knocked again on the flaking green door.

"It's you again," Dolores said letting her in.

Jyoti noticed the dusty corner window was cracked open. A bit of fresh air trickled in. The floor was swept. The magazines were piled up. And no dirty cups or plates were laying around randomly.

"What do you want now?"

Jyoti braced herself. "Dolly, I didn't expect you here. I'm lucky to have found you. I've missed you. It's not my fault if your resentment with our parents forced you to leave home. Perhaps we're meant to make amends and be sisters again."

Jyoti waited for a reaction but didn't get any.

"You kicked me out yesterday. So, I've come back to see if we could talk."

"About what?" Dolores sneered.

"About what's hurting you?"

Dolores looked skeptical, nonplussed. "You don't know shit about me. I don't need your lecture."

Jyoti shifted her weight from one leg to the other. "I've helped people who didn't even know they needed help. You're preoccupied with self-destructive traits. You say I'm a meddling fool, but Dolly, believe me when I say everyone in this building has noticed your rude, crude and self-abusive behavior. They're the ones who convinced me you needed help. Why can't I help my sister?"

"People in the building gossip about me? I don't even know them! How is it their business to meddle in my personal affairs? How dare you all tell me how to live my life! Who gives them or you any authority?"

"I came to help a stranger but found my sister. I'm trained to help, so why wouldn't I help you? Before I leave, I just want to say one more thing. As a social worker I've watched many self-destructive individuals. They live miserable lives. They actually have a choice to change but they don't. They end up losing all they could have in unimaginable ways."

"How do you mean?"

"One such person lost his business overnight. Another woman was absentmindedly crossing the road and was run down by a bus. The third fed her baby on a windowsill and let the child fall. On and on it goes. You may think it's sheer coincidence, but believe me, nothing happens without our actions. Karma accumulates and turns into fate. It's hard to mend our ways because of our own past deeds. But it's harder to clear our mind of bad experiences. I can help you if you just let me."

Quite suddenly Dolores stood as if Jyoti had struck her on the head with a hammer. "And today you came to save me?"

"Not save you, Dolly... help you."

"You want me to throw you out the window?" Dolores shrieked, clenching her fists, gritting her teeth. "How dare you spy on me and come to my house!" She shoved Jyoti out the door.

Jyoti felt limp with a hollow pit in her belly, as if all her energy had been sucked out. With her shoulders stooped and legs that felt like noodles, she held the stair railing to descend. With every exhalation she tried to breathe out what she had seen and heard, and with every inhalation she tried to draw in some sanity.

Once again, Jyoti reported back to the knitting club. They encouraged her. They convinced her something was developing, and she needed to go back to heal the woman. After all, Dolores had not immediately slammed the door in Jyoti's face. At least she had listened.

Three weeks passed. Jyoti returned to convince Dolores the folly of living her present life and to revive her love. Before she knocked, she noticed the front entrance swept.

Dolores cracked open the door. Jyoti expected her to shriek, "Get out," but she didn't.

"Well?" Dolores asked.

"May I come in?"

Dolores opened the door all the way.

Jyoti stepped forward and stood behind the half open door with her hand on the knob. "Dolly, I can't let this go. I thought I would try one last time to help prevent tragedy from happening. Please work with me, Dolly. Let's make friends. Please tell me you'll change your attitude before something terrible happens."

"Who do you think you are? God?"

Jyoti was dismayed at Dolores's consistent rejection. "No, I don't think I'm God. I know you're my sister, and we can be sisters again, happier and healthier than what you are now. I'm trying my best to help!" Jyoti wiped her face with the end of her scarf. "I love you, Dolly. I want to help you!"

Suddenly a disheveled man hurried through the door, gaping it apart. He didn't see Jyoti. Sweat dripped from his chin. Great smears of perspiration stained the armpits of his shirt. "Did you pack my stuff? I'm leaving after dinner!" he barked.

"I grilled lambchops," Dolores said as gentle as a lamb. She seemed transformed. "Where are you going?"

"I can't continue this sham. Miranda's had enough of months of foolery. She's not going to wait any longer. I'm leaving you for good!"

Dolores stepped closer to him.

"No, don't touch. You disgust me!" he shouted.

Dolores dropped into the recliner.

Jyoti felt cemented to the floor.

Beggar Woman

The thrill of spending a few weeks in my husband's city of birth and childhood excited me each time we arrived in New Delhi. The capital enticed me with its subtle scent of amaltas trees lining the streets with their deep orange blossoms. I could smell the white jasmine even before my husband and I landed at the Indira Gandhi International Airport.

Women as well as girls wore vibrant saris and salwar-kameez suits, and men dressed in kurta-pajama outfits. The jasmine circlets cascading down girls' long braids and circling around the women's chignons matched the color of the men's white clothing.

In three years, this sensuous metropolis hadn't changed. The air was intense, tangy, passionate, so different from my home in Pittsburgh, Pennsylvania, where I was raised by parents of Indian heritage. Once again, I was eager to immerse myself in the city. This time I would come to know the people better. I wanted to do something good, even if only a single altruistic act. I strengthened my resolve before landing at the airport.

During my last visit, I had wandered the local art galleries alone, pacing crowded craft stores, bargaining for outfits, jewelry and gifts for my American friends. And in the evenings with my husband, we had sauntered through the historic monuments of Old Delhi and New Delhi and savored lavish meals.

Once back in our Pittsburgh home, I had spread my loot on the bed. Owning those things did not stop my craving for more. I hung my new outfits in the overstuffed closet and added new footwear to the racks already lined with sandals and shoes. But an uneasy emptiness spread through my mind as I stored the new garnet necklace, bracelet, bangle and ring set in the jewelry box next to pieces I had never even worn once. A feeling of emptiness spread through me and lingered for days if not weeks after my last trip.

I sat at the edge of the bed and closed my eyes. Images of beggars flashed in front of my eyes: men's unmatched tattered shirts and pajamas yellowed with age and browned with dirt. The sight of begging women's disheveled and dry hair visible from the holes of their unwashed scarves, the hands, with dry skin and dirty nails, asking for a coin to fill their hungry bellies made me sick. After a day of reflection and mostly guilt something in me said, "*Even if all your desires are fulfilled, your hankering will never stop. Fiend of craving is bound to gulp you alive one day!*" I resolved to give away most of the treasure I had accumulated. Within days, I had gifted most of it to friends and relatives.

This time it was going to be different. I would fill my empty heart with the joy of generosity and kindness. Seated in the back of a taxi I smiled to my husband. Bumper to bumper cars, bicycles, two-seaters, four-seaters and pedestrians shared the road with stray dogs and an occasional cow grazing alongside. No one followed lanes. Paper and blue and pink plastic bags littered the roadside, fluttering in the slow wind. I thought of our home in America, impeccably clean. Except for a touch of the bouquet from a candle I light every morning, or the aroma of the food cooking in mustard oil and hot spices several evenings a week, the house is mostly odorless as are the homes of friends and distant families. Even neighborhood streets and the malls where I shop have no odors.

My attention was brought back to the present by a young girl selling jasmine circlets for embellishing long braids and chignons. I asked the taxi driver to stop just long enough for me to buy one. As I rolled down the window its sweet whiff floated in. "Twenty rupees," the flower girl said. *That's thirty cents*, I calculated in my head. I handed her a fifty-rupee note and said she could keep the change. She stepped back with a smile and folded her hands in gratitude.

I inhaled the heavenly scent and let the circlet lay in my hand. The stink of urine drifted in before I rolled up the window. Our taxi picked up speed. Two men dressed in white riding on a two-wheeler passed by. Our driver honked at those who crossed through traffic even where there were no stop lights. A woman draped in a bright yellow sari rode a motorbike with a girl in a school outfit seated behind her. The girl waved at me. I waved back as the babble of honking high-pitched horns and the smell of diesel fumes and burning kerosene pierced the air.

At a traffic light the taxi came to a sudden stop. A beggar girl, not more than twelve, knocked at my window. She pointed to her mouth with her five fingers touching. "I am hungry. Give me some *paisa*, mother! God bless you, mother. Give me some *paisa*!"

"Madam, don't open the window!" Before the taxi driver finished warning I had already rolled it down, my hand on the clutch of my purse. The sound of some Bollywood song on a radio flooded in.

"That's okay!" I said looking at my husband who nodded in agreement. "A girl so young shouldn't be hungry."

I handed a fifty-rupee note to her and rolled up the windowpane.

Within no time a swarm of beggar children appeared at the window.

"Madam, hungry!"

"Mother, give me a *paisa*!"

"Madam, please!"

"What did I say?" the taxi driver rebuked.

The traffic light turned green and he sped up until he had to pause and wait for a guard to open the main iron gate of Royal Rajdhani Hotel. A high wall that ended at the top with glass shards and metal blades and barbed wire surrounded the building's grounds. About ten feet away a beggar woman, carrying an infant wrapped in rags, conjured up from thin air.

She stepped closer. "*De datta ke nam*! Give in the name of God! Have pity, *memsahib*! My baby is hungry! My breasts are dry. I haven't eaten for days. Please, in the name of God, give me a *rupee*! Have pity!"

I pulled out the remaining bills and coins in my clutch purse and was about to hand them over. I looked into her eyes as she was looking into mine. She looked familiar. I noticed the hairy mole in the middle of her forehead. A small cry escaped my throat and the coins spilled out of my hand. As if in panic, the beggar woman hurriedly collected them and scuttled away. I was stunned.

The opening gate grated against the concrete. Our taxi drove past the guard and stopped at the main entrance. My husband paid the driver. An attendant picked up our luggage and we followed him to the reception desk.

"What's the matter?" my husband asked as we walked inside.

I was dumbfounded. I did not reply. A smiling concierge asked me how I was. I fumbled for an answer.

"What's wrong? What happened out there?" my husband asked.

"Did you see that?" I replied.

"What? The beggar? You will see worse. Don't let it get to you."

"The same woman, the same baby just shriveled and shrunk." My voice was but a murmur.

"The same what?"

"The same woman," I said, my lips trembling. "Now I remember. The same woman who shoved a baby in our faces three years ago."

"Oh, come on," he said. "You are jet lagged. All wretched beggars look the same—especially their infants. Come on, let's check in."

"You check us in. I'll be back." I followed the long and isolated driveway and peeked through the bars of the gate to look for her. But she had vanished, off to some other street, some other hotel.

I returned to the front desk, but I could not get rid of the woman's face, the big hairy mole, the baby. The panic in her expression and the image of the shrunken tiny head haunted me. I remembered those enticing eyes and her dirt covered lips. In three years, her face had weathered a decade, the mole now bigger and hairier.

Who was she? What circumstances had forced her to beg? The infant couldn't be the same. What happened to that baby? Would things ever change for her? Once a beggar always a beggar? Where does she go when nights are freezing cold or scorching hot? What does she feed her children?

A few days later at High Tea in the hotel's Rose Garden my husband caught me brooding. I was neither eating my favorite cucumber and Amul cheese sandwich nor munching on spiced cashew nuts.

"Not the beggar woman again? Eat something!" he said.

"I don't feel like it. And yes, the beggar woman."

The room's ambiance tried to transport me to Mughal Gardens in the valley of Kashmir. Soothing santoor music joined water cascading in a fountain, while red rose petals floated at its base. The music and the setting did their best to pull me out of my unease.

My husband was used to seeing beggars. They were at every place we visited. Whenever I asked how one got adjusted to the presence of the poor living in misery right next to the high mansion walls, he would answer, "Eventually we all get used to them."

My expression must have silently repeated the same question. He kissed my hand and added, "If you had been raised in this country, you too would have learned to accept these contrasts." He took a bite of a cheese and cucumber sandwich.

Perhaps he was right. Born in New Delhi, he had emigrated to the United States after college. I was born in the United States, however, and raised in comparative luxury. Exotic India was a land of extremes; shabbily built mud huts stood in the shadow of palatial houses. High walls with iron gates and manicured gardens separated the two worlds. People drove their Mercedes and Impalas through shanty towns without ever giving these contrasts a second thought.

"Don't you feel guilty?" I asked. "Doesn't it cause you emotional discomfort? How can you enjoy this sandwich?"

"We've half a million beggars in the country— some richer than you and I. I'm not making this up, believe me," he said. "How many times am I going to feel pity or guilt? Don't be silly now. Let's enjoy ourselves."

"I just can't get rid of her stare, her gaze. There is something about that woman I can't let go."

"If you don't get out of this mood, you'll spoil the fun we can have together each evening." He refilled my cup with my favorite Darjeeling tea and offered me a sandwich. "You have been talking and thinking about this woman since the moment we landed. For the first time we have decided not to visit my relatives so we can see the city like tourists. Let's do that! I do my work in the mornings, so you can do what you want then—write, visit art galleries or museums or shop at the Janpath market. Afternoons and evenings, we spend together. Okay?"

"Have I been so obsessed?"

"You know this woman could be any beggar. They all look the same. You can't worry about them all."

"True... true..." and I dropped the conversation.

But the guilt and agitation refused to leave. During the morning hours while my husband went about importing handicrafts, I set out to find her. I stayed close to the hotel and strolled the roads and zigzagging lanes. On busy street crossings, I bumped into several beggars seated next to signal light crossings, shaking their cups, making noise with a few coins to attract attention. Not far from them a sweet looking boy performed a popular film tune on ektara, a one-string instrument. On the other end of the street, a man sang to the beat of a damaru held in one hand, and with the other he made a monkey dance by gently tugging a rope tied to its neck. Modest means of earning livelihoods. I could see how they felt pride in their work while earning mere coins from their talents.

More than ever, I was determined to find the woman and help her in any way I could. I stopped and gazed at every beggar woman who carried a child. But I could not find her. After a couple of days, I realized my husband was right. There were thousands who needed saving.

Before returning to my room, I stopped at the guard shack. "A beggar woman lurks here at the front gate. Have you seen her lately?"

"There are many. I don't know which one you are asking about," the guard replied.

"The woman with a hairy mole on her forehead."

"Oh, her!"

"Has she been begging here long?"

"At least eight years. She was here before I came."

"Do you know her name?"

"*Bikharan*, the beggar woman, is how we know her. But I've also heard her to be Sheela? Let me think... Shama? Shanna? Sure, Shama. Why do you ask?"

"Do you know anything about her baby?"

The attendant's nose crinkled. "No, Madam. I don't go near them. They keep themselves in a dreadful condition to incite pity. They do not bathe or even clean their faces. The fouler the better," he laughed.

I smiled awkwardly. "So, you haven't seen her infant?"

"I always avert my gaze if I can."

I passed him a hundred-rupee note. "If you see her would you call my room #815?"

"Certainly."

I turned to go back inside but then I remembered. "One more thing," I said to the attendant.

"Yes, Madam."

"How does she enter the front gate? How does she manage to beg right in front of the hotel?"

"She has her ways."

"And no one shoos her away?"

"Something about this one... What can I say? Even the hotel manager doesn't object much. She comes and leaves."

For the next few days wherever we walked, rode buses, drove in taxis, I looked around for the beggar woman without my husband noticing.

And then one day at dusk as we came out of a nearby movie theater, turned a corner munching aromatic sweet pan, this woman shoved a bundle in our faces and cried in Hindi, the language I too spoke, "*De data ke nam!* Give in the name of God! Oh, *memsahib*, have mercy! Help my baby and me..." She stopped. Her eyes met mine. She spun around, let a fearful cry from her mouth and ran.

I gave chase, gathering my breath and yelling, "*Thehro*! Stop!"

She began to run faster.

"*Ruko*! Wait!" I tried to keep up with her.

She ran still faster. I lost her. She vanished.

I slowed and waited for my husband to join me.

"Is that her?" he sounded excited, his emotion resonating with mine.

We walked about a mile and turned the corner toward a market. The aroma of masala tea wafted from a street stall. There at one table sat the beggar woman raising a cup of tea to her lips. Her bundle of joy was placed on the chair next to her.

I nudged my husband with an elbow and pointed to her with my gaze. We sat several tables away. My heart pounded. He ordered two masala teas. I sipped mine until the pace of my heart slowed. Then I got up and walked to her table.

"Shama."

At my voice the woman jerked. Tea sprayed from her mouth and she fell into a spasm of shocked coughing, then thumped the bundle of swaddling clothes.

"How old is your baby?" I asked realizing now that there was no baby.

Instead there was a hush.

"How do you know my name? Why are you following me?" Her voice seemed wounded. "What do you want from a wretched beggar woman?"

I patted her back. "It's all right," I said. "Consider me a friend."

She raised the bundle of swaddling clothes, looked up at me and blurted again, "What do you want?"

"Can I sit down? I want to help you."

She relaxed and lay back the bundle on the chair facing away from me. She nodded and looked at me with suspicion.

My face must have looked sympathetic because the tone of her voice turned friendly. "That's kind of you," she said. "The way you have been following me I thought you wanted to report me to the police. The guard at the hotel said you were looking for me. What do you want?"

"First, I would like to know your story. That's a ragdoll with a real looking face. Isn't it?"

"What do you think?"

"I don't know. I've been wondering."

"It could be a baby boy. But what do you care?"

"Are you his mother?"

She turned away, gently thumping the bundle and mumbling something.

"What? What did you say?" I asked.

"Sometimes I carry an infant, sometimes a bundle of rags!" She turned to me. "Today is the ragdoll day. My baby boy is sick at home."

"I'm so sorry to hear this."

"Don't feel sorry for me. I have been doing this for ten years. This is my living. I have been taking my babies out, until they grow up and start begging themselves."

"Why do you do this? Why do you let your children beg?"

"Because I was *born* into it. My father was a beggar and his father before him. As soon as I could talk, my father jabbed his fingers in my ribs and said, 'Time to start, girl! Play an ektara, shake a cup, learn to dance, teach a monkey tricks, the sooner the better'."

"He encouraged you to beg?"

"Why not? I earn more money than my cousin who is the principal's clerk in a school, or his father who is a peon in a government office. Many of the people I know are domestic servants. Now that is as humiliating as it can get. But me? I am my own boss. My mother did not beg; she stayed home. One day my father ran away with another woman. Mother washed her sorrows away in her tears while she begged with me beside her. One day as we happened to pass by a big hotel, we saw a group of foreigners coming down from a tourist bus. To our surprise they called us and gave to us unasked. Since then we have refined our way of begging and we make double what domestic servants make. We know the bus schedules, the days and times they arrive. Carrying my infants, real or imaginary, was my mother's idea."

"Hmmm," I said aghast.

"No one before you has noticed me or looked right into my eyes. Thousands and thousands come. They give and then shoo us away. No one before you looked at me the way you did the other day."

"What about the locals?"

"They consider begging a disease. And they hate us for it."

"Do the police know or harass you?"

"They know about us but seem indifferent."

There was a long pause.

A door hinge shrieked like a soul in torment as someone went out. In the moments of silence that followed I could hear the pitter-patter of rain. Unnoticed, my husband had moved to a closer table.

"What I can't understand is how you got the courage to hold out your hand to beg for the first time. Didn't you feel humiliated?"

"Isn't that what all people are trying to do?" she asked rhetorically. "I have skills to beg and I use them. It is just like any other businessman selling his skills or goods."

"Aren't you cheating people?"

"I'm not cheating, *behen* sister! People believe they earn spiritual merit by giving. Some have so much money they try to wash off their guilt and sins by giving alms to us poor folks. I use those sentiments in my favor. People feel good about themselves if they give away a little. Some feel pity, even gratitude at the expense of our plight. They feel good... and we make money."

I continued to listen attentively, searching her face. This emboldened her.

"They may wince away their noses, yet they give, more than a pittance. Besides, *bhagvan* has given all foreigners more riches than they can spend in this lifetime. They look at me and the baby and feel guilty or blessed or... whatever they feel for having so much. The dirtier I am, the more I act as a suffering destitute mother, the guiltier and more blessed they feel. Without fail they generously open their purses."

At that moment, I realized it was not only the hairy mole that had caught my attention years ago, but also the unforgettable glint in her eyes. Now I saw it again. What a fool I had been! "But begging is not good for you, is it?"

"What is so bad about begging? I don't steal. I don't harass. I'm not a pickpocket. People give to me willingly. Do you see the difference?"

I said nothing.

"The best kept secret for begging is Royal Rajdhani Hotel," she continued with a smile.

"And for fear of being spotted you have been keeping away from the hotel?" I asked.

"Yes. I was afraid you might report me to the police." She picked up the bundle and stood. "A group of American tourists is arriving there tonight."

My husband was sipping his second cup of tea nearby. The beggar woman placed her bundle on his table and touched her palms in greeting. The three of us walked through the drizzle toward the hotel.

At that late hour, mobs of people were coming in from the airport. There was a long line at the receptionist's desk.

Before I left, I had to ask her, "Is this the first time ever?"

"What? That a tourist found me out?"

"Yes."

"You have a sharp eye," she said.

"I'm a writer."

"You won't write about me. Would you?"

"No," I answered. "At least not for many years." (It has been a decade since. She would forgive me now.)

We were a hundred feet from the hotel. I pulled out a 5000 rupee note, about a hundred dollars, from my purse and offered it to her. "From a sister."

"God bless you," she said and accepted my gift.

"Take care of yourself," I answered.

"In a year I'll save enough for us to return to my village."

"Us?"

"Oh, my son!" She turned and pointed to a young man on a bicycle, texting on his phone. "He is a college student. Every evening he waits for me to give me a ride home. Pray for me, *behen*!"

I squeezed her hand and walked quickly to the hotel entrance where airport buses and taxis overflowed with international tourists.

Behind me I heard the beggar woman, her voice dramatically altered. I turned and saw her trot forward holding out a cup in her hand.

"*Memsahib, de datta ken nam*! Give in the name of God. Have pity, *memsahib*!" she cried.

I heard the coins ring in her cup as more cars came. People spun down their car windows as the beggar woman cried, "*De datta ken nam, memsahib*! My babies are hungry! My breasts are dry. I haven't eaten for days. What am I going to feed them? Please in the name of God give me a *rupee*! Have pity!"

With mixed feelings of sorrow and goodness I followed my husband to the top step, and then to the elevator and into our room.

"You are something, my love!"

I stood on my toes and kissed his cheek as my heart filled with the joy of well-being and generosity.

Unfulfilled Dream

From the moment my daughter Kala became conscious of her surroundings I carried her to places where she was exposed to art, museums, galleries, and craft shows. I carried her in a baby sling close to my heart, then in a baby carrier on my back, later pushing her in a stroller through exhibition halls. And when she began to walk, we held hands and strolled through the parks and galleries filled with artwork. At home with Kala seated on my lap, I flipped through pages of illustrated children's books, books about world art and individual artists and talked to her about colors, textures, shapes, lines and forms.

Her own first works were stick figures of me, her dad, and herself in an empty space. These were followed by drawings titled "My Family" with three of us inside the house, at the mall, at the zoo. She was so good with details; ten lines graced each hand, the sofa and the television, even flowers posed in a vase. She was beautiful, gifted and imaginative. Her future was filled with possibilities. There was no reason why she couldn't blossom into a great artist.

Kala was seven when one day as she dabbled with a brush and jars of poster paints, I said to my husband, "Look how well she paints!" He didn't look up. But I was excited. I walked over to the sofa where he was seated, stood behind him and gently turned his chin in the direction where our daughter labored.

He watched her dab orange pigment and apply new paint next to earlier red strokes. She followed the yellow with blue, turning it green, then orange, red, blue until the shape turned muddy purple.

"What's the big deal? All seven-year-olds paint this way," he said turning back to his reading.

"There is something amazing about her use of basic colors!"

"Looks like a big mess to me," he muttered without a second glance.

At the end of fourth grade, Kala brought a painting home from school and held it up for me to see. "Great job! Who is it?"

"Me."

"I love it!" I turned to my husband and said, "Look at her self-portrait. She is so talented. I can't wait for her to grow up and become a great artist."

He nodded then turned to her. "Come here, give me a hug." They hugged. But he didn't say a word about her painting.

"Don't you agree?" I asked.

"About what?"

"About her talent."

"My agreeing or disagreeing is meaningless."

As she grew, her interest in art began to fade. Thirteen-year-old Kala's drawings and paintings did not garner high merit. But *all* her artwork couldn't be excellent, could it? Her middle school had art class as part of their curriculum. I was excited to hear that. But she was not. In high school she continued to study art "for my sake," she often reminded me.

By the time Kala was fifteen she lived in a world of her own. Her attitude changed. A distance grew between us. But her relationship with her father developed into a warm friendship. One day I saw her mouthing, "Practice, practice, practice!" to her father, mimicking me. Their eyes met. Both giggled. I was hurt.

Kala was normally gentle with a quiet voice. She began to avoid eye contact with me and on rare occasions would burst into temper tantrums. I regarded her over-sensitive temperament shift as growing pains. During her senior year there were days when she did not paint at all, or even sketch, making me nervous.

Having read and reread the biographies and autobiographies of world-famous artists that I had purchased for her, I realized that almost all the role models those books presented were emotionally intense, unpredictable in their behavior, and they were temperamental. What did they do with their feelings and emotions? They poured the tides of passion into their art. There were so many instances when they too did not create for long durations. So what if Kala didn't paint when she was not in the mood? I came to realize this as characteristic of a budding artist.

When Kala casually commented that she had started to take pleasure in her high school art class, I exhaled a sigh of relief. "But why doesn't she talk much or pay attention to her appearance? She looks unkempt," I confided in my husband.

"Perhaps the reason for her silence, her tantrums, is that you are always nagging her about something or other that has to do with art... She may or may not want to continue."

I felt a twinge of losing a dream.

He continued. "As for her not talking much, why bother? You make up for her lack of words."

He had said this in mirth, yet I did not appreciate his humor. He noticed that I was not pleased. "Jokes aside, she writes quite well, even in Spanish. Why do you insist upon her focusing on art?"

"How do you know about her writing?" I felt kind of left out.

"Her grades in language arts and Spanish are excellent."

One day I saw Kala holding a stack of college applications. I smiled and wished her luck. Later, while in the middle of filling them out, she declared, "My first choice is to major in Spanish and minor in English and art. I love the Spanish language."

I could hear my heartbeat. "But you are talented in art!" I blurted.

"You choose, darling," her father butted in. "If you want to major in Spanish then you should major in Spanish."

My husband believed that if Kala became an artist, she would have a hard life. He insisted we should let her choose her major.

Choose? Isn't it the parents' responsibility to gently push the child toward a desired path—the path they are skilled in—and make sure they work hard at it? Isn't talent cultivated by training and practice? Her father disagreed with me on all accounts. But I persevered. I continued to mold her into a life most suitable to her.

Fortunately, Kala was accepted at a state school with a strong art department. The tuition was not exorbitant, but I would have to work to cover expenses for lodging and the additional cost of art material. Kala reluctantly agreed to major in art and minor in Spanish. I searched for a job and was hired as a bank teller. I didn't have the heart to tell her that I was not working to pay for a Spanish minor.

On a Saturday afternoon, having cleaned the house the whole morning, I closed our bedroom door and lay down to take a long after-lunch nap. I was woken with a jolt when Kala burst into our bedroom. "Mom, the monthly art expenses have increased. Materials cost too much. I can't manage with what you give me."

My body was still tired. My mind disoriented. "At least say hello." What was wrong with her? In addition to distancing from me, her behavior was changing, her manners deteriorating.

She sat at the edge of my bed and explained that in the second semester of the sophomore year the students were expected to use oil paints on canvas. Oil brushes, oil paints, stretched canvasses, all that was expensive.

Her grades were average but her demands continued to increase. In the second semester of junior year Kala claimed the class was expected to travel around the country to visit national museums and historic art sites. Some we catered to, some we refused. It was not that I did not want her to travel and expand and enrich her art experiences; it was that we didn't have extra savings to spare. She threw a couple of tantrums and we succumbed.

Before the start of her final year, Kala's report card showed that she had accumulated more credits in Spanish than art. It hurt my ego. I avoided confronting her in hopes that she would make up the remaining credits through her final portfolio.

Before the semester ended Kala came home with her suitcase and art paraphernalia. A surprise visit?

"Isn't it early for you to be home? Are you done with final exams?" I hoped to God she had not come home for good, before finishing the first term of her senior year.

"Oh, I did the work, but I don't think I'll go back to college."

"But why? Only one semester left for you to graduate."

"I feel suffocated, Mom. Already too many years wasted."

"What? Wasted!" Unable to contain myself I screamed.

She did not respond. She carried her easel and paintbox and walked to her room.

Why can't she be like normal people with normal reactions?

I carried the suitcase to her room. "Don't think about returning now. The final year is always fun. It's summer break anyway. By September you'll be ready to return," I said partly to myself and partly to her.

"No matter what you say, Mom, I'm not finishing the art degree." Her chilling words gave me shivers. She said she hated the atmosphere at the art college. For some reason the university town "stultified" her, blocked her. "After all, Gauguin went to Tahiti; Mary Cassatt went to Paris. Van Gogh made his best works in Arles. Creativity flourishes away from congestion and familiarity. The uninspiring routine deadens imagination."

I wanted to shout, say something, but her body language warned me against it.

My husband and I accepted her decision as it had come at a comparatively convenient time, but both of us felt uneasy about Kala's future. Why would she abruptly give up?

"This is the result of your desire to turn her into an artist."

"My desire! What about your responsibility in this whole scenario?"

"Well, if she were a boy, she would have helped me with all the chores I do—mow the lawn, trim the bushes, clean the car. I'd have made a boy sweat. But you didn't teach anything to this girl. Wasn't it your responsibility to insist that she sweep and mop the floors and dust the furniture? Why did you discourage her from cooking and cleaning? I don't know what's gotten into you. You keep insisting that she spend all her time doing artwork."

I didn't know how to respond.

Then he added, "If she were a boy, I would have encouraged her to study a major that would get her a paying job."

My husband learned about an art camp. The ad boasted of two world-renowned artists as teachers. Students could stay for six months and earn one semester's worth of college credit. I begged Kala to join. When she agreed I was so excited that I cried.

The camp was not exorbitantly priced. A wealthy art connoisseur had donated the Mansion in the Woods, and students could use the studio and lodge in the house. They were required to submit paintings made under the tutelage of the teachers but had to pay for their own food and help maintain the grounds.

I was in the kitchen unloading the dishwasher when Kala came home. "Back again! What are you doing here?" I pretended to be firm.

My heart bled as I stared at my daughter, weary, unsure of herself, carrying her easel and a box of art material, suitcase at her feet. "Why didn't you call? I'd have cooked a nice dinner for you." I presumed she was home for just one night. It had only been four weeks since she left for camp.

Wrinkles creased her eyes, like an unfolded dress pushed to the back of a drawer. "Mom, they use resident artists as manual workers. Can you believe that?"

"But that was one of the conditions for admission, remember?"

"I do! But the 'work' they want us to do is to clean bathroom floors and toilets, clean the dirty dishes, mow the lawn, trim the shrubs. I just can't take it anymore." Her lips curled then she turned her back to me to pick up her suitcase.

"What can't you take anymore? Tell me?" I wanted to hold her tight. I wanted her to feel close to me the way we did when she was younger, when we did art-related things together. But she jerked away from my touch.

I hardly recognized her. Some strands of hair were dyed bright pink. She had a nose ring and thick wooden sticks in her earlobes. After she removed her leather boots and leather jacket, I saw words written on the back of her t-shirt in a language I could not read. In the same script was a tattoo on the nape of her neck. I was too afraid to ask what it meant.

"Don't you want to finish the rest of the credits for your art degree?"

"Back off, Mom! You never ask me what I want, if I even like what I do. You keep dragging me along on your dream."

"Don't you like to paint?"

"Not really."

"Did you ever?" I didn't want to hear the answer, so I continued, "Why not finish the rest of your credits and at least get your degree?" My heart was breaking.

"Are you listening to me, Mother? I hate what I'm doing!"

"You cannot stay home!" I put my foot down. "Either finish your senior year or find a job."

"Sheer waste of time! How can you or Dad, especially you, tie me down to some nine-to-five job?" Before I could complete my sentence, she turned and glared at me. "Leave me alone! Why are you bent upon destroying my life! Haven't you done enough!"

"*Destroying my life?*" I thought I was in a nightmare. No, I was not. Kala was right in front of me telling me that I had ruined her life. I was dumbstruck.

At that moment her father walked in. His face flushed. He yelled, "Leave her alone!"

He asked Kala to sit at the breakfast table. She sat. He turned to me. "Isn't it time that you came to your senses? What is this obsession of yours? And why are you forcing it upon her?"

At that very moment my dream shattered. The glass castle of my desire, conjured up for so many years, crumbled onto the floor. Its shards mocked me. All hope was lost. Yes, I was obsessed, obsessed for her to become a famous artist.

But I found myself at a loss for words. I was too embarrassed to confess that I myself had a full-fledged dream of becoming an artist. I had great awe and admiration for the masters of European Renaissance paintings and Indian miniatures. I would have loved to paint like Leonardo da Vinci or Botticelli. I dreamed of making miniatures like Rajasthani and Mughal artists. But before I was old enough to attend art school I was betrothed, married and pregnant within three months. I couldn't change my past... but if Kala succeeded, I'd be reborn. All these years, I had carried that desire in my heart like I carried Kala in my womb.

I dreamed to fulfill my ambition through my daughter. What was wrong with that? I didn't want her or her father to jeopardize my secret dream. Yet, I kept my lips sealed. I finished loading the dishwasher and refused to respond to their outbursts.

A few weeks later Kala declared she wanted to go back to school to finish her senior year. She communicated this to me through her father. My heart broken and having been burnt before, I didn't get excited. I wasn't responsible for her failures and unfinished projects. Was I? She left as unceremoniously as she had arrived.

While Kala was away at school, I attended a poetry reading. That evening's guest was neither unkempt nor scruffy. He wore thick-rimmed glasses and an old-fashioned suit. He didn't look artsy at all. Friendly and polite, he told the audience that the life of artists, poets and most creative minds was not easy. The number of artists who could make a living from their art was miniscule. But they needed to make a living. "My poems can't feed me or put a roof over my head. I write during the day and work at nights. A job is essential. T.S. Eliot worked in an office, Theodore Mosley in a post office..." So and so was a schoolteacher, and so and so worked as an office secretary, he'd explained.

He concluded his talk by saying, "Anyone can learn to be a poet, an artist, a musician if you have passion, motivation and perseverance for it. But you need a job."

Inspired by his pep talk, I too began to make pencil drawings when no one was home. I sketched and drew at the kitchen table. I copied figures and faces and landscapes from old family photos and the magazines I had subscribed to for Kala. Each drawing pad I completed I hid in the closet behind my winter clothing.

In a few months, I gathered courage to paint. I had no way of knowing if they were good or bad. I was not an artist, so how could I judge my own work? However, the more I painted the happier I felt. With each painting, Kala's dark betrayal washed off canvas by canvas until I felt free of my attachment. I felt unchained from her. It often made me hum and smile.

Kala telephoned her father. I panged for her attention and affection. He said I had so badly bruised her that she did not want to talk to me. Maybe next time. My artwork helped pull me from the betrayal I felt. The more deeply I painted, the better my days unfurled.

One evening my head ached so much that I excused myself from dinner and went to bed early. I woke with hunger pangs to the aroma of coffee wafting from the kitchen.

My husband greeted me with a kiss. "Kala came home late last night!"

"She did? Oh, I can't wait to see her! Should I wake her?"

"She said she wanted to sleep in."

"Did she complete her degree?" I almost shouted.

"Yes and no."

"Did she or did she not?" I asked.

"For you the answer is yes and no. Look what she left for you to see." He beamed, pointing to two pieces of paper on the table, their reverse side visible.

I turned over the sturdier one. It was a degree in Honors Spanish, *cum laude*. The other was an acceptance letter to a job teaching Spanish at our community college.

Multi-cultural

A Chance Meeting

Two winters ago, my general manager instructed me to represent our drug manufacturing company at the annual International Pharmaceutical Conference in my city, New Delhi. The first morning, I sat next to a Japanese delegate. We heard a talk about a new drug for Alzheimer's made from an amalgamation of Indian turmeric roots and other chemicals, supported by human brain scans pre- and post-therapy.

Hours passed quickly, and it was time to stretch our legs. The Japanese delegate turned to me and smiled. I folded my palms. "I'm Mohan Bhargav." The five-foot man introduced himself as Tetsu Ishadate and bowed low, giving me a glimpse of salt and pepper hair. I asked if this was his first trip to India. In broken English, he replied on two previous visits he had visited Mumbai, Bangalore and Calcutta but never New Delhi.

At lunch, I saw Ishadate seated with delegates from other countries. "May I join you?" He pointed to an empty chair next to him, and I sat down.

He savored each dish that was served, asking its Hindi name and if I thought it was tasty.

"Paneer pulao, aloo chole, gobi... Not as tasty as homemade," I said.

"Are you a good cook?" someone from the group asked.

"Not me, but my mother is."

During our lunch conversations, I discovered that Ishadate was keen on Indian architecture. He said he planned to stay an extra day to visit local historic monuments. He also wanted to know about my job and family. I told him I had been working for my current employer since graduating from Delhi University five years earlier, and that recently I had purchased a two-bedroom flat where I lived with my mother. As we ate, several other Japanese delegates came over to say hello and greeted him as Professor Ishadate.

On the second day of the conference, I asked the professor if he slept well. He said he felt well rested and ready to hear about more groundbreaking research and innovative drugs being introduced to the market. That day was similar to the previous, positively affirming the future of pharmaceutical companies, filled with new information about drugs claiming to cure diseases. I took meticulous notes because I would be required to present these to my boss about what I'd learned.

Afterward, Professor Ishadate asked if I could recommend a tour guide for his last day in India.

"But you can't see everything in one day," I exclaimed.

"Only important buildings," he said. "Next time, visit more."

"What about the three evenings between now and then? Visit one monument each evening, then on the last day, see the remaining ones. That way, you can fit in all the important sites within the time you have."

"Hmm—tour guide meet me in the evenings?"

"I'll take you around," I offered. For some reason, I felt like spending more time with him.

Ishadate was taken aback. "Thank you, but no trouble for you!"

"No trouble at all! How many times in my life will I get a chance to be a Japanese professor's tour guide?"

"Yah… yah… thank you very much!" He bowed several times and laughed heartily.

For the next three evenings, he sat on the backseat of my Honda scooter as I drove him to see the local monuments. It was June and the temperature hovered between 105-110 degrees Fahrenheit. Although the evenings were a few degrees cooler, hot wind blew our hair and the sun scorched our scalps.

The first evening we visited Qutab Minar, the second-tallest freestanding tower in all of India. Constructed in 1192, its red sandstone is inlaid with white sandstone decorations. The professor looked up at the tower from the ground, admiring its outer wall decorated in arabesque style with quotes from the Quran.

"Very, very elegant!" he said. He took pictures and was impressed by how the wide base narrowed at the peak. Then, together, we climbed the 379 spiraling stairs to the top of the tower. For his age, he ascended energetically. We admired the panoramic view of South Delhi, which looked Lilliputian from a height of 240 feet.

The second evening I drove him to Humayun's Tomb, the garden-tomb of the first Mughal emperor. Designed by a Persian architect, it was commissioned by Humayun's widow, Empress Bega Begum, in 1569. Ishadate pointed out that the exclusive use of red sandstone gave the monument an aristocratic look, and yet its geometric symmetry imparted serenity. I translated signs and boards written in Hindi. In return, I received lessons in aesthetics. Our sightseeing together seemed like a good bargain.

After only two evenings, I felt our acquaintance had developed into a friendship. I offered to treat the professor to sugarcane juice, a local drink, and he agreed. At the street vendor's stall, he drank a few sips to please me, but I could see he did not like it. Too sweet for the Japanese, who do not include desserts with their meals, I supposed. So instead I drove us to a place for green coconuts. This time he found the juice refreshing and relished its flavor. Then he half-joked that a spicy meal following that drink would be most enjoyable.

"I didn't think you would like spicy food."

"Why?" He raised his brows.

"Because Japanese food is so mild."

"Reason I like spicy," he laughed.

On the third and last evening of the conference, we went to Jantar Mantar Park, a Hindu monument with thirteen astronomical structures. Built in 1724 by a Hindu maharaja, Jai Singh II, the primary purpose of the observatory was to compile astronomical tables and to predict the movements of the sun, moon, and planets. Professor Ishadate made me pose in front of Samrat Yantra, a sundial seventy feet high, 114 feet long, and ten feet thick. He wanted to photograph its 128-foot hypotenuse, which parallels the earth's axis and points toward the North Pole. Then we posed together and let a passerby take our picture.

We made our way to Misra Yantra, the monument that determines the shortest and longest days of the year. It indicates the exact moment noon occurs in various cities and locations, regardless of their distance from New Delhi. "Remarkable, quite remarkable," he said and asked me to take his picture in front of it.

His keen interest in Indian architecture and admiration for the monuments we visited made me ask him about Japanese Zen temples. I had glanced at them in books and been intrigued by the Zen gardener's ability to merge his skill with nature and how natural beauty was maintained and manicured for a unique aesthetic.

"Nature and gardener come together," he said.

Did he mean that the gardener skillfully cultivated natural beauty? Were they gardens or temples? I asked. He said they were the places where time stopped. "Me and nature, one," he declared. "Harmony between people and nature. Walk in garden, drink tea." He looked at my confused expression, and added, "You visit garden and know better!"

I could not experience Zen gardens by listening or looking at books. Perhaps someday I might visit Kyoto and Tokyo, I dreamed.

It was late in the evening, and we were hungry. "Why don't we go to a *dhaba*? You like spicy food," I suggested.

"What is *dhaba*?"

"A roadside eatery. The one I want to take you to is known for its *gol gappas*."

"*Gul goppas*?"

"*Gol gappa*! It is a hollow, crispy dough the size of a golf ball. Very light. You pierce a hole at the top." I made a gesture of holding the ball with my left hand and pointed my right finger at its top. "You fill it with spicy liquid and eat it. Very spicy!"

"Good! Okay we go," he said with a glint in his eyes.

We drove to a shop in Safdarjung market. The seller sat cross-legged on a wooden platform under a canopy. In front of him were two earthenware vessels three feet in circumference. At this cooler part of the day, we were the only customers there. After welcoming us, the seller handed each of us a paper plate, grabbed a *gol gappa* from a mound of balls in a large wicker basket, pierced it with his finger, dropped in a few chickpeas, filled it with the sweet lemony-peppery juice from one of the vessels, and served a mouth-watering ball first to our Japanese guest and then to me.

The professor watched as I crunched the crispy ball in my mouth and gulped it down. Then he too slugged his down. The taste exploded in his mouth, and his eyes widened, his lips stretched, and he sucked in air. But he did not say, "No more, thanks!" Instead, he extended his plate for another... and another and another. He kept gulping and sucking air, smiling all the while.

We ate, sucked air, and smiled a dozen times until sweat beaded on our foreheads. The seller filled the thirteenth *gol gappa* with chickpeas and spicy liquid and offered it to the professor. But he shook his head, kept his plate on the side table, and patted his belly. "Very tasty!" he complimented.

I paid *gol gappa wala* a little more than what we owed him for the two-dozen balls of heaven.

"Very tasty! Funny to eat!" the professor said as we rode back to his hotel.

Since I had been taking him sightseeing each evening, I told my mother that on the last day I might bring him home for dinner.

Ishadate wanted to buy gifts for his family, so on the extra day he'd added to his stay in New Delhi, I drove him to Connaught Place, the most vibrant business district of New Delhi. I parked my Honda scooter in CP's outer circle, and we crossed the road to the inner circle. With each store's best wares displayed in bay windows, we window-shopped under a canopied path, and the professor looked for gifts that would interest his family.

As we strode from one window to the next, he and I talked about many things: the conference, pharmacologists and scientists we had met, historic monuments we had visited for days, and a little about Japanese monuments and Zen gardens. As we walked by Kwality Restaurant, the guard opened the door for us to enter. The aromas of lunch wafted through the door.

"Hungry, Professor?"

"You, too?"

We had lunch at the restaurant where the food was spicy and the prices reasonable. He insisted on paying the bill, but eventually allowed us to go Dutch.

By late afternoon, he had purchased several silk scarves and ties, a woodcarving of Ganesh—the god of beginnings, a bronze statue of Nataraja—the god of cosmic creation and dissolution, a stone image of the seated Buddha, one gold bracelet, and a pair of gold earrings. Satisfied with his purchases, I asked if he would like to visit the Red Fort, a famous Mughal monument. But he said his flight was early the next morning, and he did not want to exhaust himself.

"What about an early, home-cooked dinner?" I asked. He looked pleasantly surprised and thanked me; then I drove him to my house.

It had been a long, hot and humid day. We were sweating when I knocked at the front door. My mother opened and greeted Mr. Ishadate by joining her palms. I had told her about my new friend— more than she wanted to know. He reciprocated her greeting by bowing several times. She ushered us into the drawing room and asked us to be comfortable and cool ourselves. Then she returned to the kitchen.

We sat on cushioned wooden chairs under a ceiling fan that ran at full speed, our wet shirts drying, our bodies cooling. My mother returned with a tray holding two glasses of freshly squeezed cold lemonade.

"What mother cooking?" Ishadate asked after she returned to the kitchen. The aroma of roasted red pepper and cumin seeds hit our nostrils.

"Frying spices for some *dal*. Would you like to watch?" I asked.

"She will mind?"

"No!" I called, "Ma! Can we watch you cook?"

"Kitchen is not clean!"

"He doesn't care about that! He just wants to see how you cook!" I called back.

"Okay, come in," she said.

The kitchen was so small that we stood close behind, flanking her as she rolled out rounds of *puri* with dough she had kneaded earlier. One *puri* was deep-frying in hot oil, turning golden and puffing up at the surface.

"Mother of *gol gappa*! Yah?" he mused. "This how *gol gappas* made?"

"What is he saying?" my mother asked.

"He says they look like large *gol gappas* and wants to know if this is how they too are made," I translated.

"Yes, exactly! Only bigger." She strained the *puri* and gently pressed another that was frying in the oil.

I translated what she told me for our guest.

Not wishing to crowd my mother in the hot kitchen, the professor returned to the drawing room, and I followed. How else to entertain him? I switched on a twelve-inch black-and-white television set. A news anchor delivered his report, but the image scrolled in quick succession then went kaput. The screen started to snow.

"Purchased it from a friend." I smiled sheepishly as I adjusted the antenna. "Secondhand! Does this often." I tapped the top and slapped the sides several times. Usually, that did the trick, and the image would stabilize. But this time it didn't work.

The professor said jokingly, "Machines tick when you kick. Right?" We both laughed. Embarrassed, I turned off the television. He must have a large-screen color television at his home. After all, Japanese manufacture the best televisions in the world.

My mother set the dining table, which had been pushed against the wall between the kitchen and drawing room. She called us to eat. When Professor Ishadate pulled out a chair for her, she giggled like a schoolgirl and said in Hindi to me, "Tell him I'll eat after making a few more *puris. Garam, garam khao*, eat them warm!"

When I translated, he hesitated before sitting on the chair I had pulled out for him. On a steel plate, Ma placed two *puris*, a serving of aromatic rice with green peas, a bowl of *moong dal*, and a bowl of cauliflower. I showed him how to use pieces of *puri* to scoop *dal* and morsels of cauliflower florets. He learned quickly and had no use for a spoon and fork. When Ma served more *puris*, he used them to eat rice.

We talked about good Indian restaurants in Tokyo where he often dined with his wife and children. When their children and grandchildren visited, they made it a point to have a meal at their favorite Indian restaurant. Then Ma came in and asked if she could get us anything. Usually she and I ate together, but when I brought a friend for dinner, she did not join us, preferring instead to eat later.

"Mother's food—most tasty. Thank you for your trouble!" he said, looking at her, and then asked me to translate. Before I could do so, my mother said she understood.

Before leaving, the professor again thanked my mother for a delicious meal. She folded her palms in return and thanked him for coming.

I drove him back to the hotel. Before going in, he held my hands in his and said, "Thank you! Thank you for hospitality! Please visit Tokyo someday!" I thanked him for the invitation and went home.

Almost two years passed. One morning, my boss called me to his office. He congratulated me for being on the list of Indian delegates invited by the University of Tokyo for that year's International Pharmaceutical Conference. My expenses would be paid in full, but he was puzzled that Professor Ishadate had requested a two-day leave for me after the conference. Did I know this professor?

I reminded him that I had been the professor's tour guide when he came to the international conference in New Delhi.

At the Tokyo airport, a man was holding a placard with my name. I introduced myself. He bowed and said his name was Yamamoto. He was going to be my guide during my stay in the city. As we drove toward the conference hotel, he did not say who had engaged him or arranged my stay. Before dropping me off at my hotel, he said I was to meet Professor Tetsu Ishadate that evening.

Several hours later, Yamamoto came back to pick me up. We drove for a half hour through the heart of Tokyo and stopped in front of a tall building with a sign that read *Ishadate Pharmaceutical Industries*. As we entered through the front gate, I found myself walking into a strikingly different atmosphere—bonsai trees reflecting in miniature waterfalls and ikebana arrangements aesthetically placed on pedestals in front of floor-to-ceiling glass walls.

Riding the elevator with my guide, I nervously looked at my reflection hoping I was presentable. When we exited the elevator, a door came into view that read *Tetsu Ishadate, CEO*. An attendant opened the door to a luxurious office. Yamamoto beckoned me to go in while he waited outside. The attendant closed the door, and I recognized the man seated behind a large table. Ishadate walked toward me with an extended hand.

"How are you, Mohan?" he said. We shook hands and he bowed. He had the same smile and twinkle in his eyes that had charmed me the first time we met. I noticed our pictures from Jantar Mantar on the shelf behind him.

"Fine! I am fine, Professor! Thanks for your recommendation!" I replied.

"Thank you, you come! Mother, how is she?"

"She is fine and sends her regards," I said as I looked at the beautifully paneled walls. "I thought you were a professor."

"Part-time only. This full-time job," he said, tapping on the table. "TV working?" He smiled.

"I got it fixed," I said sheepishly.

"Sorry, Mohan! I attend important meeting in Osaka." He bowed his head.

"You won't be at the conference then?" I was hoping to spend some time with him.

"Mr. Yamamoto show my office," he said, and instructed the man to give me a tour of the facility.

My jaw fell as my guide showed me the working robots their company had built to efficiently and safely dispense drugs. The manufacturing facility was a world in itself. The robots were capable of scanning barcodes on medications and retrieving drugs for patients.

Yamamoto, I learned, was an assistant manager in the company. He said, "Most of the credit goes to the professor and his team for their research and development. They have made it possible to improve communication between nursing and pharmacy, and also increase the safety of dispensing medication from the pharmacy to the patient's bedside."

Seeing my enthusiasm, he took me to all the floors. The tour lasted for an hour, then he drove me back to my hotel.

I spent the conference days attending lectures and workshops and participating in discussions. During the evenings, in the company of a few other delegates I befriended, we tasted Japanese cuisine while networking. My task was to write two articles for my company's bi-monthly magazine. One was to be about new drugs for AIDS, and the second about the new chemotherapy capsules for blood cancer.

We ate bento box lunches that included tempura and sushi accompanied by pickled ginger and wasabi paste. I liked it but missed my chutneys and chili-peppered meals.

The morning after the conference, Yamamoto drove me to the airport where Professor Ishadate surprised me. We bid goodbye to Yamamoto and took a flight to Kyoto.

From the Kyoto airport, a limousine drove us directly to Daitoku-ji. The exquisite Zen temples I had seen in photographs were a pale resemblance to where I was standing. I had been transported to the most serene surroundings. Ishadate then led me through the outer gardens of Daisen-in. We saw monks wearing straw hats squatting on dewy green moss, clearing fallen yellowed leaves and twigs, leaving the area spotless. A stone pathway led to the inner garden where a stream's gentle sounds greeted us. On a rock in the water, a white-eye bird sat watching a Mandarin duck cleaning its beak.

A stone path led us to a dry landscape. Instead of grass, the whole garden was of stones, gravel, and rocks. A monk raked circles and waves on the white gravel. The professor explained that this design would remain until the next day when another monk would rake a new one. Seven rocks of various sizes jutted from the gravel. We sat on the steps overlooking the dry garden to contemplate what the monk had composed. The monochromatic image conjured up a feeling of tranquility. The silence and stillness grounded me, helped deepen my attention. I inhaled the air slowly and deeply, trying to take it all in.

We stayed in a nearby hotel that night, and I woke refreshed, looking forward to another day with my gracious host. After breakfast, we were driven to a forested area. We walked on a long stone pathway that led to a teahouse secluded behind the trees.

Here, at once, our connection with the outside world seemed to break. We rinsed our hands in a carved stone basin and crouched to enter the teahouse. Light filtered through the paper windows reflecting on an *ikebana* and, behind it, a scroll painting.

Already in the room was the tea master watching puffs of steam escape from the spout of an iron kettle. Ishadate bowed, introduced me to him, then sat with me cross-legged on the *tatami* floor. The tea master held a ceramic cup in his left hand and added two spoonfuls of emerald-green powder. He mixed this with steaming water by adding a bit at a time. He whisked the mixture until it was frothy, then poured it into two cups and handed them to us. We were also served sweet buns on a napkin decorated with a drawing of a cherry blossom.

In silence, we slowly sipped the tea and tasted the buns while the master wiped the utensils he had used to prepare it. Then he passed them around for us to admire: the ceramic bowl, the whisk, and the spoon. Our senses of taste, smell, and sight thus stimulated, we appreciated the simplicity and serenity of the exquisite ceremony.

That afternoon, we flew from Kyoto to the Tokyo airport, where I was to take my flight home. I thanked the professor for his hospitality and promised to stay in touch. Before departing for the terminal, we embraced. During my short visit to Japan, I had experienced two most peaceful days. They had stirred something deep within me, a sense of peace I could not explain but would carry with me for the rest of my life.

I was quite overwhelmed. The professor had recommended my name for the Tokyo conference, then generously guided me through the Zen gardens. What a magnanimous man! When he visited India, I had simply treated him the way I did because I was attracted to his charm and simple manners. As my mother often said, "We should treat our guests the way we receive our gods."

From New Delhi airport, I hired a three-wheeler to my home. My mother greeted me at the door. In the middle of the drawing room, I saw a big cardboard box.

"What is this?" I asked.

"It was delivered yesterday. The man said it is from Japan. I was surprised myself."

The box was a gift from the professor. I cut through the tape and pulled out the flaps. Snug between the packing materials was a large-screen color television.

An American Dialogue

Mrs. Susan Weiss watched as Mumta Kashkari, the sprightly bride-to-be, entered the coffee shop accompanied by her parents. The young woman ordered a strong El Indio blend from Tarrazu. Her mother got a nutty roast from Costa Rica, and her father a robust flavor from Nariño, Colombia. Mrs. Weiss stared into her own half-empty cup before they joined her at the table. *Such diverse tastes.*

After the usual greetings, Mrs. Weiss pulled out her binder of wedding planner materials. "Mumta, do you envision this event like the one we planned for your older sister? Or will you want a more traditional ceremony?"

"Can't be one-hundred-percent traditional," the father said. "So much is bound up with the native land and the people."

"I would have liked a typical Kashmiri ceremony, but now it has to be combined with rites from another religious tradition," Mumta answered.

"What she is trying to say," her father interrupted, "is that this ceremony has to be eclectic. A bit different from Meena's. Only select rites from two unique traditions."

Mrs. Weiss jotted a note on a lined yellow pad. "We could do a white canopy—like the kind they use in Jewish weddings," she suggested, "and decorate the four poles with wreaths of white jasmine."

"Yes, yes!" Mumta smiled. "I like that very much. I have seen it in pictures." The young woman glanced at her parents who didn't seem so sure.

"It may look nice with the *vyug*," her mother said, perhaps not to dilute Mumta's excitement.

Mrs. Weiss tried to recall if Meena's wedding had included such an item. "Please remind me, what is a *vyug*?"

"Remember the cosmic symbol of a circle inside a square we composed on the floor with flowers?" the girl's father said.

"Please ask the florist to make it in yellow, peach, and red rose petals," Mumta requested.

The wedding planner noted the request in her pad.

"Our marriage," said the mother touching her husband's arm, "was performed in the valley of Kashmir according to *Sarasvat* Brahmin tradition. My older sister painted our *vyug* on the floor with edible powders—yellow turmeric, red chili pepper, green dried mint, and white flour. But Meena and Mumta are changing that tradition with fresh flowers."

"What happened after your sister drew this pattern?"

"We stood on the *vyug* of powdered spices outside the entrance to my parents' house. Then my mother fed us *nabad*—crystal candy. While on auspicious ground we were enveloped with sweetness inside and out. For Mumta, the *vyug* will be in the wedding hall followed by the ritual of *posh puza*."

"*Posh puza*." Mrs. Weiss tried to wrap her tongue around the words. "I don't know if I'm saying it right. But isn't that what we did at Meena's wedding to bless the newlyweds? When the guests showered marigold petals on the couple it made some of them cry. Even the groom's family was touched... you know, even though they were from the Christian tradition." She paused to see if her words had disturbed the family at all, then hastily added, "It was so beautiful, I cried like a baby. Oooh, this is getting exciting! What else? What else?" Mrs. Weiss couldn't contain herself.

Mother and daughter looked at each other and began speaking in Kashmiri.

The father turned to the planner. "Before we go ahead with all the details, why don't you tell me how much it is going to cost this time?"

"I will detail out costs by line item, Mr. Kashkari, including the florist, the musicians, the videographer and photographer, hotel rooms, caterers, and all the other details. Just strike out the things you don't want, and I'll either suggest alternatives," she said looking at Mumta and her mother, "or delete them. Whatever you want."

"We don't want to delete any of the ceremonies we did at our older daughter's wedding. No!" The mother glanced sideways at her husband. "We may add a few more."

"Can we put a stop to this somewhere? Let's keep as many rituals as in the previous wedding, but no more. No more expense! There seems no end to this." The father moved uneasily on his seat. His wife stared hard at him.

"Daaddyyy! Let her write down all the things we are discussing, and then you can delete the ones which are over our budget."

"And then we'll consider your deletions—two against one, Daddy," the wedding planner kidded.

"Who is following the budget? There is no end to this spending," he mumbled to himself.

"Oh no, there's something I completely forgot to ask you!" Mumta said.

"What?"

"We want to find someone who can recite a few verses from the Quran."

"Quran?" Mrs. Weiss's pencil dropped on the pad.

"Yes, I did not get a chance to tell you that my fiancé is Muslim."

Wide-eyed, the planner repeated, "A Muslim fiancé!" She glanced at the bride-to-be and quickly looked into the eyes of the mother and then the father. Their expressions didn't tell her anything. She picked up her pencil and started to scribble something on the pad. "Where is the groom from?"

"Seychelles," the bride-to-be said.

"I find this very interesting—a Hindu family, one daughter married to a Christian, another marrying a Muslim... very interesting. I don't know if I can find someone. I have never done a Muslim wedding," Mrs. Weiss said curtly.

"Traditionally only imams recite suras from the Quran," the father said. "But that doesn't matter to us. We are interested in the recitation. We want our guests to hear the lyrical sounds of the suras in Arabic."

"Anyone with a beautiful strong voice can recite. It doesn't have to be an imam," Mumta said. "Do you know someone?"

Tapping her pencil on the pad, the planner said, "You know I'm Jewish."

"Of course, we know you're Jewish," the mother said.

The daughter and father nodded.

"That is not the point. We're asking if you can find an Arabic-speaking reciter," the father said.

"Have you met her fiancé's parents yet? What's his name?" The wedding planner had enjoyed planning the Kashkaris' older daughter's wedding. She had found them good-hearted and generous. Not a prejudiced bone in their bodies. Although she prided herself on mixing and mingling with people of all religions, no one from her family had married someone belonging to another religion. Her family circle was strictly Jewish.

"His name is Amir Abdullah," the father said.

"Seychelles sounds like a made-up country," she said nervously. "You need to be careful."

"You should check the atlas. Seychelles is a group of islands near Madagascar," the father said. "Are you worried about interacting with the groom's family?"

"Oh no! I'm only concerned with the usual problems," Mrs. Weiss replied. "Daily news is filled with nothing but the burning of what had once been called the Fertile Crescent. Terrorist groups who trace their lineage to this geographic area quote the Quran to justify suicide, murder, looting, rape, kidnapping... and as you must know, the massacre on 9/11! I fear for your family. Have you met them yet?"

"Yes, yes. Good people, great family. We have met them on several occasions," said the father. "When Amir's parents visit him in New York, they also come to Boston to stay with us. In any case, Mrs. Weiss, you are talking about terrorists. Why should we generalize a whole religious group because some of them happen to be terrorists? We have enough examples of domestic terrorism."

"That's a... uh... that's okay... no, it is good! I worry... how the minds of young men are being poisoned," said Mrs. Weiss. An awkward silence followed, and she gave a silly laugh. "Wait till my husband hears this. He is going to get a kick out of this wedding!" She looked at Mumta, then at the mother and the father.

"Why is that?" Mumta asked.

"Only in America would one find a Hindu family marrying a Muslim immigrant with a Jewish woman as their wedding planner. And if I remember correctly, we also had a diverse guest list at your older daughter's wedding."

"It seemed like the whole world had arrived to celebrate! Only in America!" Mumta said.

Her parents nodded.

Realizing that an hour had passed in a flash, the wedding planner said, "Okay then, I'll get back to you next week." They all stood, said their goodbyes, and left the cafe.

Later that night, Mrs. Weiss called the Kashkari residence. Mumta picked up the receiver.

"Long time no see! What's up?" Mumta was her cheery self.

At first, Mrs. Weiss hesitated, but then said, "Something has come up, dear, and I'm afraid I may not be able to plan your wedding. Please feel free to find someone else."

"No, no, no! What happened, Mrs. Weiss? We'll be lost without you! Please don't say that," Mumta pleaded.

It was as if Mrs. Weiss didn't even hear her. "I just don't feel right about this. I'd be happy to recommend someone." But then she hung up before Mumta could implore further.

A week passed. Mrs. Weiss's son, Joshua, came to visit along with his friend, Adam. Joshua couldn't stop raving about Adam's conference presentation on the relevance of Moses in the 21st century. "He impressed me with his knowledge of the scriptures and their significance during the time of turmoil, anger and hatred such as the world is going through now."

"And your son is very thoughtful," Adam chimed in. "I was going to have to bail out on visiting my parents across town this weekend, until Josh offered to loan me his car tomorrow morning."

The feeling of goodwill and peace mixed with the aroma of Mrs. Weiss's freshly baked bread. The young men suggested going out for dinner, but it was Friday. Mrs. Weiss had prepared a nice Shabbat meal of roast chicken, potato kugel, and challah.

"Our customs are similar," Adam said. "How can we not stay home to withdraw and repose and enjoy this meal?"

The four sat in the family room with glasses of Merlot and continued to talk about how differences could be overcome through familiarity and understanding. Mrs. Weiss quoted from the Torah and *Nevi'im.*

"From the very first time I met Adam," Joshua told his mother, "he reminded me of you."

"In what way?" she asked. "Do I talk like him?"

Joshua mimicked his mother's voice. *"I honor how we reserve a day of withdrawal and repose for contemplation, enjoyment and culture."*

"That's me?" Adam said and looked puzzled.

"That's exactly what my wife says," Mr. Weiss interjected.

"Now listen to this, Mom!" Joshua cleared his throat and tried to copy Adam's voice. *"One day a week, we must escape the everyday world to add meaning to our lives."*

"Does Adam say that, too?" she asked.

"That surely sounds like you, honey!" Mr. Weiss chuckled.

"Both of them talk like that, Dad. It's amazing! Adam says, *'Spiritual life decays if we fail to sense the grandeur of eternal time. Twenty-four hours of contemplative pause is important—stop doing, enjoy being,'* and the similarity is uncanny!"

Mr. Weiss laughed and clapped his hands, causing Mrs. Weiss to blush.

"God is invisible and immaterial," Adam added, "not divided into millions."

"Exactly!" Mr. Weiss agreed.

Mrs. Weiss was pleased that her husband and son had memorized what she often said.

After dinner they didn't go to the temple as usual. Instead, they continued the conversation.

"God is an awe-inspiring power!" she said. "Did you know, Adam, that when Moses went up the mountain, God showed himself to a neighboring mountain and it came crashing down, making Moses fall senseless? Yet God is compassionate and merciful."

"Quite right!" Adam jumped in. "Somehow, we have this misunderstanding that He is a stern and wrathful judge, but that is clearly a misconception. God's compassion and mercy are cited one hundred ninety-two times in the Quran, and his wrath and vengeance have only seventeen references. I believe God is goodness and power, the reason why the material world is good." Adam spoke with such pride that his black eyes glowed.

At this point Mrs. Weiss noticed his chiseled good looks. His manners were gentle, his movement elegant, yet he spoke with confidence and determination. She loved this fine young man. If she had a daughter, Mrs. Weiss would have been delighted to have him as her son-in-law. "I didn't know that Islam and Judaism had any similarities," she said.

"Both are rooted in Abrahamic religion. What I like about them is that the soul's individuality and freedom are not only celebrated, but individuality is emphasized. We believe human existence is a precious opportunity to choose the best life has to offer."

Adam continued talking about the similarities between these faiths. "When a Muslim recites *La ilaha illa'llah*—there is no god but God—the God referred to is none other than the One God of the Jews, Christians and Muslims. The God who created the universe, revealed his will to Abraham and Moses, and whom Jesus called Father and Muhammad called Allah."

"Oy vey! The same God? And how do you know so much about Islam?" Mrs. Weiss asked.

"Yes, the same God! I have been studying these religions for over a decade. Besides," Adam said matter-of-factly, "I am a Muslim."

A silence fell over the room.

Joshua and Mr. Weiss watched Mrs. Weiss's face turn pale.

"But your name is Adam," she said.

"It is pronounced differently in Arabic, but in English, it's spelled the same," he answered.

Coldness descended upon the room. For the rest of the evening, Mrs. Weiss was civil but didn't say much.

Very early Saturday morning, Adam borrowed Joshua's car and left to meet his own parents before Mr. and Mrs. Weiss were awake. When the family gathered at the kitchen table, Mr. Weiss said, "That Adam is such a nice young man!"

"Why didn't you tell me he was a Muslim?" Mrs. Weiss's eyelids were puffy. "I had no time to prepare myself."

Joshua scowled. "Why would you need to prepare?"

She lowered her gaze and took a deep breath.

"Let me ask you something, Mom," he said. "What right do we have to shut ourselves off from people simply because they belong to a different religion?"

"We meet people all the time. If we like them, we extend the hand of friendship. If we don't, we keep our distance," she said.

"She is not against anyone, Josh. She gives everyone space," his father said.

"Except if he happens to be a Muslim," Josh retorted.

"Why drag misery home?" his mother said.

"Was Adam miserable?" Josh sounded irritated. "There are many people we know well—talk about misery! I thought you were different from the rest of our family, even more liberated than Dad. Since Adam became my friend, my life is richer. I have met people from different parts of the world." He nervously tapped his leg against the chair. "I thought you too felt that about your clients, the Kashkaris. But it seems to be otherwise."

In her community Mrs. Weiss was regarded as a good-hearted and open-minded woman—accepting of people from other religions and races. After all, she had planned weddings for Hindu and Christian families. But mingling with Muslims? That was emotionally upsetting.

Joshua refilled his coffee cup and went out to the back porch. His father followed. As Mrs. Weiss sat at the kitchen table, she heard the men she loved dearly, talking and laughing. She preferred sitting alone; her heart was heavy.

Someone rang the doorbell disturbing her thoughts. At the front door stood a police officer. "Hello?" she said.

"My name is Officer David Mallick, ma'am. Is this the Weiss residence?"

"Yes, what's wrong?"

"I have some bad news about your son."

"But my son... he is here."

"Was someone else driving his car then?"

Her hands shook. "Wait a minute, please! Why don't you talk to him?" She called out, "Josh, please come here! This police officer wants to speak to you."

While Joshua and Officer Mallick exchanged words, Mrs. Weiss felt cemented to the ground. A shiver passed through her body. She couldn't hear. She couldn't sit. She couldn't scream. Her lips felt numb. She just stood there looking at her son and the policeman.

"Mom! Mom!" Joshua was covering her shoulders with a shawl. "Sit down!" He moved her to the sofa, helped her sit and shouted for his father to come in. "Dad, Adam was in a car accident."

"Is he okay?"

"He was killed, Dad." A lamenting cry burst out from Joshua. He let go of his mother's hand and sat down next to her.

His father's legs shook. He sat on the chair next to his wife and began rubbing her back.

"So sorry for your loss, sir! Madam!" the officer said and then added, "I'll need someone to come with me to identify the body."

After Joshua left with the officer, Mr. Weiss made her a cup of coffee. They both felt mute, didn't know what to say. Adam's image, vibrant and alive, reeled in her mind. How his face glowed, how his black eyes shone as he spoke. How passionately he used his words that mirrored her own thoughts. She marveled how, through a short encounter with the fine young man, she had unwittingly crossed an ocean—one small step closer to the Muslim faith. Her heart was overwhelmed with a mélange of emotions. She did not know how to unravel them.

How was she to combat this strange new darkness? She'd had similar feelings when she met the Kashkaris for the first time. Hindus? Who are they? What do they believe in? What do they think about family? About parents? About children? Yet they turned out to be lovable, honest, generous people. Organizing their daughter's wedding was one of the most pleasurable events of her professional life.

Joshua stayed a few extra days with his parents as he saw them more grief-stricken than he might have expected. "Mom, a memorial service for Adam is being held at the Monroeville Mosque where his parents live. Would you and Dad like to attend?"

"Should we?" she asked. Even the thought of joining strangers for such a heart-wrenching event made her belly crunch. At the same time, she somehow felt guilty for what had happened, guilty that she grew fond of him at their first discussion and guilty that suddenly a chasm cracked open when she heard that he was a Muslim.

"It will make you feel better. Since Adam left us you have not been yourself. Being with his family and close friends may help heal the pain."

Joshua's words rang true. Yes, for her to heal, entering a religious place may pay some sort of penance.

The words seemed reluctant to leave her lips. "I will attend."

As they entered the front gate of the mosque, they were led to separate sections—Joshua and his father with the men and Mrs. Weiss with the women. Sounds of lament and sobs echoed above the hush.

The imam, an older man with white hair and beard, stood in the middle facing the gathering. In a thunderous voice, he began to recite in Arabic, a language she had never heard. Mrs. Weiss was fidgety. She did not know what to do or how long it would last.

With a questioning glance, she turned to the woman on her left who was wearing a sky-blue-and-white hijab.

"He is reading *fatiha*, the first verse from the Holy Quran," the woman said.

Mrs. Weiss faced front and tried closing her eyes to concentrate. But to no avail. She turned to her right. A woman with a purple scarf tied around her head smiled and offered a white handkerchief from her handbag, gesturing for Mrs. Weiss to place it on her head.

Reluctantly, she wrapped the cloth over her hair and whispered, "Thank you!"

The collective focus of the gathered people was on the recitation. So she too closed her eyes. In the darkness, Adam's face appeared. She sighed, remembering his elegant manners and the motherly feelings he had aroused in her. The sounds of Arabic words streamed through her, replacing Adam's memory, his image dissolving into the phonic vibrations of the imam's thunderous voice.

The recitation had a soothing effect. When the melodic sounds stopped, she opened her eyes and saw the imam step back. A young man took his place and introduced himself as Irfat Salaam. A minute's silence ushered in a serenity that affected all. A calm overcame Mrs. Weiss.

Dressed in white pajama and shirt, Irfat said he would recite verses of the Sufi poet, Rumi, in English. Mrs. Weiss became attentive.

"I will be with you in the grave on the night you leave behind your shop and your family." The young man's words were like pearls in a necklace. "When you hear my soft voice echoing in your tomb, you will realize that you were never hidden from my eyes. I am the pure awareness within your heart, with you during joy and celebration, suffering and despair." It was as if Adam were speaking directly to her. The feelings he had left behind that were still with her stirred.

"Do not see me through haze. See me clearly, see my beauty without the old eyes of delusion." Was he talking of the kingdom of God within? She understood the language of the poet.

The young man continued, "What kind of gossip-house have you opened in our city? Close your lips and shine on the world like loving sunlight."

So what if Adam was a Muslim? Her eyes welled with tears. She pulled the handkerchief from her head to wipe them. The two women flanking her turned, but seeing what she was doing, returned their attention to Irfat Salaam.

The imam spoke the final words, thanked the audience for their attention and asked them to gather for a simple lunch. At that point, the Weiss family decided to leave.

During an hour drive home, Mrs. Weiss was lost in her thoughts as were her husband and son.

"Mom, may I help you prepare lunch?" Joshua offered.

"Thanks, but first I have to make a phone call." She flipped through her wedding planner notebook and dialed the number. "Mumta, this is Mrs. Weiss."

"I know who you are! So good to hear your voice."

"I'm sorry, dear, for whatever I said to you last time. I don't even remember now what words I spewed. I called to let you know that I'll be available to plan your wedding. How is Amir Abdullah? ... I hope you have not found another planner yet… and would you still let me?"

Mrs. Weiss heard Mumta laugh. "Mrs. Weiss, I was waiting for you. I knew you'd change your mind. And Amir is fine, thanks for asking!"

OLD-FASHIONED ROMANCE

Unrequited Love

In the last fifteen years I've changed from the devoted son who welcomed the opportunity to take care of my elderly mother to a man whose anger murmurs in his belly when she calls. She gave birth to me, nourished me, took care of me when I was sick. Now she needs my complete attention. I understand this intellectually, but emotionally I am spent.

"Avatar. Hold my hand, son. I will fall!"

"You are fine, Mother," I assure, as she limps out of the car to flop into the wheelchair. I grip her shoulders now turned boney. Wrapped in six yards of silk she gives whiffs of talcum powder.

I have heard good things about Residential Lake Hotel, its staff and service, so I rented a studio apartment for the summer to celebrate my birthday, and hers as well. A change of scenery might help us both.

"You're bruising my shoulders," she says, her voice devoid of emotion.

"Sorry, I'm helping you sit!" I try to suppress my irritation.

With her eyes closed and head bent she adjusts her posture. When she looks comfortable, I trundle her to the front entrance on the narrow sidewalk.

"Don't run me into the bushes," she grumbles.

I remain quiet.

"When did you get bitten by the travel bug?" she says out of nowhere. "I've told you a hundred times we're better off at home." Despite the biting words, her tone is neutral. An outsider couldn't guess she is annoyed.

"We'll have a good time," I say though my irritation is increasing. I don't expect her to be thankful. Gratitude is not one of her qualities.

"We? I came for you. Didn't want to disappoint."

"Thanks?"

"But what is the point of a vacation? Curbing desires is good for your mind and soul. I've always taught you that hopping from one place to another is a sign of restlessness."

"But I enjoy going to new places, learning about new cultures, meeting people." I try to be cheerful and keep my blood pressure from rising.

"Learn to curb your cravings while you're young!"

I ignore her and tell myself not to let her words vex me.

As a young man in college, I hitchhiked from city to city, trekked through wilderness and climbed mountains. Travel taught me things about myself I wouldn't have otherwise known. The wanderlust bug bit me long ago. After graduation I dreamt of far horizons, but by the time I saved enough money, my father died of a massive heart attack. Mother was devastated. As her only child, I became responsible for her. For the last fifteen years I have looked after her, yet this two-week holiday badgers her.

I remember covetously watching my best friend Arun's mother hug and kiss him during overnight school excursions and birthday parties or when he told her about getting high marks on an exam. I never got that sort of affection. But she is the only mother I have. I must ignore her whining and cynicism.

A charming woman greets us at the entrance and points us to the concierge desk. I turn back to look at her, but she is welcoming other guests. I wait for the room key.

"How nice of you to bring your mother for rest and relaxation," I hear someone say. It is her now standing behind me. "Will your wife be joining us?"

"Just the two of us," I answer, and she glides away.

"Here you are, Mother," I say once we arrive in the studio apartment. "Nice. Well-lit."

"Don't get attached," she comments indifferently.

I order room service lunch for her and return to the lobby. The concierge hands me a map for scenic treks around the hotel. I am about to leave when again I see the woman who greeted us earlier. I was distracted before, but this time her smile beguiles me.

"May I help you?" she asks.

"No, thank you. I have what I need."

"May I ask you something?"

I was already captivated. "Sure."

"Why do your eyes look so sad?"

Her blunt question takes me aback. Startled, I mumble something undiscernible, wave goodbye, then turn and descend the front steps.

Several days pass. I am in the lobby admiring a mural, a panoramic view of the lower Himalayas, somewhere near Bhutan, the happiest place on earth. Snow-laden mountain peaks and golden temple tops float above the forest pines. Miniature figures of lone travelers with baggage on their backs journey narrow paths as musk deer and golden langurs roam the jungle. In the foreground are flowering bushes with bees and butterflies. A red-headed trogan and black-rumped swift feed on branches of fruit-laden trees near grasshoppers and ladybugs.

I hear my name announced on the overhead speaker. "Mr. Avatar Johar, please come to the concierge desk."

"Did you call me?" I say to one of the attendants.

"Your mother wants you in the room," the man replies.

I turn to walk back to my studio and hear a female voice say, "If you like, you can enjoy the mural while I go attend to your mother." It is the blunt young woman with the beguiling smile.

"Thanks for the offer," I say. "A delightful landscape, isn't it?"

"Why don't you travel to Bhutan and see it in real life?"

She has hit a tender spot. I extend my hand. "Call me Avatar. And you are?"

"Jasmine. I've been assigned as your butler. Please don't hesitate to let me know if you need anything."

I thank her and leave to attend to my mother. When I return, Jasmine is still in the lobby. We chat. She is lively company. When and why I shared my dream of traveling the world, I do not recall. "I will include Bhutan on my itinerary. I also want to go to Paris, Rome, Mumbai, Beijing, Tokyo," I say to her. "For so many years I have saved brochures, maps, flight schedules, hotel listings. I know the goings and comings of every vehicle over the seas and in the sky. I get goosebumps imagining myself in foreign lands, like a pilgrim."

Journeying to distant horizons excites her, too. I feel our meeting has potential to develop into an unbounded friendship. Across several working days we sneak in a few chats over cups of coffee. She asks about my responsibilities toward my mother, as if worried about the impossibility of fulfilling my wanderlust. I try to explain how old people turn into children, demanding attention, love and care.

"She will not live forever," I say.

Jasmine replies, "Neither will you."

She gazes at my face for a few moments, then clears her throat. "Don't mind my saying so, but she needs to be weaned off of you."

I don't mind. I need a woman like Jasmine, who will honestly tell me how things are. I may be fulfilling a son's responsibility, but I also know my mother has started to take advantage.

On the day of our departure, we bid goodbye. Mother is happy to return home though Jasmine's expression is different. "Why do you look so sad?" I ask, feeling my heart ache.

"Look after yourself!" she says. "Will you return next year?"

"Love to," I reply, my shoulders slouched as I push the wheelchair toward the exit. I feel her eyes staring into my back.

For my mother's eightieth birthday, I insist we return to Residential Lake Hotel for the summer. Jasmine is now assigned to the concierge desk. She greets us with open arms.

On our birthday I invite Jasmine for cake. She agrees and brings two gifts.

"Mother, I want you to meet—"

"I know who she is." I ask Jasmine to take a seat, but before she can select a chair, Mother says, "I do not want to have *help* join us on our birthday."

The words jolt me. Jasmine turns to stare into my face as if asking, *Didn't you check with her before inviting me?*

I had. Not once but several times. But Mother remembers only what she wants and utters words when they hurt most.

I swallow my embarrassment, my rage.

Jasmine thanks me for inviting her and leaves abruptly.

"Good riddance!" Mother spits. "I don't want to celebrate my birthday with a doorman."

"Woman, a receptionist."

Dinner is brought in but I have lost my appetite. Mother eats with gusto and asks why I am not doing the same.

We cut the cake and wish one another a happy birthday. When Mother goes to bed, I carry the rest of the cake to the lobby where I find Jasmine.

We sit in the restaurant and I order Colombian coffee, her favorite, and apologize for my mother's behavior. "I am tied to this woman in flesh and blood."

I cut a piece of cake for her and put a spoonful close to her mouth. She eats it shyly. Then she feeds me. I am famished and thankful since I did not eat with Mother.

"It's uncanny," she says. "You look just like her. It seems you were made from exactly the same mold."

"I've been told that before."

"But your temperaments are worlds apart."

"Why do you say that?'

Her silence awakens me to certain realities to which I had not paid attention earlier.

I look straight into her eyes and say, "One day soon, I am going to ask you to marry me."

"We don't know each other that well!" she exclaims. "Plus, your hands are currently full."

The following summer my mother is sick and we can't travel. Jasmine phones to say she is praying for my mother, which surprises me considering how rude Mother had been to her. Before the conversation ends, she says something that makes me love her more. "I often think of old age. I feel sorry for your mother. She brought you up with love, and her presence in your life partly made you who you are. Since your father's death she is lonely and unconsciously makes herself physically and emotionally dependent on you."

I completely agree.

"But," she continues, "you don't have to be with her day and night. Try to lovingly persuade her to think about a daytime caregiver."

The following summer we return to the hotel. I trundle the wheelchair to the entrance. Mother is more shrunken, her senses of sight, hearing and smell slowly shutting down. She gets up late, lays down most of the time and goes to bed early.

Jasmine and I steal an hour here, two hours there. We hike the narrow paths through the wilderness in the vicinity of the hotel. We saunter around the lake behind the building, and after she is done with her job we dine together.

One day as we sit on the bank of the lake surrounded by pipal and neem trees I ask, "Do you have siblings?"

"No. My parents were dedicated professionals. They were too busy to have more children," she answers, looking into the distance.

"They seem to have paid full attention rearing you."

"Lucky for me that when I was twelve, they were covered to their heads in work. I was also interested in what they did. I kind of met them halfway."

"What do you mean?"

"Mom is a psychiatrist and Dad is a psychologist. I would sit quietly listening to them talk with guests—mostly their colleagues. They discussed and debated human behavior in the living room, at the dinner table and over dessert and coffee in the library. By the time I left for college I understood the basics of human relationships, how they develop, how to maintain them... and how to stay out of trouble."

"That is a useful thing. What did you study in college?"

"Psychology and Communications. Even then I was in the habit of mulling things over before falling asleep. If something did not make sense, the next day I'd ask my teachers for clarification the way I asked my parents when I was younger."

"How did you end up working at this hotel?" I had been curious since we first met.

"I traveled for many years. Married impetuously, and it ended badly. Then I wanted to work at a place where I'd meet people from around the world. This job was easy to get. You see, my parents are part owners of this hotel."

I was struck that Jasmine had been married before. She said the experience had been terrible. She had decided never to marry again... until she met me.

The last day of my stay, I urge Jasmine to join me and Mother for dinner at the hotel restaurant. "My mother is not the same person she used to be. Her failing body has calmed her down. She doesn't react to people or things the way she did several years ago."

Jasmine says she will be happy to join us.

When she arrives, my mother and I are already seated. Though smiling, mother eyes her from head to toe, questioning her very presence. The table is quiet while I order food: Jasmine's and my mother's favorite dishes. Jasmine insists that I order my favorite dish as well.

"I happen to like the things you like," I say. This pleases her. But in the presence of my mother the rest of our conversation feels contrived.

When Jasmine leaves to freshen up, I sip the wine and nibble at tandoori shrimp. She returns and when the food arrives, I recognize two of my favorite items though I hadn't ordered them. Jasmine smiles with a twinkle in her eye.

We savor the wine and eat leisurely. The chitchat, sometimes spontaneous, at other times stilted, makes us both feel good. At the end of the meal, she extends her hand and I shake it. She places my hand between her palms, and thanks me for dinner. When she says, "Goodbye," I have separation pangs.

I feel I am drifting away, lost without an anchor. "I'll come down to see you a bit later. Will you wait for me?" I mumble to her back.

She nods and walks away.

In the room, I bid Mother goodnight and race down the staircase to the lobby.

"Your mother doesn't look too good," Jasmine says.

"She is very sick. She won't survive long."

"I'm sorry. She does take a toll on you."

"I agree."

"My heart hurts... especially when I see no gratitude, no generosity, no smile on her part." Jasmine suddenly stops and says, "I'm sorry, Avatar! I think I had too much wine earlier and blurted out something that I should not have."

The moon is full as we walk outside. Holding hands, we pace silently around the lake. Once in a while she squeezes my hand or gently rubs my hairy arm and then holds it tenderly. A feeling of joy bubbles up in my heart. I want the walk to last forever.

At one point I let go of her hand, turn to face her, hold her by the shoulders and kiss her on her lips. She kisses me back. I put my arms around her waist and hold her tight. A current of passion passes through my body and her kiss wets my lips, making me forget where I am.

The next morning, I help my mother into the taxi. As I pull the suitcases to the exit, I see Jasmine walking toward me.

"I thought you were off today," I smile.

"I am. I came to tell you something."

I leave the suitcases and step closer to her.

She hesitates for a few moments but then reaches for my hands. "I have waited all my life to meet someone like you—dedicated, vulnerable yet determined. I love you, Avatar! I can't wait any longer. I do want to marry you."

I do not reply. How can I marry her when I am taking care of my mother fulltime?

Seeing my expression, she turns and leaves. Hopelessly, I load the taxi as if going to my own hanging. I love Jasmine. And she loves me. But my mother, whom I love despite herself, can't stand Jasmine. As her only son, it is my responsibility to keep her emotionally and physically safe and comfortable. I can't shove her into some nursing home and leave her in the care of strangers.

Poor Jasmine has fallen in love with someone who is not physically available. What a psychological prison my mother has built around me!

For the next two summers Mother is in and out of the hospital. I call Jasmine to inform her. Then when we finally are able to return to the hotel, even before checking in I whisper to Jasmine, "Feels good to see you finally! How are you?"

Covering her face with her hands, Jasmine begins to sob.

"What's wrong?"

"Avatar, don't—" Jasmine cries.

"Here." I hand her my handkerchief. "Listen, Jasmine. I've decided to make living arrangements for Mother. Sometimes she recognizes me, sometimes she doesn't. I can no longer take care of her. So, what do you say?"

"I met someone. I'm so sorry!" Jasmine says, her eyes brimming with tears.

"Jasmine, madam. Please come to room 555!" the maid's panicked voice calls the concierge desk. "It's terrible. I think Mr. Avatar Johar is dead! Hurry, madam!"

"Call an ambulance! And summon the doctor!" Jasmine hangs up and races to the elevator. As if night birds had been startled from their nests and blocked the light of the full moon, everything goes pitch dark. *No, no, Avatar cannot die. He was not the one supposed to die.*

Jasmine flies into the room and sees the mother seated in her wheelchair. Avatar is prostrate on the bed.

Jasmine puts her ear to his nose and touches his chest. He is still breathing.

Sitting at the edge of the bed she holds his hand and wipes her own tears. She knows that deep in his heart he wanted to run from his mother, from the world. But he couldn't. Instead, he decided to leave them. The empty bottle of sleeping pills lay on the nightstand.

Avatar had not breathed free air all his life. And now this!

The attempt to kill himself makes Jasmine angry, but when she looks at his face, she sees a wingless bird staring through the ceiling at a sky through which he has never flown.

She holds his hand and looks into his pale face. She feels a painful tenderness in her heart.

The doctor arrives.

"I'll never forgive him for this!" Avatar's mother declares. "How could he do this to me?" She is fully alert, repeating, "How could he?"

Through the winter Avatar continues to call Jasmine, writing long letters but never asking about her marriage.

One spring day in the hotel lobby Jasmine is checking in some guests. One of the regular hotel staff members sees me alone and says something that makes me laugh. For years I have not laughed that wholeheartedly.

Then, someone hugs me from behind. When I turn, it is Jasmine. I'm practically beaming.

"I came to see you, Jasmine. One last time."

"How are you, Avatar?" She tries to hide the tears welling in her eyes.

"Everything's great! Come have a cup of coffee with me."

We drink and she makes me laugh. I ask about her husband.

"The relationship didn't work out," she confesses.

What a relief that is for me!

She gazes at me and says, "How refreshed and youthful you look."

"Jasmine," I whisper intensely, leaning forward. "Let's fly to Rome tomorrow!"

"Rome?"

"Not Rome? What about Bhutan?"

"Bhutan sounds good."

"Let's get married! Will you marry me? Say yes, Jasmine. Will you?"

Jasmine gazes at me with her radiant face. Does she know how much I love her? Did she have dreams of marrying me the way I have about her?

She takes my right hand and holds it between her palms. Looking into my eyes, she shakes her head.

"What? No?" I say, surprised.

"I'll marry you. But I won't go to Rome with you."

"Why not?"

"Avatar, I don't think you should marry so soon after you have become free. You don't really want to marry now."

"Don't I?" I blink.

"No! You need to live by yourself for some time. Experience what it is to be free, Avatar. Travel alone." She looks so determined. "When you come back, if you still feel you want to marry me, I'll wait for you."

"Since I first laid eyes on you, I have wanted to be with you, Jasmine. All these years I waited so that I can spend the rest of my life with you. Now you don't want to come with me?"

"First, learn to be happy with yourself," she says.

I gaze at her face then gently pull her closer. With one hand on the nape of her neck and the other on her cheek, I give her a kiss to erase the memory of all other kisses she may have experienced before.

When we separate, she cannot move.

I watch her lovingly and whisper, "I'm not going anywhere without you, Jasmine. From now on you and I are one. Wherever you go, I go."

Suddenly she hugs me again. A current of pleasure passes through my body. In the fullness of the moment my frustrations and stress are replaced by the heart filled with love. With Jasmine's head over my thumping chest and her arms around my waist I feel certain we will not only marry but love one another for the rest of our lives.

A HIKE THROUGH THE WOODS

The early spring air was fresh as we hiked beside ancient banyan trees that had planted their aerial roots across centuries. They stood guard over the low hills, their foliage at places so dense it covered the sky. Further down, emerald ashoka and golden amaltas vied in their beauty. Some were entwined with purple morning glory or pink clematis and others with wild trumpet vine and butterfly pea. As the sun rose higher, parrots and pigeons flew to the ground to peck at insects and seeds.

At a clearing on our narrow pathway, a peacock appeared from nowhere to show off its iridescent plumage, enlivening the small space. The thought of returning and spending another day in such surroundings sent a wave of delight through me.

"We'll go on a different hike today," my husband announced. "You'll love it!" Every year he would discover at least one new place for us, away from the hustle and bustle of the city, in a forest through which ran a tributary of the Ganges.

"Great!" I said, excited after two long monsoon months.

We parked our brand new 1963 Fiat and stepped into a manicured entrance to the forest. I inhaled deeply as we leisurely strolled under a scented canopy of intertwining yellow and magenta bougainvillea. A passage of some hundred feet ended abruptly, leading to a pebbly path that trailed toward the slopes of the low hills. Blossoming pink primrose, yellow button-weed and white daisy bushes came into view. As we ascended, green ferns rubbed our ankles.

The climb was easy. From above, we could see the stunning river gorge below. My husband smiled contentedly. He was equipped with an umbrella that he'd insisted upon carrying. I held a water bottle.

We chatted about this and that until we reached a clearing that branched into two pathways. The marker was broken off its stake. But trees marked with yellow squares were there to guide us. "Should we take a left or right turn?" I asked.

"We can go either way," he said. "Though it branches into several smaller treks, the path is more or less circular. If we stay on track, we will end where we started." He sounded certain.

We continued on the unpaved rocky path, chatting for a while, becoming quieter with each step until lost in our own thoughts. Brisk walking gave rise to the warmth that swathed me in sweat. I took several gulps of water and handed my husband the bottle.

We must have walked two or more miles when we heard distant thunder. Clouds overcame the sun and the sky grew dark. It began to drizzle. I was now glad my husband had insisted on carrying the umbrella.

Suddenly, we found ourselves in the middle of a storm. We sprinted down the path. But when wind joined the torrents of rain, it seemed they were bent on beating us. Should we wait? Go back?

"It might get worse before it gets better. Let's wait for it to pass," my husband said. We stood patiently under the umbrella. He looked up at the trees. "Weren't we following the yellow squares?"

I noticed a red circle on the trunk he was looking at. "We missed a turn," I said.

"We must have!" he replied sharply.

"You said it was a circular path. How could we take a wrong turn?"

"I'm not the boss here. Why didn't you notice it when we took the wrong turn?"

"But you are the boss, with your sense of direction."

He didn't respond. I was sure we would soon spot a tree with a yellow square. We had gotten lost before, but then weather conditions had not been like this. We decided to retrace our steps. The downpour grew heavier. We stood still under the umbrella, close together, his hand on my shoulder.

Wind gusts increased and changed direction. It blew so hard the umbrella flipped and slipped from my husband's grip. We watched it fly away into the sky until it vanished.

The storm soaked my husband's hair. His face looked pale and his eyelashes dripped. Mascara ran down my chin and my black hair became soggy like a wet bird. I ignored him as I noticed the bright orange of my cotton shirt smearing my arms and white jeans.

New watercourses formed around us. Gushing forcefully, rivulets joined together to create unrestrained streams. They carved grooves in the mud, flattening the ground foliage and exposing pebbles. It was the kind of rainstorm that drowned memories of all previous storms we had withstood.

We waited and waited for it to calm. After what seemed like ages, the wind slowed a little, but the torrents had no intention of ceasing. The storm seemed to bleach the landscape; the scenery turned into a blurry black-and-white photograph.

After half a mile, to our combined relief, my husband spotted a tree painted with a yellow square. Our pace quickened. But a mile later our path was blocked by a huge fallen tree. He noticed my frustrated face but didn't say anything. We turned back and took a different path, hoping it would guide us to our car.

"Look!" he said, pointing to two fallen criss-crossing trees. "Didn't we see this on our way here?"

"Yes! How much farther?" I noticed my pruning fingers.

"I don't know," he said. "One mile? Ten? A million?"

"Why don't you know?"

"Why do you always expect me to know?"

My entire body shivered. "When will the rain stop?"

"Be patient! I remember seeing a couple of shelters on the map. I'm sure there is one somewhere here." He looked around. There was none. "If you imagine hard, you might be able to conjure one up," he joked.

"Are you saying this to make me laugh? If you are, it isn't working."

"I'm trying to lighten the mood. Why should I be the one to cheer us up?" he cried in exasperation.

I didn't like myself for being sullen and irritable. I had turned his jolly mood sour. But my limbs were cold, and I was exhausted. It had been four hours since the beginning of our hike. Our usual trekking time was never more than three hours. Too fatigued to continue, I slumped against the trunk of a fig tree. He hunched next to me. The ground was muddy. The earth seemed to be melting. I felt water rushing through the channels underneath my bottom.

Dripping rain mixed with the chilled wind. In a shallow grove about ten feet away, I noticed a dead peacock upside down. A shiver ran through my spine. I turned my head away. Thick fog appeared and made it seem colder.

"This tree is of no help," I said. "The raindrops are beating on my head. I feel sore."

"As they are on mine. Today I forgot to wear my hat."

"I wish I was wearing one, too." My nest of hair was of no use under the hard rain. "Oh, how long will this torture last?"

He turned to me. "Imagine yourself walking under the summer sun. Okay?"

"What?"

"Imagine a glittering golden fireball in a cloudless blue sky."

"Okay." I humored him.

"Close your eyes! Feel dry clothes on your skin. We are listening to our favorite music, drinking hot tea and eating *garam* cheese *pakoras*."

I closed my eyes and tried to imagine the pleasant picture he had sweetly painted for me. "I can't. I tried."

"Try again!"

I did not respond.

"You will forget all this once you are home under the warmth of a quilt. You can lay there as long as you want. I'll make dinner tonight."

I spotted another dead bird, this time a pigeon. What was next?

We got up and continued to walk.

"Of all the days, today I forgot to bring my compass," he said. "I'm getting sick and tired of this."

"Try to keep calm," I said. "Imagine a summer landscape, dry surroundings... the way you asked me to do." I tried to be kind. But then I heard thunder.

"Look at me! Water is coming from each pore of my body. The tips of my fingers have begun to freeze." His palms had turned wrinkly and white, his fingers tinged in blue. This worried me.

"Look at those blue bolts of lightning!" I said.

"Where? Where?" Before he raised his head, they were gone.

We walked over dozens of puddles.

"There it is!" he shouted and began to trot.

"There is what?" I fell in with his steps.

"Our car!" he yelled as he raised his hand to shield his eyes from a rush of rain.

I could see a yellow blob at the edge of the parking lot. It had to be our Fiat.

"Thank God!" I shrieked.

We smiled at each other.

"Finally! Come on!" he said.

"Let's stop at the first *chaiwalla* we see and order tall glasses of strong and sugary milk tea!"

"Whatever you say, madam!" He chuckled.

We began to sprint. The blob grew bigger, its yellow brighter.

"Remember when we got lost... in the hills of Mount Abu in Gujarat... under the heat of the summer sun, sweating like pigs? I hated the sun that day, the way I hate this rain."

We reached the car laughing. "Don't we have some almond chocolate left?" he asked as I rested my hand on the passenger door handle.

"Yes, we do!" I smiled, water dripping from my parted lips. "Open the door quickly, please."

He put his key into the keyhole.

"What's the matter?"

"The key doesn't work! What the...?" he yelled.

The windowpanes were misted. I wiped the glass and looked in. My breath fogged it again.

He cleared the water dripping on the pane and looked harder. "This is not our car!" he said. "There are tennis rackets on the backseat!"

"Not the brown bag with almond chocolate? Our beach towels? The duffle bag with dry clothes?" I asked, almost crying.

It thundered again as the rain poured harder. Water ran down his balding head and on my washed eyelashes.

"Can't you somehow open this door? Can't we sit inside this car for a while?" I pleaded.

"And go to jail?" He looked at me through the curtain of rain.

"So where is our car? Where is the *other* parking lot?" I realized it was as much my fault as his. But instead I growled, "How far?"

He walked a few paces looking up the hill and toward the river. "Not far—maybe a mile."

"Not far? A mile?" I repeated his words in frustration.

"Don't scream at me! We could wait here for the owner of this car, then get a ride."

"What if he's camping somewhere? He may show up... or he may not." I sighed, realizing the folly of this hope.

"We have to keep walking." The raindrops got bigger and the rain harder.

"I hate water!" I said.

"It won't take more than half an hour to reach the other lot," he consoled.

"Half an hour for one mile?"

"In this weather, yes!" he emphasized with his usual confidence.

"What if our car went down the river and floated away because of a landslide? We were parked at the edge of the hill, remember?" I shuddered at the thought.

"Why such negativity?" He began to lose his temper. "We'll have to get there to find out, won't we?"

"I'm tired! I'm tired of this weather. I'm tired of these thundering clouds. This rain. I want to eat almond chocolate, and drink hot tea with cheese *pakoras*."

He pulled me closer, kissed me on my watery lips, held my hand and began to jog. "We'll be okay," he said.

I prayed.

We had been walking for five hours now. The sky was getting dark. The evening was setting in. I was worried about our safety.

"I've got to sit, take a break," I moaned. "Oh, God. I wish we could sit under a banyan tree but the roots might hide creepy animals. I don't see anything else big enough to protect us from these torrents."

We did find a tree. Not exactly the kind I had imagined but close enough. Big drops of water struck my neck as I rested my head on my knees. Something crawled on my skin. A creepy touch. I leapt up and wiped my face, neck, arms and legs, sneezing, coughing and choking.

He stood up beside me. "Let's make a move. It's getting dark!" he said.

"Just leave me here," I moaned. I must have momentarily lost my mind. "You go!"

"I've no energy left to argue. It is not safe here—coyotes, foxes and who knows what else." He pulled me forward. "Let's go."

"I can no longer feel my fingertips."

He turned and rubbed my hands between his palms, one by one as I watched him. "Okay?" he asked. "Are you ready?"

I nodded. In our sneakers we plodded through the sludge. "How long?" I asked.

"I guess fifteen more minutes."

"What? I can't hear you. Speak louder!"

"Can't you hear anything?" he said.

"What?" Rain had finally numbed me to the bone. "You go ahead. I don't think that parking lot is this way. And even if it is, our car won't be there. I'll just sit here under this tree." I stopped and was about to sit down.

He held me by the shoulder. "You can't give up now after walking for more than five hours!"

"Just shoot me! And then go!"

"I would if I had a gun." He was who he was. "Stop this drama!"

"Drama? How much more dramatic can it get? If you find the car, come and fetch me."

"It is getting dark. Remember that rope bridge? Let's walk up to that point, then you can sit and I'll bring the car."

"I can't, I just can't. Please have mercy!" I had nothing left in me.

But then I saw his point and dragged myself behind him. We floundered our way through streaming water and slushy puddles and strewn broken branches. I was fifty feet behind him. I managed to cross the rope bridge then stopped and leaned against its wooden post. Through the thinning veils of water and dim light of early evening a parking lot came into view. My legs felt weaker than a minute ago.

"Is this our lot?" I shouted.

"Looks like it."

"Are you sure?"

"Yes, I'm sure!" he shouted and sprinted now. I saw him slip and fall. Quickly, he got up and then wiped his hands on his muddy pants. He turned back to look at me, smiled sheepishly and stepped carefully. I could barely see him. It was almost night.

There were streams of water rushing through the lot that had not existed when we arrived. My heart beat faster as a yellow Fiat came into view. My pace quickened as it became larger and familiar. I ran, ignoring the puddles as rain fell on my flailing arms.

My husband stood next to the driver's side, too nervous to insert his key into the lock. I looked through the window and saw a brown bag lying on the backseat.

"Definitely ours!" I shouted.

He put in the key, turned it and twisted the door latch. When it opened he whooped triumphantly— the loudest I had ever heard him. He sat for a moment, closed his door and beamed at me from inside.

"Come in," he said.

"Unlock my door," I screamed from the other side.

"Oh, sorry." He let me in.

The torrents had turned to a light shower. On the backseat were the towels, the brown bag of chocolates, and our duffle bag.

With his palms over his eyes my husband exhaled, then pulled the towels from the back and handed one to me. We dried our wet hair, faces and arms.

The rain slowed down to a pitter-patter on the windowpanes. "Start the car!"

"Off to the teashop," he said, turning the key. The engine groaned. Then nothing.

"What was that?" I asked. He tried again. This time there was a click and then nothing.

"Don't tell me you forgot to turn off the lights... again?" I shuddered.

He hit his forehead against the steering wheel several times and cursed in desperation.

Book Lovers

From inside her haute couture women's store Lily spotted a man in blue jeans and a white shirt. He was gazing at colorful scarves displayed in the window. He walked in.

"May I help you?" she asked.

"Something for my mother's birthday," he replied pleasantly.

His smile captured her. She was smitten.

She reached across him for a magenta silk scarf and draped the fabric over her shoulder.

He pointed to the blue silk scarves arranged in the next pile. "What about this one?" He pulled one out and placed it on her other shoulder. "I'll take it."

"Good choice," she said and asked him to follow her.

Lily rang the sale and handed over the bag to him. "Nice to have met you. I'm Lily Brooker."

His gaze rose to take in the low-cut neckline of her mauve georgette dress, the pearls at her throat and earlobes. "Lily Brooker, you say? Any relation to the famous Virginia Brooker?"

"She was my great grandmother. I called her Momma."

"Oh!" he said with a mysterious smile then thanked her and left.

What was that all about? Lily wondered. Virginia Brooker charmed all kinds of people. Her library, now inherited by Lily's granddad, included many irreplaceable volumes. Momma herself was a cultivated woman, a voracious reader, an avid collector, and patron and friend of writers.

While growing up Lily had spent many weekends and summer holidays reading beside her out in the garden, on the deck or in the library. Momma often said, "The most precious thing about a good book is what is between its covers." Whether it was vintage or that year's Booker Prize winner, whether its front cover image was stunning or intriguing or it was plain red, to Momma that all was irrelevant.

Lily wished she had asked the man for his name. *Well, if I'm destined to know him we'll meet again someday.*

That someday turned out to be the following month when she was invited to a dinner party at her store owner's home. The guests were from diverse professions—artists, musicians, writers, journalists and others. A bit shy at first she mingled, listened to what people were talking about and laughed with them. A man joined them. He looked familiar. Oh, yes the blue scarf guy.

"I'm Edward." He shook hands with several people but when he reached for Lily's hand he stopped. "Lily Brooker, right?"

"Right."

"Good to meet you again, Lily."

She liked the way he said her name.

"May I bring you something to drink?" he asked.

"I can get it myself." She walked with him to the bar and ordered a glass of Cabernet.

"My favorite drink," he remarked.

They sat down. She couldn't believe her luck. "I wonder what else we have in common."

"Well, I like to read and write. Do you read?"

"You like to read? You would love Granddad's library," she said excitedly.

"You mean Virginia Brooker's library?"

They chatted about Momma and her library and how Granddad always kept it locked. They chatted until the host announced that dinner was ready.

Before leaving the party Edward said to Lily, "I enjoyed your company. Would you like to meet again?"

"I too had a wonderful time."

Edward pulled out a business card from his wallet. "Any time or day convenient to you after work."

Lily read the card. *Edward Smith, Editor, Arts and Letters*, with a phone number underneath.

"If you don't mind coming to my office, we can go any place you like."

"It's not too far from where I work." She put the card in her purse and waved goodbye.

Waiting in the reception room of Edward's office, Lily picked up a recent issue of *Arts and Letters* magazine. She was pleasantly surprised to see Edward's stamp-size photo at the upper corner of the editorial page. Flipping through the pages of text and artwork she hoped to find something that would interest her. She turned to the contents page but still didn't find anything worth reading. Before placing the magazine back on the coffee table, its back cover attracted her attention. It showed an ad for a writer's retreat in Hawaii. She had vacationed on the big island with her family during several summers.

That evening Edward wanted to know everything about Virginia Brooker. Nothing about Lily. She asked how he selected material from the hundreds of submissions he received. He told her that his desire was to be a writer. He had been writing a novel for years and was nowhere near finishing it. He intended to complete the manuscript during a retreat in Hawaii.

The two started to date. They met for cocktail parties at friends' homes or just the two of them for dinner. With her Barbie Doll looks, people often wanted Lily around. Edward seemed to laugh at her jokes and enjoy her company. Lily found him simply amazing. He might be unkempt and absent-minded, but she couldn't help falling in love. Whether they were having a cup of coffee or a quick lunch, he talked about books, about his favorite authors and, if she asked, about the draft of his first novel in progress. No one was like Edward in her family... except maybe her grandfather.

Several months passed. Lily did not read as much as when she was with Momma. But that had been a long time ago. Slowly she too began to get excited about Edward's readings when he seemed to be submerged in what he was reading or writing. She too plunged into his fictional world and floated on the surface of a pool, pond, ocean wherever he would take her. An ordinary dinner date felt enriched by his passion for literature and love of words.

Lily decided to invite Edward to meet her family the following month on the day of their annual gathering. With so many people it wouldn't seem strange that she had brought a friend. She imagined introducing him. How handsome he was but how he didn't give any importance to his looks. How much knowledge he had and yet how humble. She'd say, *"Edward is just a friend. I admire him as an intellectual,"* and, *"He simply does not care about things most people care about. When he is writing or editing he is so absorbed in his work that he forgets to eat, bathe or sleep. He amazes me. He is so smart!"*

At their usual Saturday dinner date, after they had ordered their favorite wine, Edward said, "Tell me something about your Momma."

"I may have already told you she corresponded with Kipling, Woolf, Lessing, Neruda, Tagore, and authors of that caliber. Some of their handwritten letters are now framed and hanging in Grandpa's study."

"They handwrote letters to her?"

"I guess because she wrote to them in longhand. Her letters and their replies are now family heirlooms."

"That is amazing." Edward nodded over his wine glass, genuinely impressed.

"I'm visiting Granddad and the rest of my family next month. Would you like to come with me?" She so desperately wanted him to agree.

"Who's coming?" he asked.

"My three uncles, their children and grandchildren."

"What do your uncles do?"

"The eldest is a banker. He's coming with his wife and the children..." Lily paused. "I'll introduce you to all of them on Saturday. It's our annual family luncheon. That's why I want you to come." She looked into his eyes with the infatuation of a teenager.

He picked a roll from the basket the waiter had just left on the table, and slathered butter on it while her leg shook restlessly.

"Where is this gathering going to take place?" he finally asked and took a bite.

"At Granddad's house where the library's located."

The following Saturday, when Lily went to his apartment, Edward greeted her at the door. His pants were stained and his shirt wrinkled. "Did you forget we're visiting my family? Why aren't you dressed?"

"No. I didn't forget. I intended to do a load of laundry but ran out of time." Edward snickered and locked the door behind him. "You don't like what I'm wearing? You want your family to like me as I am, don't you?" He tried to lighten the mood.

Lily ground her teeth. But what he said made sense. "That's all right."

At the parking lot he unlocked the car, got in and said, "Come on. Hop in, Lily."

At first both remained quiet until they crossed the city limits. Then she put on some classical music and chatted about this and that. After more than an hour's drive she pointed to a house in the distance. He made a sharp turn off the road into a concealed entrance. The long driveway was flanked by a cream gravel border that turned into an expanse of mowed grass. The hedges were scrupulously clipped.

They got out of the car. But instead of walking up a flight of steps where tubs of red and white geraniums greeted them leading to the front door of the mansion, Lily led him around the house and asked him to wait on the back verandah. When she returned, with a white shirt and khaki trousers, he stood with a jerk.

"Here, change into these!" she said. "They are Granddad's."

Edward looked uneasy and hesitated. After a minute's thought he agreed to try them on. Garbed in half-size smaller clothes, at least he looked respectable. He followed her to the front of the house and up the flight of steps and inside.

The drawing room overlooked the garden. Dozens of people stood holding glasses with beverages of various hues. They cried out greetings and liberally gave hugs and kisses. Introductions were made, hands were shaken, smiles given.

Edward looked uncomfortable in the well-creased pants an inch above his ankle and the shirt a little tight around his chest. But Lily was relieved when he responded to other people's queries with poise as she introduced him to immaculately dressed men and women in rayon silk dresses or trim pants.

"If you're a writer and an editor, you'll love the library," said the banker.

"Oh, the library," said the banker's wife as if trying to remember something.

"A journalist, right? Intriguing job," said the president of a construction company.

"I'm not a journalist. I am editor of a magazine, *Arts and Letters*," he clarified untucking his shirt. No one recognized the magazine.

"And how do you see your career developing in the future?" one of them asked.

"I like what I do. Haven't thought much about my future."

With Mimosas and champagne, people began chatting louder. Lily's father raised his voice for Edward's benefit. "My father keeps up his mother's legacy. She knew all sorts of famous writers. You'll find it more interesting than my daughter does."

Though Lily was talking to her cousins, half of her attention was on her father and Edward. She turned and said, "Daaaddyyy!"

"I'm not criticizing you, baby! To tell the truth, I'm not a great reader myself. Your grandfather is in a different league," he indulged her, then turned to Edward. "The collection is indeed wonderful. One section is dedicated to extremely valuable and rare books."

"Sir, I'm sure you know this, but your father's rare and extensive collection is the envy of the literary community..."

"I didn't know that. But thanks for sharing." Lily's father seemed genuinely pleased.

"The whole house is stuffed with books," Lily's mother chimed in. "What we'll do with them eventually, I hate to even think."

On the sofa, sat the grandfather with a slight humped back. He was thin and undistinguished, but once must have stood tall.

"Here is Edward, the writer I told you about," Lily introduced.

"Editor!" Edward reminded. He held out his hand.

The old man took it and then slowly let it drop. "Why are you so late?" he asked Lily.

"Sorry, Grandddad. But not too late, only fifteen minutes... Traffic."

He shooed her remarks as if a fly and said, "Let's eat. Go tell the cook."

The eldest son sprang forward to help him get up.

"No, leave me alone. I can manage." He frowned then turned to Edward. "I want to talk to you. You sit on my left and you sit on my right," he said to Lily. "The rest can sit wherever they want."

Lily helped pass around bowls of creamed tomato soup and platters laden with stuffed quail, asparagus spears and grilled potatoes. Scrubbed and manicured hands served themselves. Lily admired neatly cut and brightly polished nails picking up bits with a fork or spoonful and putting the food into mouths.

The grandfather sat hunched at the head of the table. Slowly he unfurled a white napkin and talked loudly to another grandchild halfway down. "Sixth grade now? What are you learning?"

Each time the old man made some remark, they all quietened dutifully, smiling tolerantly at what he had to say.

The girl took a quick look at her father.

"Tell him which subjects you're studying," he encouraged.

"Yes, Granddad, we are learning English, math..."

While the kid was still speaking, Grandfather turned to Edward. "What do you do?"

By this time everyone knew, yet he responded, "I am an editor of an art magazine."

"None of these people read. What do you think about them?" Grandfather glared at his family who were busy gossiping and eating. "Do you read? Do you have a collection of books?"

"I've a small collection but mostly I read on my iPad."

"I can't stand the new gizmos and gadgets. I only cherish properly bound books."

Others talked about the books they had heard of but not read.

"A famous editor and writer once told my mother that her collection was the finest he had ever seen. All first editions. My mother read the manuscripts of many writers who eventually grew to be bestsellers and award winners. She was the first reader of a few poets who are famous now. But that is history."

"What is your fondest book-related memory of your mother?" Edward was curious.

"When an appraiser came to evaluate her treasured books. He appraised the first edition of *Don Quixote de la Mancha* by Miguel de Cervantes for $500,000! I couldn't believe that a measly yellowed book would be worth that much." He pointed to the almirah behind him. "Then he appraised several even more valuable. They're all stored here behind me," he said pointing once again to the wall.

Edward admired the cabinet. "Have you held the la Mancha volume in your hands?"

"I have no such desire. Haven't touched even a single one of Mamma's 'gems'."

"Have you added a new volume to her collection?"

"No. I plan to sell them, make a profit and then donate the remaining ones to the local library. I'm just a custodian of the books."

Edward eyed the people talking amongst themselves. The woman sitting next to him said, "Granddad, we had a small library when I was young. It was the reason I inculcated the habit of reading and became a librarian."

Granddad nodded with disinterest.

"Which book have you read recently?" Edward asked.

"*Great Gatsby*, perhaps the third time—such a thought-provoking book," she said excitedly.

"Third time! Why?"

"So many lessons—how Gatsby woos Daisy with his palatial home and lavish parties and yet ultimately fails to win her affections. None of the people who attend his extravagant dinners show up at his funeral. It's a hair-raising read. Look at my goosebumps." She pointed to her arm.

"Money can't buy love," Edward whispered.

She smiled and said, "Did you grow up in a household filled with books?"

"No, but my mother took me to the neighborhood library on weekends."

The woman seated opposite said, "I have never been inside a library building!"

Grandfather nodded then turned to Edward. "Did you not have books of your own then?"

Edward answered slowly. "I was allowed to borrow three library books each week. However, it has been my deep desire to collect books."

Granddad became thoughtful and took a good look at Edward. As a few moments passed Edward moved uneasily in his chair, perhaps trying to figure out why his host was scrutinizing him. But he couldn't.

Plates were cleared, dessert served and then the coffee was brought into the library. Women chatted. Men wanted to light cigars, but as always Granddad forbade smoking in the library.

"Ah, good! Now is your chance to look at the famous family collection," Lily's uncle said to Edward.

The library was as large as the drawing room, its walls paneled and lined with glass-fronted cases.

The whole family gathered there, sitting on leather sofas or perched on the arms of chairs.

Aunts asked Lily's mother if her daughter was serious about Edward. She replied, "Oh no, she's prone to passing fancies." A few of the women looked at Edward. He glanced and flashed smiles. Their conversation broke.

Lily's mother carried a cup of coffee with a dessert biscuit and walked to Edward. "Here, enjoy!" He thanked her, placed the cup on a table farthest from the bookcases where leather-bound, gold tooled books were shelved.

The grandfather pointed around the room as he said, "On all six shelves is everything from 1900 to 1950. The next three cases contain 1951 to 2000. And the last three cases are hardcovers and paperbacks published in the twenty-first century."

Edward tried to open one of the glass doors. Lily, standing behind him, said, "They're all locked. But Granddad has the keys."

The grandfather pointed to the 1900-1950 section at the far end of the room. "For his sake I unlocked a few cases this morning."

Edward crossed the room and began to browse. Kipling, Tennyson, Hardy, Trollope. Each spine had the stiffness of a new book. The flimsy pages clung together. He put one book back and tried another. The same thing again—a creaking spine and tacky edges unopened through the years. From shelf to shelf, he sampled books arranged according to size.

"Mind you," the grandfather prodded, "put things back in the right places. But enjoy!"

"Certainly. Thank you for letting me handle these."

Edward took down Tagore's, *Gitanjali,* illustrated by the author himself, and placed it on a side table, then Kipling's *Kim* caught his attention. He pulled that out and held it in his left hand. With a smile on his face, he read, *Autobiography of Anthony Trollope*, and took out that one, too. He kept the pile of books on his left and sat down in an armchair to read a few passages.

From the other end of the room Lily walked briskly back to Edward. She felt the piercing gazes of the guests on her back. "You can't just sit here by yourself!" she whispered.

"Just getting acquainted with these treasures. Oh Lily, how I wanted to have these books... Look, Lily—Kipling, Tennyson, Hardy, Trollope!"

She kept her voice low. "When you have your fill, join in some conversation. Mix and mingle! Chat! Don't read now!"

"Why not?" Edward said. "We are in a library. If not here, then where?"

"You've come here to meet my family, be with them, get to know them. Books can wait." Lily turned pale and flung a glance toward the staring faces and then turned back to him. "Please... really?"

"Your family must come here to read often. They will understand. Won't they?"

She rolled her eyes and didn't answer.

"The only reason I drove here was to see this library, to touch these books, to have the pleasure of meeting the man responsible for this collection." With each word the volume of Edward's voice rose.

"What is it, Lily? What's the fuss?" Granddad called.

The whole room fell silent.

Lily walked closer to Granddad. "Just asking Edward to mix and mingle and not read right now."

"If the boy wants to read, let him!"

Lily's shoulders slouched. "I invited him to meet the family."

"Lily, the reason I came here was to see the collection."

"I didn't think you would actually do nothing else but that."

"Geez, I wasn't going to read the whole time."

She glared at him.

"I think I should leave," he whispered to her.

"Please stay," she said.

He walked to Lily's mother and said, "Thank you for the lunch. It was lovely." Edward headed for the door, then turned and waved to the room. "Nice meeting you all, goodbye!"

Lily followed helplessly as he simply walked out of the library, through the living room, vestibule, down the staircase, and onto the driveway. She did not stop him.

As he was walking over the gravel down the drive, he turned around and said, "You want to drive with me back to the city?"

"No thanks, I can get a ride with someone." Her heart was heaving. She wanted to drive back with him, but the ego nailed her motionless.

During the following weeks Lily made no attempt to get in touch with Edward. She wanted to but had no excuse to do so. Granddad had been asking her to bring her beau back to his home. He had taken a fancy to the boy and wanted to get to know him better.

"He is not my beau, Granddad. When I see him, I'll tell him," she replied each time he asked.

When Granddad continued to pester her about bringing him back, she said, "What is it that you want to talk to Edward about?" He wouldn't say but smiled and nodded to himself. No longer able to postpone Granddad's invitation she reluctantly called Edward's office.

"May I speak with Edward," Lily said to his secretary.

"Of course," she said. "Please hold."

The first words Lily heard from Edward were, "Lily, I'm so sorry about my behavior at your granddad's library. I've been thinking about you since the day I drove back alone. I thought you would never want to see me again."

His voice and his words delighted Lily but she curbed her excitement. "I called because Granddad is pestering me about you. He wants to see you again."

"Really! Why? When?"

"Whenever?"

"Would you come with me? Would we drive together?"

"You can't drive by yourself?" She gave him her granddad's number. "Call him before you go so that he'll be home."

"I don't want to go without you."

"Then don't go!" she said but felt miserable.

The following Saturday Edward called Lily. "I'm overwhelmed with your granddad's decision. I don't know what to say or how to thank you for this."

"What decision? What are you talking about?"

"Seriously? You don't know?"

"I've no idea."

"He plans to bequeath Momma's library to me. To me, Lily! I can't believe it!"

To her own surprise Granddad's decision greatly pleased her. Momma would agree. Edward had a passion for books. He submerged himself in them, in words, in literature. He drank, ate, breathed books.

"Good for Granddad! And great for you!" Lily pretended not to care.

"Please Lily, don't talk like that. I had no idea why he wanted to see me again, alone. I thought he was interested in *Arts and Letters*, perhaps wanted to buy the magazine business. I really didn't know. Please don't be angry with me."

She realized she loved him, loved him very much.

"Are you there, Lily? I can't wait for us to go to Hawaii. If you would come with me. I'll purchase two tickets for the retreat. Would you go with me, Lily? Lily, please?"

Revenge

The train whistled. It shunted, shuddered and began to move. I felt as if I was under some spell—feverish and roused with only one thought in my mind, *Revenge!* The train screamed a shrill whistle and picked up speed.

She thought herself to be sexy and smart but to me she was conniving and loathsome. What would I say to her if we were face to face? How would I make her regret the way she treated me? Would she even remember destroying my tender childhood and precious teens? Would she feel guilty or repentant?

I remember the first time I mentioned my mad desire to take revenge on my stepmother to my husband. I had been crying. My eyes turned red. I was seated at the edge of our bed when he came and stood at the door.

"What's going on?" he asked. *"Are you enraged? Again?"* He sat next to me rubbing my back. I nodded. Each time something triggered her image a destructive emotion stirred my heart. A memory—the scent of my birth mother's perfume, an old photograph, an excerpt from my father's letter. This time it was the voice of my father's sister, Janaki,

who often called to say hello. *"You are trembling."* My husband put his arms around me, pulling my head closer. *"You must clear your mind of whatever junk it is filled with. This is not healthy."* He kissed the top of my head. *"You can't go on fearing and hating someone for the rest of your life. It is like holding hot coal in your hand. It will burn you but won't hurt her."*

I wiped my eyes, trying to recover from the bout of my craziness and realizing the truth in what he had said so often. What I was doing to myself was insane and had to be stopped. But whenever a trigger dug deep into my growing-up years, a fossil came to light that incited my hatred. I relived the moments—no... days, weeks, months—thinking of the time when my father remarried immediately after my mother's death. The triggers turned me into a teenage girl. Momentarily anger controlled me. It took quite an effort to calm down and be my normal self. It didn't happen often, perhaps once or twice a year, but when it did it jolted me out of my normalcy, and my husband had to take the brunt of it.

"I want to kill her!" I screamed when he left the room to brew tea. He was in hearing distance. *"She must be paying for what she did to you,"* he yelled back. *"Ugly witch!"* I cried.

I adored my birth mother. I idolized her. And suddenly one day when I came home from school, to my puzzlement, many friends and relatives were gathered. Aunt Janaki came running toward me, hugged me tight and as gently as she could told me that my mother had died. I refused to believe her. I ran to my mother's body. She was covered with a white sheet, only her face visible. I touched her cheek; it was cold. Numb, I sat next to her lifeless body. It took me years before I accepted the reality of her death and to convince my heart of the absence of her warm touch. My father remarried long before I could absorb the pain and sorrow of my loss. While I pondered why a stranger would sleep on my mother's side of my parents' bed, my father wanted me to call this woman "Mom."

My father's new wife was nothing like my mother. She never uttered affectionate words or made physical gestures of love. My mother was loving, caring and kind. She loved to prepare our favorite dishes. She watched television with us. She was spontaneous, natural. But my stepmother had one face with my father and another with me. She was blunt and watched her favorite shows behind closed doors. I hated her. Aunt Janaki asked me to be patient. She tried to convince me that I was not giving my stepmother a chance. What did she mean? How do you give someone a chance to show motherly love?

But I tried. I would walk up to her, hug her, kiss her, but she didn't respond. When I looked into her eyes begging for her love, some warmth, I sensed indifference, distance, at times even hate. Within a couple of years of living with her my desire for affection shriveled. I packed the memories of my mother's love in my heart for savoring and safekeeping.

Occasionally, when I needed permission from my stepmother or asked her a question, the only reply I got was, "No," "Nope," "Can't be done," "We don't do that," or when she wasn't sure if she could negate me by herself she would add, "I'm not sure if your father would agree." If I looked disappointed, she smirked. If I looked satisfied, she would say, "What was that again?"

I stopped asking.

"I don't want to go," was my answer when she dragged me along to adult parties that were excruciatingly boring.

"You can't stay home. If we are going, you are going," was her parrotlike answer.

I was twelve or thirteen and no other guests brought along their children. I either watched television or played with the babies who were being watched by a sitter.

The parents drank, smoked and laughed more than necessary. She demanded "perfect" behavior from me but never showed what perfection looked like.

My father traveled often. When he was away on his business trips, she tried to control everything I wanted to do. I felt smothered. I spent my free time climbing and falling out of trees behind our house, breaking and bruising my limbs. Amongst trees I felt at home, safe and protected. On weekends I did my homework, my reading, and lunched amidst those trees.

When the three of us were together we rubbed each other the wrong way. She called me "Know-it-all" or "trouble-maker" because of my rebellious behavior. At school I misbehaved often and was sent to the principal's office. This offended my father and drove his wife crazy. Yardsticks were cracked on my back and arms so often that welts formed. I always wore long-sleeved blouses to hide the bruises.

Adolescence was a nightmare. At fifteen I fell in love. When she found out she said, "You are possessed by the devil! You need to be exorcised. You better not come home pregnant." She didn't have to worry. I was so sheltered that I didn't even know how one got pregnant. Through her church group she came to know that my best friend was pregnant. She stopped calling that girl by her real name and referred to her as "your-friend-the-whore."

I looked up to the girls in honors classes—confident, multi-talented and smart. I dreamed to be like them—to be in honors classes, win debating awards, participate in piano recitals. By the time I graduated from high school I had lost all interest to struggle and strive. My desires and abilities were drowned in the sorrowful tides of my mother's loss and obliterated with discouragement from my stepmother.

The thought of being a mother terrified me. Even imagining having a child gave me chills; I'd sweat profusely and feel like an insecure teenager who was being welted by sharp words of cynicism and intimidation. The antidote of my husband's love had managed to scab the psychological welts and slits.

Willy-nilly I grew, went to college and got a certificate in counseling. At this time, I left my father's house never to return. My father would call and often leave messages, but I never returned his calls. I would get news about them through Aunt Janaki. But after she passed away that connection also got severed. In time, we lost all contact.

I met my husband when I worked part-time in an art supply store. At the end of every month, he'd come to buy supplies: oil colors, charcoal sticks, sketching paper, linseed and turpentine oils and whatever he needed as an oil painter. One day he asked me out. I accepted.

We began to date regularly and enjoyed our conversations. At one such warm meeting I told him about my nightmares.

"Many people have nightmares," he said casually.

"They don't get up sweating and screaming and shouting, 'I'm going to kill you!'"

Obviously, he was curious. "We may utter horrific words in our sleep, plan terrible things in our dreams, but we don't actually do them in daylight."

"Even when I'm awake I want to kill her."

"Who do you want to kill?"

"Someone you don't want to know."

"I want to know."

Then I told him about my stepmother. I did not give too many details. But slowly I began to share an episode here, another there, from my young adulthood. He listened attentively with concern. "If that's how you feel, we won't keep any relationship with her." I realized he had no idea about the depth of my feelings.

"And one more thing," I said. "I don't want to have children." My confession abruptly ended our conversation. I realized this only much later because afterward we kissed and said good night.

He did not call after that evening. And he did not call for months. I thought about the reason and understood why he would not want to continue a serious relationship with a woman who would not want to have children. The separation pained me. But I did not blame him for not staying in touch. I did not want any children because I was afraid I wouldn't be a good mother. He loved children.

One evening he surprised me by coming over to my apartment with a bouquet of roses. I was ecstatic. I invited him in for a cup of tea. We sat facing one another. After we had finished talking it was as if we had never broken the friendship. He held my left hand and kissed it tenderly. "Don't worry about having children," he said. "The more I thought about you not wanting to have children, the more I realized the folly of not seeing you because you don't want any. I have missed you so."

My eyes welled up. I had been feeling guilty for being abrupt about what I thought without respecting his choice of wanting children. I wanted to hold him tight, never letting him go. But overwhelmed with emotions, hearing his feelings for me, I was unable to move. My hand still in his, he slipped a ring on my finger and said, "Will you marry me?"

We got married that year.

I had lost and then found a man who was confident in his masculinity and comfortable with his own feminine nature. He showed me how to love, to pay attention to my own needs, listen for the cues and clues my body sent. And not to dwell on what had happened to me growing up.

After a couple of months of our marriage, what I was afraid of happened in the middle of one night. He heard my screams and jumped from his side of the bed. He walked to my side, woke me and held me tight. Then with my head close to his chest he calmed me down. My screams subsided but I started sobbing. He turned on the lights, fetched a glass of water and helped me take a few sips. With a napkin he cleaned my eyes and nose and said, "Walk for a few minutes until you are fully awake."

Then for one whole year, nothing. I thought the marriage had cured my fright. Yet I experienced two nightmarish bouts with decreased intensity. My husband, level-headed and self-possessed, never lost his cool. His unconditional love was turning me into a calmer person. I hoped for a complete cure with his genuine understanding and love.

Year passed. I experienced a terrible nightmare, the worst my husband had witnessed. The next morning, he was hell bent on knowing all that had happened to me during my childhood and teens that still caused me such suffering and pain.

One by one I brought to light the festering emotions that until then were hidden in the darkness. I told him what I had never told anyone before. I narrated the toxic and turbulent events that had resulted in guilt and hatred but I had done my best to swallow or push down. I narrated incidents of abuse that I could neither suppress, consciously control, or forget. I told him how grateful I was for his love, his understanding and his concern for me. I told him how his being beside me had helped expunge the poison from my heart and almost clarify the mind.

What I didn't know was that by verbalizing and rethinking, instead of expunging these thoughts, they had intensified. I must have looked horrified because he stared at my face.

"Why don't you confront your stepmother and tell her what a mess you have become?"

I raised an eyebrow.

"Well, nothing else seems to work. You must confront the root cause of your problems."

"No way! I hate that woman!"

I dug deeper into the mine of my memories. From blurry images emerged a clearer picture of an angry hateful fifteen-year-old. She was drenched with years of snide remarks and rude insinuations. It felt raw, the cause of such pain.

He kept nagging me. Every time he got a chance he would ask, "So when do you think you will be ready to meet this woman?"

I did not know what to say. I simply stared at him.

Disgusted, he got up and left. He stopped talking to me.

The following week, I told my husband that I had decided to meet her. He smiled faintly and said, "Trust me. You will be free." Then he added, "Don't drive. Go by train. I insist."

The day turned into dusk. The train attendant handed me clean sheets and a pillow for the night. I lay down but was unable to sleep. I sat up as the big raindrops splashed the cold windowpane and hit the train with a bout of thundershowers. Against the dark sky I saw my face reflect on the windowpane.

"Fool! Where do you think you are going?"

"To confront my tormentor!"

"What is the purpose?"

"Revenge! She destroyed tender years of my life with insults and vitriol. She squeezed out my self-esteem like pigment from a tube of paint and left me shriveled. She stole my self-confidence during critical years of my youth. Don't you see the bruises, black and stale yellow, that cover my body and my heart?" I moaned, pitying myself.

The train whistle shrieked. Behind the glass the nightscape rolled by.

"Why confront her now? It has been decades since you left home," the reflection asked.

"Because memories keep reeling in my mind all the time."

"All the time? Really? What memory is coming now?"

"Like the first night after they returned from their honeymoon. Having showered I put on my favorite pajamas with monkeys hanging from tree branches and styled my hair. When I walked into the room where she sat with my father, she took one glance at me and snickered, 'You look like a boy!' I felt I had slipped and rolled in mud. Those were my favorite pajamas. The first time I wore them my father said, 'Come here, my monkey. Give me a hug.' But that day he did not even look up from the newspaper he was reading. I expected him to say something or at least smile at me. He agreed with everything she said."

"Do you have any other memory?"

I was too sad to remember anything.

"Oh I got one," the reflection said. *"On your twelfth birthday she promised to buy you the Monopoly board game. But she did not keep her promise. Instead, she brought you a flowering cactus that you knew she wanted for herself. You reminded her about the game. She pretended as if she did not remember. 'Look how pretty the cactus looks here on our kitchen windowsill'."* A rare occasion when she used "our."

The raindrops struck hard on the reflection on the cold glass. It asked, *"What other memories do your bruises hide?"*

This time I did not have to think hard. I said, "She stared at me from head to toe whenever I walked to them when they were seated together. I think he was afraid of her. Afraid she would leave him if he uttered words of affection to me. The gestures of his fatherly fondness had disappeared. It was as if I no longer lived in that house, as if I was as dead as my mother."

I saw my loveless stepmother's face replace my reflection. The glass pane reflected hatred, anger, jealousy. How would she react to that face after thirty years?

By early evening the storm faded. The train wailed as it stopped. I picked up my duffle bag and purse, got off and walked out of the train station. I didn't need a taxi. I remembered those streets and lanes. I walked over the bridge, crossed the river and walked through the zigzag roads toward town. The setting sunrays painted everything rage red.

Lush green leaves were touched by golden rust. Brown roofs peeked through the treetops. A stray dog followed me to my neighborhood. The rose window of the church burned with jealous orange rays. Nothing but the emotional demise of my enemy circled my mind.

The neighborhood was dark by the time I reached the street where my childhood house stood; where she, I was sure, continued to live. I turned the corner and walked four blocks to a single streetlamp. I stood still for a few minutes to look across the street at the two-story house that was staring at me. A cloud of viciousness peeked through its windows.

I felt old, stupid, tired.

I faced her house where I had lived. The house she had somehow managed to swindle from my father. Before he died, he had left her and lived alone in an apartment on the other end of the town.

I walked up on the porch and read her name on the mailbox.

Did she have any children? Did they live with her? Did she have grandchildren?

I rang the bell. I could hear my heart pounding.

Would she recognize me? Would she remember my name?

No one answered the door.

I rang the bell again.

The doorknob rattled.

I crossed my fingers. My heart continued to hammer.

The door opened.

An old woman bent with age stood there, whitehaired and wrinkled. Blinking. Gazing at me.

"Yes?" she said.

I stood there for what could not have been more than a minute. But too many things happened in that minute.

I saw her sickly, wrinkled, sunken face.

I saw her deteriorating, shrunken body.

I saw her bent with old age.

I had seen her when she, in heels, towered over me at five-foot six inches.

Nature had turned a glamorous woman into a waxen head, a healthy one into a shrunken body. Old age had ravaged her looks.

Now I towered over her as I stared and gasped. I was a robust forty-something with a few strands of salt in my peppered hair.

She had lost most of hers. She looked a hundred plus and smelled of funeral.

I was in good health.

I no longer wanted to kill her, psychologically or physically, even if I could. I wanted to gaze at her as she was at that moment. Just to stand there and look at what she had become. That's all! Lonely, sick, old and miserable.

Her eyes flew up and down my body, not even close to how she used to glare; her mind squinted at the woman who shadowed her door. She lifted one hand and put it over her mouth in a kind of wonder. Her lips trembled. At last her voice, so small, so frail, so nervous blurted out, "You look familiar. What do you want?"

She seemed to age with each moment of my staring. By the time I was done ogling hard at her she was one hundred twenty years old. The universe had already taken revenge on her.

I turned and walked down the steps and reached the street before she called, "Who are you? What do you want?" I heard her voice for the last time before she hesitantly closed the door.

I walked behind the house and looked up at the window where I had lain every morning for the first sixteen years of my life. I waited long enough for my young self to come down to join me. When she did, I said to her, "Let's go! Let's make the best of this life. Let's not treat ourselves or anyone else shabbily."

A long way off, I looked back. All the lights of the house were lit. It was as if after I left, she had gone around and put them all on. I walked, listening to the sounds of the crickets and into the darkness of the river. I crossed the bridge and walked up the stairs leading to the train station. With my young self settled peacefully within me, I rode the train out of town and back to join my loving, adoring husband for the rest of my life.

INSPIRATIONAL

SECRET HEALER

Young Saras waited until he felt sure that Dhaniram had stopped breathing. The boy jumped off the bed and ran through the kitchen door. He dashed past the blurry confusion of big and small houses, the water pump, the zigzag street shops—the tea stall, the cobbler, the grocer, the cloth merchant—all shut down for the day. He kept running as crimson streaks of the setting sun reflected like blood in the whites of his eyes. He ran on the paved road that turned into a narrow mud path flanked by thorny succulents. He ignored the bloody scratches the horny cacti made on his shins and calves.

When he came to the foot of the range of hills, he ran up where young bushes were shadowed beneath large pines and maples. Reaching the bald hilltop, he stopped near a single bare tree. The sun that had blazed the whole day became ash. Heaving and panting, he leaned against the tree trunk, sweat dripping from his forehead and neck, his vest buttons slipping from their worn-out holes to reveal his dark skin.

A cough rattled in his throat; he spat and wiped his mouth. With his sleeve, he pulled back the thick shock of dirty hair from his forehead. His clammy pants, several sizes too big, had not been washed in weeks. He had not bathed in days. He could not rest lest they come after him. He ran down the other side of the hill, lost his balance, and plummeted into a shallow pool. His bruises and cuts smarted.

He dragged himself onto the dry bank and felt a bloody gash on his forehead. His ribs throbbed, but the excruciating pain paled in comparison to the fear in his pounding heart. He raised his head to see if anyone had seen him. Through blurred vision he saw a silhouette approach. Panic struck his soul. He muttered a curse and lost consciousness.

The old man carried the boy to a hut and laid him on a charpoy. He pushed the small bedstead close to the warmth of the hearth and sat on the edge to clean the boy's bruises and cuts and dress them with an herbal salve he had concocted. He bandaged the boy's bleeding forehead and wiped his body clean with a solution extracted from marigold pistils. Finally, he covered him with a cotton quilt.

As the old man gazed at the half-conscious boy, pity and affection stirred his heart. What could this boy be running from? He tucked the quilt under the boy's feet and chin and walked out to the porch. There, he lay down on a makeshift charpoy for the night.

Saras floated in and out of consciousness. All night, his head throbbed. His ribs ached. His wounds smarted. He touched the bandages around his head and chest. *Where am I? How long have I been lying here? Who brought me here?*

The morning light filtered through the window. Saras heard the door open and quickly hid his face beneath the quilt.

"Are you awake?" the old man asked.

Does he know? Has he summoned the police?

"What is your name?" The old man stood next to his bed. Saras did not move.

"Would you tell me your name, son?"

Saras shrank underneath the covers and remained still. The old man sat at the edge, on the opposite corner of the charpoy. Saras jerked away from him.

"How can I take care of you if I don't even know your name?"

"Why do you care?"

"Because you were hurt, and I brought you to my home."

With squinted eyes, Saras examined the room— the white walls and mud floor. His arms crossed against his chest. His neck stretched, he turned his head toward the wall.

"Did you dress my wounds?" he asked.

The old man said, "I did."

"And change my clothes?" Saras turned on his side and saw the lush vegetation outside the window.

He tried putting his feet on the floor, but the pain made him moan.

"Yes," the old man nodded.

"Why?" he screamed. "Go away!" Then the boy writhed in pain.

The old man got up at once.

"Ahhhh..." Saras whimpered, lay down again, and turned to the other side.

"You are hurting," the old man said. "You should feel better in a few days. Thank God your wounds are not too deep."

Saras watched the old man leave the room. He had a peaceful face and a gentle voice. Was he pretending to be nice, or was his heart as kind as his voice?

After a while, he re-entered with a stainless-steel plate laden with food. "I brought you something to eat." He placed the plate next to the bed. "You need to get your strength back." He turned to leave.

Suddenly, Saras said, "Who are you?"

"People call me the Healer of Plants," the old man said without turning to look at him. When Saras did not respond, the man left the room.

What does he want from me? Saras tried to raise himself but fell back on his pillow with a whimper. Hunger prompted him to try again. He sat up with a moan, propping himself against the pillow. He picked up the stainless-steel goblet filled with fresh milk and gulped it down. He placed the plate on his lap, gobbled up morsels of pan-baked roti mixed with vegetables, and topped it off with hot tea. The sugary tea reminded him of his mother's breakfast brew. Tears welled in his eyes. He slid back down under the quilt and started to daydream about the sweet memories of his early childhood.

It seemed ages since Saras awoke to the rooster's crowing and followed Baba, his father, to the riverbank. From the bank, he would jump in the Tapti River, wash his body, rinse his mouth, and watch his father offer an ablution to the rising sun. After washing themselves, they would fill two plastic buckets and two vessels—one brass and the other terracotta—with water. On their return home, Baba would hang the two heavier buckets at the ends of a long bamboo stick that he balanced on his shoulders while Saras balanced the water-filled vessels on his head. Only recently had Saras begun carrying vessels, sometimes even a third smaller one on top of the other two. Just a year ago, he had frolicked as he walked next to Baba, hitting stones with a stick. Year by year he had been given more responsibilities.

Once back home, Ma served them pan-baked roti and dal with such seasonal vegetables as brinjal, pumpkin, or zucchini that she grew in a small garden patch behind the house. She brewed milk-tea fit for the gods. While they ate, she bundled their midday meal in a cloth napkin—roti, mango pickle, a piece of onion, and green chili. They sipped their tea as she ate her morning meal. The three of them would leave their home at the same time—Saras with Baba to herd cattle and Ma to the river to bathe and wash clothes, pans and pots.

Every morning, Baba and Saras gathered the cattle from the sheds and pens behind their landlord's homestead. The dust flew as the animals scurried through the wooden fences. The bells around the cows' necks tinkled, and flies danced up and down the buffaloes' noses and backs. Baba led the cattle with a long cane stick and yodeled as they approached the pasture. But those carefree days came to an end when Saras turned thirteen.

One day, as Baba was yodeling, he was seized by a bad cough. Saras held his father and settled him on the ground. Before the cattle had time to scatter, Baba felt better. They continued to walk toward the low purple hills where the pasture was greenest. In bare feet, they walked miles going one way until the sun was at its zenith.

Saras's favorite place was the mango grove where the cattle busily grazed and lazily chewed their cud. Baba sat down against the trunk of the largest mango tree and kept watch. As Saras unknotted the bundle of their midday meal another bout of coughing attacked Baba. Saras thumped his back, gave him water to drink, and laid out their lunch. The two ate in silence. When they finished, Saras looked at his father's tired face.

"Why don't you lie down, Baba?"

"I think I should, son."

"I'll watch the cattle from the top of the tree."

Baba patted him on the back and lay down to rest, and Saras climbed the trunk of a mango tree until it branched. He made himself comfortable there, his legs dangling on either side of a sturdy limb as he plucked a mango and peeled its leathery skin with his teeth. The sour fruit made his mouth salivate. He took a bite, and then another and another, until his mouth felt raw. *In a month or two, the green fruit will turn gold. I will be able to bite into the juicy fruit like a monkey and feast on its sweet flesh.* Imagining this, his chafed mouth watered.

He looked into the distance—the various shades of green expanded and extended into purplish-gray hills against a background of blue. He began to hum a tune. Slowly turning his head he took in the view and dreamed of the days when he would have his own herd of cattle, like Baba. Better still, he would live in the city like Chacha, Baba's brother who visited once a year.

From the ground below, Saras heard Baba coughing again. Climbing down, he collected as many mangoes as he could fit in the pockets of his short pants for his mother to pickle.

As sunset approached, Saras felt a tinge of sadness. He did not want the day to end. But his father was not well and needed rest. The two walked together until they reached a pond. Baba continued to cough as he waded knee-deep into the shallow water to gather the cattle who had cooled themselves before returning home. When the sun neared the horizon, it was time to yodel the herds back to their pens and sheds.

At supper, Saras watched from the kitchen door as his parents talked in whispers. Baba's cough had subsided. The flames from the hearth glowed and danced on their faces. Ma set out steel plates and filled the steel bowls with dal. She had saved all of the sour mangoes that he'd brought for making hot pickle except for one, which she turned into savory chutney. He joined them as she rolled out, baked, and served warm roti to him and Baba. Then she ladled second helpings of simmering dal into their bowls. Only after serving them the seconds did she eat.

"Sleep well, my son. Tomorrow is the day of merrymaking; it's Krishna's birthday," Ma said before he fell asleep. Saras hoped Baba would feel better so that they could leave early in the morning for the temple as they did each year.

As far back as he could remember this was the only holiday they celebrated away from home, at the Krishna Temple, the pride of the town of Ramnagar.

Very early the next day, Saras was glad to see his parents in a good mood. Dressed in their festival finery, the three of them rode a bus to a stop at the center of Ramnagar, then trekked to the temple. Saras walked in the middle, the swoosh of his mother's starched red and green sari echoing the rustle of his father's white kurta and pajama. Closer to the temple, they joined the throngs of people who had arrived for the celebrations. Walking in rhythm with the river of people, Saras focused on passing through the hurrying crowd and taking a look at the images of the Lord Krishna and goddess Radha enshrined in the temple's inner sanctum.

One by one, Baba, Ma, and Saras rang the bell hanging at the temple entrance. As they made their way through the main hall toward the womb chamber, they heard the priest blow the conch. They stood in line until it was their turn to hand in their offering of bananas, a coconut, and a box of sweet laddu to the priest. Closer to the door of the inner chamber, Saras gazed at the images of Krishna and Radha and took a closer look at the blue statue of baby Krishna that had been placed near the feet of the two deities. The priest applied vermillion tilak to each of their foreheads and gave them a teaspoon of consecrated water to sip. He broke the coconut and removed its creamy pieces, then added them, a banana, and a few laddus to a tray over-laden with offerings from other devotees. The offering thus blessed, the priest returned the rest to Baba. Saras and his parents joined the devotees already seated, facing the inner shrine and singing songs of love and devotion for the baby Krishna. They ate the blessed food—a banana, a piece of coconut, and a laddu each—enjoying the familiar songs. When they finished eating, they joined the chorus.

Late in the afternoon when they arrived home, they savored some more laddu with Ma's brew of sweet tea, as delicious as the tea the old man had prepared for him.

The superficial cuts on Saras's body were better in a few days, and the deeper cuts had begun to heal. From the window he watched the old man working in his farm-like garden from early morning until sunset. His savior's profile reminded Saras of his uncle who lived in the big city. *When Chacha is older he will look like this man whom people call the Healer of Plants.*

Chacha was Baba's younger brother. For years, he had worked in the big city. Once a year, he would stay with Saras's family for a holiday. He was muscular and healthier than Baba, with eyes, nose and lips that attracted women's attention. Baba often remarked how Saras looked more like Chacha than him.

Chacha dressed like city Maliks, suited and booted during the day, and in loose pajama and shirt at night. If Saras brought him hot tea holding the cup with his sleeve, Chacha would lovingly rebuke, "*Abe gamdi,* oh villager! What is this? Why don't you use a tray?" Or when Saras walked in bare feet, Chacha would call out, "*Abe gadhe,* oh you donkey! Are you a boy or a monkey?"

"Chacha, how can I be a donkey and monkey at the same time?" Saras would argue in good cheer, making his uncle laugh.

Saras enjoyed Chacha's stories the most. They were vivid and wonderful narrations about Maliks and Bibijis, the city dwellers he mingled with. He described their fine clothes and fancy footwear and their dining habits and discussions at the dinner table as they enjoyed meals of roasted chicken, goat kabobs, aromatic rice pilaf, syrupy jalebi, and mangoes from Varanasi.

⁕

The day after their trip to the Krishna Temple, Baba's health deteriorated. He was unable to keep food or drink down. When Chacha got the news, he came for a surprise visit and was saddened to see Baba cough incessantly. That week, Chacha helped Saras herd the cattle.

Day by day, the family observed Baba's energy diminishing. Chacha could not stay any longer. His job with Dhaniram compelled him to return to the city lest he be fired. After he left, Ma expressed her worry about money to Saras. Without Baba herding the cattle, how were they going to survive? Saras assured her that he could herd the cattle himself. Without a word to his father's employer, as Ma was certain the employer would not hand over such responsibility to a thirteen-year-old, Saras herded the cattle, and day after day brought the animals safely home.

On payday, when Saras went to collect his wages, the employer gave him his father's monthly earnings. The man inquired about his father's health, as he had heard he was not keeping well. Saras said he was getting better and would be able to return to work soon. On his way home, Saras met a family acquaintance heading toward his own home.

"So sorry to hear about your Baba," the man said, patting Saras on the head.

"What about my Baba?" Saras halted.

"Ummm. You didn't know?" The neighbor looked confused. "Ummm! Your father was really sick, son!" With his palm on Saras's head he tried to console.

"He only had a very bad..." Saras began, but seeing the expression on his neighbor's face, he stopped mid-sentence and ran as fast as he could.

Outside his home a crowd had gathered, and he heard cries and moans coming from inside. When he entered, he saw Baba's body laid on the floor and Ma sitting cross-legged next to him. She asked him to pay his last respects to his father. Saras pressed his palms together and bowed down. But then he fell on his father and sobbed on his chest. Chacha, who had been summoned back by a neighbor, picked up Saras, made him sit next to his mother, and covered the body with a white shroud. Saras hugged his mother and cried bitterly.

Before sunset, the cremation services were over. The next day, Chacha performed the last rites in the presence of a priest. Saras saw how sad and worried Chacha was about him and his mother—nephew and sister-in-law. He suggested that Saras get a job in the city. Otherwise, how was Ma going to pay for the funeral and manage the household?

Ma was darning Saras's socks. He stood tall and asked his uncle, "What kind of work will I do?"

His hand on Saras's shoulder, Chacha sat down on a charpoy and asked Saras to sit next to him. He looked Saras in the eye. "You can work at my employer's home. He is not the best person to work for, but he is looking for someone to help his wife clean and cook."

Ma stopped darning. "Are you asking him to work as a domestic servant?"

"I don't want to live with a stranger. I don't want to be a servant." Saras squirmed in discomfort.

"What's wrong with serving? You get to live with a nice family, the food is free, and you earn money and save it for your ma."

Ma put her head down on her knees and sobbed. Saras patted his mother's back. She wiped her eyes with the loose end of her sari and said, "Have mercy, Chacha. He is too young!"

"Thirteen!" Saras said with pride.

"Now he works herding cows from dawn to dusk earning a sack of grain and perhaps a five-rupee note per month," Chacha said.

Ma picked up her darning. "That is enough to feed us. God bless Baba's employer—he has agreed to keep him," she said.

"If they gave him half of what they gave my brother, that would have been something, but five rupees?" Chacha said.

"They will; eventually, he will earn more when he is a bit older," Ma said. Sitting beside her, Saras placed his arm around her shoulders.

"How do you plan to pay the debt of the last rites and the cremation, hun?" Chacha asked.

"I will find a way. I'll work. We'll work!" Ma insisted.

"As you wish," Chacha said and dropped the subject. That evening, he gave his sister-in-law some cash and returned to the city.

The local grocer knew Saras's family well. Out of sympathy, he hired Ma to grind spices. She was to do her work in a shed behind the store. From dawn to dusk, day after day, she turned the millstone round and round grinding turmeric and ginger root and whole chili peppers into powder, only stopping at lunch for a meager meal.

Even after a year of grueling work, she was only able to pay half of the interest they owed the moneylender. The debt kept increasing. Saras worked as hard as his father had, but he did not receive more money, only more grain. The landlord said he was still too young to do his father's job, although Saras knew he did as much, if not more.

Each evening, Ma came home with her face, arms, and sari covered with powdery dust and smelling of mixed spices. Without bothering to change, she prepared the evening meal, making enough to save for their morning and noon meals the next day. They ate, and then Saras helped her wash clothes and dishes. With each passing day, Ma's eyes darkened and her cheeks hollowed. Lamenting her husband's death and forced to grind spices to pay her debtors, she seemed to be fading away. Finally, exhaustion took over.

One evening, Ma did not return home. Saras waited and waited, imagining all of the awful things that might have happened. Anxious and restless, he could no longer sit and wait. He went to look for her at the grocer's shop where she worked. He found her where he expected—behind the store and under the shed, where the air was filled with the biting scent of spices. She was motionless, her legs splayed around the grinding stone, her head bent, and her hands fallen from the wooden handle. She was covered with yellow, red, and beige powder. Saras knelt and laid his head on her back, embracing her the only way he could. The warmth of his mother's lap had turned cold.

"Where have you gone, Ma?" he wailed. "Where will I go? What will I do without you? Oh, best mother ever!"

He realized he was all alone and would have to fend for himself.

Chacha arrived for the funeral. With solemnity, he conducted the last rites for his brother's wife as he had done for his brother. He consoled his nephew the best way he knew how, by trying to make him laugh. But Saras had forgotten how to laugh as he watched Chacha efficiently take charge of his family affairs. Seeing this made him feel hopeful; there still was someone in the world who cared about him.

Chacha sold what little belongings the hut contained. The money he received was used to pay off the moneylender, and what was left he kept safe for Saras. Three days later, Saras, with a bag on his shoulders, and Chacha, dragging a tin trunk, went to the bus stop. The sun that had made the green mangoes golden was now searing the narrowly paved road. Chacha walked with military strides. The soles of Saras's bare feet—more accustomed to sauntering and galloping through meadows and marshes—burned on the concrete. They rode a bus to the train station. On the railway platform, they sat on Chacha's trunk and waited for the train to arrive. Saras blew on the soles of his feet to soothe their burning as Chacha tenderly caressed his head. Finally, the train arrived and carried them to the city.

Under the glare of the sun, in front of a large building, Saras stood behind Chacha as he unlocked the door of a ground floor flat. They entered a dark room with a small window that had been closed since Chacha left. When Saras's eyes adjusted to the darkness, he found the dwelling smaller than the space in his village home. This was no big city house. It was a dingy room with a cooking corner and a common outhouse at the back. As both of them were hungry, Chacha cooked rice and dal on a kerosene stove. There was no fancy chicken, no goat kabobs.

"Let's eat," his uncle said, "and leave for Lala Dhaniram's home right away. We don't want him to be home when we are there." Hurriedly they ate, and when their hunger was satisfied, they left for Chacha's employer's house. To make the half-hour walk easier for Saras, Chacha gave him his rubber slip-ons that were two sizes too large.

They arrived in front of a brick house plastered with yellow paint. It was the biggest house on the street. Under the roof of the front porch, Chacha smoothed his hair, took a deep breath, and knocked at the door. Minutes passed, and no one appeared. He knocked again.

"*Thehro Bhai!* Wait! What is this, so much knocking, knocking? Can't you wait?" a stern voice said. The face of the plump woman who opened the door did not look as stern as her voice sounded. Saras stared at her face and neck, which was adorned with a thick gold chain that shimmered on her tomato-colored sari.

"*Bibiji*, Mistress, I brought my nephew to work for you," Chacha said to Dhaniram's wife, his hands folded. Flashing a glance at Saras, he said, "Greet your mistress."

At once, Saras joined his hands. "*Namaskar*, Bibiji," he said.

"Too young. Too dirty," she said, scrutinizing Saras from head to toe. "Looks like a villager."

"He is from the village, Bibiji. He just lost his mother. But he works like a grown man."

"Does he know how to clean and cook?"

"He is very smart." Chacha grinned, rubbing Saras's back. "What he doesn't know, he quickly learns, Bibiji."

"How much does he expect to be paid?"

Saras turned to look at Chacha.

His uncle smiled sheepishly. "Who is asking to be paid? Check him out first. But I'm sure you wouldn't want to pay less than one hundred."

"A hundred rupees!" Bibiji said, both hands on her hips.

"He will do what you ask him to do and do it well," Chacha said, almost begging.

Bibiji rubbed her chin with two fingers and said, "You want me to pay you or him?"

"I will come to collect his salary. I will put it in savings until he is old enough to manage his own money. But please give him a little monthly pocket money."

"I don't want him running around in the house," Dhaniram's wife declared, and then turning to Saras, she warned, "Keep to the kitchen, all right?"

Saras nodded. But he was not sure what she meant. What was he expected to do in the kitchen all day?

Chacha looked gently upon Saras. "He knows his place. He will stay in the kitchen. He learns fast, Bibiji. I am telling you, he is smart..." Chacha's voice trailed off.

"Say goodbye to your uncle," Bibiji ordered. "Then I'll show you where the kitchen is."

Saras did not want to say goodbye. He did not want Chacha to leave. He turned to his uncle pleadingly, but Chacha gestured for him to follow his mistress. "We will stay in touch. I don't live far away," Chacha whispered to his nephew and left.

Saras hesitated before giving him a quick hug, holding back tears. In a minute, Chacha was gone.

"Come on. I don't have all day!" Bibiji called.

He turned and followed her.

Bibiji led Saras through a wide corridor, passing two closed doors on the right. The kitchen door was the second on the left. She showed him utensils, ingredients for making tea, spices, vegetables, rice, wheat, and varied dals in plastic boxes with lids. She put some water on to boil, asked Saras to make tea, and left. Saras sat down on the kitchen floor and cried until the bubbling water evaporated by half.

Bibiji returned to the kitchen, looked at Saras's face, and asked, "Do you even know how to make tea?" He shook his head. She emptied the over-boiled water in the sink, boiled fresh water, and taught him to make tea. She gave him a cup to drink and took one for herself to her room.

When she returned with the empty cup, she handed him a towel, a used bar of soap, an oversized old shirt, pants, and vest. "Wash up thoroughly, dry yourself well, and put on these clothes."

"What should I do with my old clothes?"

"I'd burn them! But if you wish, wash that filth. And hurry up; there is work to be done."

He returned to the kitchen cleaned up, and Bibiji pointed to a corner and said, "This is your place. Sit there until Malik comes and whenever you have nothing to do."

A hot bath after the long journey soothed Saras and he fell asleep quickly, for the next thing he knew he was lying on the floor in the dark kitchen, cold penetrating the worn-out brown blanket. A fly buzzed noisily and settled on his nose. His stomach was growling. Where was he? What day was it? Then he remembered. He had ridden a train with Chacha, who had brought him here. With an acute pang of separation, he softly called, "Ma! Ma! *Hai Ma!*"

During the following week, Bibiji showed Saras how to peel, cut, and cook vegetables, prepare steamed rice, and make dough for roti. He followed her instructions, at first clumsily, but in time learning to assist her. He stirred vegetables, kneaded dough, and rinsed rice for steaming. Bibiji did most of the cooking. He washed the dirty dishes and swept and mopped the floor.

Saras was glad to sit down in his corner. It had been a long day. He dozed off. A bombardment of angry words between Bibiji and a man awakened him. That must be Malik Dhaniram back home. Saras had fallen asleep once again after a day of manual work. Growls from his stomach joined the sounds of shouting from the bedroom, one loud, the other shrill. He got up and found a plate set with the food he had helped prepare. He greedily ate everything and went back to sleep on the floor.

Several weeks passed. Saras thought of his uncle before going to sleep and after getting up. One night, thinking of Chacha kept him awake. One moment he was missing him, and the next moment someone was poking him in the ribs. "Wake up! Wake up!" Bibiji's grating voice called. "You sleep like a pig. What kind of servant are you?"

"Send me a cup of tea," Malik yelled from the bedroom.

Pulled out of his sleep, Saras rubbed his eyes and tried to adjust to the dawning light. He had watched Bibiji place the kettle on the stovetop. By now, he knew how to brew a good cup of tea.

While waiting for the water to boil, Saras scanned the kitchen. Burnished brass pots with black bottoms were on the bottom shelf. On the upper shelves, plates, pans, and aluminum tumblers were stored. Underneath the counter were sacks of flour and lentils. Plastic boxes lined the floor. He stepped softly into the corridor that separated the bedroom and drawing room from the kitchen and bathroom. At one end, on a plastic rope, hung heaps of folded shawls, quilts, and blankets.

At the end of the corridor, in a glass almirah, a display attracted his attention. On a wooden tray were set a teapot, teacups, and saucers of shiny white material. He gently opened the glass door and touched their glossy surfaces, rich and smooth. It had the feel of the city, and this made his mind wonder what exotic things the other rooms contained. He tiptoed to the door facing him. Through a chink in the wood, he looked at his employers: Malik reading the daily paper, Bibiji curled under a sheet with a pillow over her head. He peered through the doorway down the hall and saw two ornate chairs and a third that could seat three people. The chairs were arranged in a circle. In the far corner of the room, he noticed a table with a medley of knickknacks and photographs. On the walls hung family pictures and calendar images of gods and goddesses. The sound of Malik loudly clearing his throat stopped him in his tracks. He ran back to the kitchen. Puffs of steam emerged from the bubbling kettle.

"Oh, Saras! Saaaraas, is the tea ready?" Bibiji called from the bedroom.

His heart beat faster. "In a minute, Bibiji." He prepared his fine brew and took two steaming cups to the bedroom.

He gave Bibiji, who was now sitting up in her bed, a cup and handed the other to Malik. For the first time, Saras noticed his employer's skeletal body and birdlike face, the rough skin and long nails on the hands that held the daily paper. "Namaste, Malik," he said. For a few moments, Malik stared at him with a grin that made Saras uncomfortable. Then he went back to his paper. Saras noticed Malik's feet, his heels on the floor, and his toes in his slippers. Malik nodded without looking at him and continued to read the paper.

Every morning, Bibiji was at Malik's beck and call as he bathed and dressed for work. That day, he was to have breakfast with someone in a restaurant but did not stop giving orders to Bibiji until he left the house. She closed the door behind him and looked relieved. "He gives me a headache even before my day begins."

Saras sat on a slab facing the kitchen faucet, scrubbing the breakfast dishes. As the water ran, he gazed at the soiled water flowing out to the open drain through a hole where several mosquitoes buzzed. It reminded him of the herd of cattle drinking water knee-deep at the end of the day. The memory made him homesick.

A slap on his head jolted him out of his remembrance. "Are you dumb? I don't pay you for daydreaming, but I do pay for that water. Do you understand?" Bibiji poked his shoulder.

Saras quickly withdrew his gaze as he nodded and mumbled a few words. Then he got busy with what he was doing.

⌘

Within a few months, Saras had learned to make beds, serve food, and buy groceries. Besides brewing good tea, he cooked vegetable and chicken curries, rolled roti, and put *tadka* in dal. Bibiji even taught him how to bargain for vegetables and fruit at the market. Soon he was able to negotiate prices with shopkeepers. He tried his best to be a good servant, so he could not understand why he never pleased his mistress or master.

Another month passed. Saras began to ask Bibiji about Chacha's welfare. Did Malik see him every day? Why had he not visited? Could Saras go visit him? When he brought up Chacha during the rare moments Bibiji talked to him, she either changed the subject or said something like, *"These days, who has time to visit? If he could, he would. If you go to see him and he is not there, then what would you do?"*

When Saras continued to press Bibiji, she said that Chacha would show up sooner or later if for nothing else but to collect Saras's salary. That made sense to Saras. He knew Chacha loved him and would appreciate his hard-earned wages. He decided he would give most of his money to Chacha and keep only a portion of it for himself. But was it possible that Chacha was so tied up with his work that he had forgotten his nephew also lived in the city?

At the marketplace early one afternoon, Saras had bargained with vegetable and fruit sellers so well that he couldn't wait to share the good news with Bibiji. Instead of entering the house through the kitchen door he usually used, he came through the front room where Bibiji and Malik were seated, with the bag of vegetables in one hand and a bucket of milk in the other.

"Oh, you stupid orphan!" Malik barked before Saras could open his mouth.

"You donkey! Look at your dirty feet," Bibiji said.

Saras felt hurt. He had taken off his sandals outside the door and made sure his feet were clean.

"If you ever enter through this door again, I'll break your legs. Understand?" Malik warned.

"Are you a *sahib*?" Bibiji said. "Haven't I told you to use the kitchen door, slow brain?"

Saras walked out and re-entered through the kitchen, his shoulders stooped and his head bent. He dropped the bag and bucket on the floor with a thud and cried his heart out. But who was listening?

The following week, Saras swept all the rooms and was mopping the bedroom floor. He bent to rinse the mop in a bucket filled with phenyl solution, but when he picked up the bucket and tried to straighten himself, he wrenched his back. "Ma!" escaped his mouth. Beads of sweat broke out on his forehead. With his sleeve, he wiped them away and sat on a nearby chair.

"Oh master, may I bring you a cup of hot tea?" Bibiji said sarcastically. "When will it sink into your brain that the only place for you to sit is the kitchen floor? Get up from that chair! It is not meant for you."

As she took a few rupee notes from her purse to pay the milkman, Saras sat staring at her. He tried but could not get up right away.

"You thief! Don't stare at my purse," she cried and pulled the purse strings tight and knotted them twice.

"Bibiji, I am not! I can't get up. My back suddenly gave up."

"Don't behave like an old lady. Go sit in the kitchen until you feel better."

Ignoring his pain, Saras forced himself to get up and wobble to the kitchen.

An hour later, Bibiji called, "Oye, Saras! Saraaasss! Have you died?" She called again from her bedroom in her grating voice. Saras still did not respond. "Oye! Do you want to become an orphan?" she yelled.

"I am already an orphan, Bibiji. You can't make me one!" Though he was in pain, he smiled at his reply and felt good about it. If she said anything in response, he did not heed it.

Late afternoon, just before teatime, Bibiji called him to come to her room. He stood near the doorframe. "Have you seen my gold chain?" she asked.

"No, Bibiji, I haven't." He was standing against the doorframe.

"Don't lie to me! Who else could have taken it?"

"I don't know." Saras shrugged his shoulders.

"Malik will break each and every bone in your body if you don't tell me the truth."

"I am telling the truth, Bibiji. I don't know."

"I'll summon your uncle and send you back with him."

The past ten months had felt like hard labor camp and solitary confinement combined. Saras had begged Bibiji and Malik to let him visit Chacha, but they behaved as if he had been sentenced to a lifetime of imprisonment with only a little time of freedom to buy groceries. He could not leave his kitchen cell. Saras wished that Chacha would appear through some miracle. Or that he could visit him. But how?

At that moment, he saw Bibiji shaking with anger, walking restlessly to and fro. She cried, "I know you took it! Where could it have gone? Do you want me to call the police?"

From the corner of his eye, he saw her staring at him. He stared back, wishing she would go away, disappear, or fall dead.

Suddenly, Malik appeared. Arriving home half drunk and earlier than usual, he pointed wildly at Bibiji. "You! You daughter of a landlord! Throwing gold chains down the drain?" He was holding an almost-empty bottle of liquor in one hand while, with outstretched fingers, raised a muddied gold necklace in the other. "How many times have I told you not to take off your gold chain when you bathe? You forget it. It falls on the bathroom floor and washes out with the water... and here it is."

Bibiji stood speechless. The chain must have drained along with the water from the bathroom floor to the open drain outside. Malik spouted verbal filth at Bibiji. She pushed and shoved her husband to their bedroom and closed the door.

That night, Saras thought about ways to run away if Chacha did not come to get him. He had tried to please his masters, to keep them from abusing him. In the process, he had grown sullen and pallid. As he sulked in self-pity, a plan popped into his mind.

A couple of days later, Malik came home in the evening demanding that Bibiji fry potato chips for him. At the sight of golden potatoes, the smell tantalized Saras and his mouth watered. After his masters had eaten their fill, Bibiji brought the leftovers to the kitchen and saved them near the stove to supplement their dinner.

Glistening with oil, the fried potatoes enticed Saras. He couldn't resist and ate one. Its flavor teased his taste buds, and he ate another and then another. Before he knew it, the plate was empty. As he was wiping his mouth with his shirtsleeve, Bibiji appeared at the door.

"What happened to the chips? Did you eat them?"

Saras did not know what to say. Bibiji called Malik to the kitchen to teach Saras a lesson. Malik came, heard what had happened, and slapped Saras hard. Then he dragged him through the kitchen and out of the house and bolted the door shut.

Saras was locked out, left alone in the dark, cold night. Begging for mercy, he knocked and cried saying he would never do it again. But it was as if his master and mistress were deaf. So he lay down in the verandah close to the front door. In the wee morning hours, and only at the milkman's coaxing, did Bibiji finally let Saras in.

Back in the kitchen, angry, hurt and scared, Saras thought that his life as a servant was as inevitable as the sunrise and sunset. Malik would continue to beat him and Bibiji would continue to insult and humiliate him. "Where am I to go?" he cried. "What am I to do? I wish I were dead!"

The next morning, he awoke to the same hellish life, but in that dark cloud was a streak of light. This was the day when Malik's friends were gathering for the evening. A pleasant sensation rose in his heart as he served tea.

Every few months, Malik's friends came to the house to drink, smoke, talk, laugh and play cards. Saras had enjoyed watching the men interact. Some of them had been nice to him, patted his back, smiled at him. Some even secretly put a rupee or two in his pocket.

As soon as the guests arrived, Saras served tea. He took pride in serving the hot brew that they enjoyed drinking. He heard guests gathering as he strained the sugary, milky tea into the shiny white teapot. He had placed the pot on a tray painted with bright red roses and arranged six shiny white cups and saucers around it. He picked up the tray and scurried to the drawing room.

As he was about to enter the door, Malik screamed, "Oyeee, Sarasssss!" and Saras trembled and slipped. The teapot, saucers, and cups smashed to pieces and scattered on the floor. The scalding tea splashed Saras's legs and arms. He got up, his soul knotted in fear, and picked up the shards, trying to salvage the unbroken pieces. Bibiji ran to the drawing room and watched in shock. From out of nowhere, Malik came and kicked him, and kicked him again and again.

"Forgive me, Malik, forgive me!" Saras shrieked from a fetal position on the floor, his hands covering his face.

"Forgive you? Yesss! Yesss! I'll forgive you, you son of a pig!"

Malik picked up a cane from a corner of the room and struck Saras with it, blow after blow as Saras begged for forgiveness. Malik's actions shocked the other men, and when Saras's nose started bleeding, Kumar Malik intervened. "Stop hitting him! He has no one in this world, and you know it!"

In the midst of the pain, Saras thought of his uncle. *Is Chacha dead?* Dhaniram was still focused on hitting. Kishore Malik rebuked, "Let it go, Dhani! Do you want to kill him and get hanged?"

It was only then that Malik stopped. Kishore Malik pulled Dhaniram from the boy and forced him to sit on a chair. He saw Saras's nose dripping blood, his forehead bleeding. Kishore Malik asked Bibiji to fetch disinfecting lotion, a bandage, and medicated cream.

He led Saras to the kitchen and made him sit on a chair. Saras felt his flesh smart and his bones stiffen. He looked thankfully at the kind man. Kishore Malik squeezed his shoulder and said he would make him well. He tended to Saras's bruises and helped him gulp two white tablets with water. Then he wrapped Saras's worn blanket around his shoulders, patted his head, and told Saras to rest; afterward he left to join the others.

Saras tightened the blanket around himself and remembered what Kumar Malik had said. *Has my chacha really gone? Am I an orphan?* Yet, exhausted and with the medication in his bloodstream, he succumbed to sleep.

Saras dreamt that his mother had kept a full tumbler of hot sugary tea balanced on the side of the hearth. Its warmth spread a queer delight through his body. When he woke, he was glad that his mother and father were dead because he didn't want them to live in this cruel world. Hate surged in his soul—a hatred of which he had not thought himself capable.

Several days after the tea incident, Bibiji was comparatively calm, and Malik indifferent as usual. The only thought that circled Saras's mind was how to run far away. He remembered the day he had arrived at Chacha's one-room dwelling and the meal his uncle had cooked that sunny afternoon.

Saras heard Bibiji snore. She had announced that she was shopping that day but complained of a headache. She must have decided to postpone her outing. Saras gently opened the kitchen door, walked out of the house, and shut it tight behind him. He crossed the lane and walked up the hill. For the first time in almost a year, he walked through the city without a task or errand at hand. The warm rays of the sun massaged his numbed skin and aching body. He looked up and let the sun caress his face and shoulders. He rubbed his arms, hands, and put his palms over his face. He remembered how his mother had massaged him with mustard oil under the morning sun. His eyes welled with tears as blood turned his ears red.

The walk through the bazaar bombarded his senses. There were wafts of open drains and decaying vegetables. Then the pungent smells of spices and meats and the sweet aroma of fruit and pyramids of sweet mithai teased him. Under the full sun, the grocers had arranged fresh vegetables, rainbow-colored dals, white flour, and red chilis. The sights made him forget his misery. The meat seller had threaded skewers with chicken pieces to roast over burning charcoal while his assistant baked tandoori roti and stirred tamarind chickpeas simmering on the coal-burning stove. A plate of fresh lemon wedges, green chili peppers, and red onion slices were ready to decorate lunch platters. A man waited to buy an early lunch. Saras's mouth watered, but he was in a rush to reach his uncle's home.

Huffing and panting, he arrived at Chacha's doorstep and saw it padlocked. Outside the door, on a jute charpoy, sat an elderly man smoking bidi. He was wearing a white dhoti and shirt and a pagadi—an elaborate turban.

"Who are you looking for?" he asked.

"My chacha," Saras said.

"Mehnat Ram?" the man asked, coughing.

Saras nodded. "Yes! Yes, him!"

"Sorry, son. Do you not know he died many months back? Poor soul!"

"How? How did he die?"

"Run over by a truck. Poor, poor man!"

So it is true. My chacha is dead!

"What happened to his things?"

"His master, that Lala Dhaniram, took them. He said the man had no relatives alive."

"Oh, Chacha! Oh, Ma! Oh, Ma!" Saras leaned his back against the door, wailing. He dropped onto his haunches. With his arms around his legs and his head on his knees, he could not stop crying.

The old man stood up, walked through the door into his house, and moments later returned with a lunch thali. Saras was still sobbing.

"Stop crying, son. Here, eat something."

Saras looked up and wiped his tear-stained face with the sleeve of his tunic.

"Where are your parents?"

"He was my only living relative." Saras stood up.

The man pointed to the place next to him on the charpoy, gave Saras a clean rag to wipe his face, and silently watched him eat.

At many times during the last year, Saras had thought of running away, and the only place that had come to his mind was Chacha's home. Where would he go now? He would have to return to the place he had run away from. Malik and Bibiji may beat him, but he did have a place to sleep and food to eat. His heart ached at the decision he had to make. What other choice did he have?

The old man rubbed Saras's back, uttering a few words of solace. Saras cleaned the plate, thanked the man for his concern and for the food, and dragged himself back to the house he hated.

Thoughts of revolt and fury possessed him. If he ran away, they would call the police, bring him back, and treat him more cruelly than before. The root of his tongue was bitter. *I hate you, Dhaniram! I hate you, Bibiji! I hate both of you! One day, I'll tear you to bits!*

When he returned, no one was home. He seethed in his misery. Thoughts of revenge continued to race through his head.

Someone kicked at his ribs. Startled, Saras stood up and smelled a waft of stale alcohol. Malik, with a lecherous grin, was bending over him. He squeezed his shoulder, and mumbled to Saras to bring him a cup of tea.

Saras woke, made the tea, and took a cup to the bedroom. As he was setting the cup on Malik's bedside table, Malik turned and said, "C-c-ome heeeere, you… little pig! Loook at me!" A red scarf was loosely tied around Malik's neck.

Suddenly, with a lusty grip, Malik grabbed Saras's arm and dragged him onto the bed.

"Come… sit here!"

"No… Malik! No!" Saras tried to free his arm.

As Saras pushed Malik's hand off, the sheet pulled away and Saras saw Malik's erect penis.

"Let go of me, or I will kill you!" Saras yelled. But Malik seemed possessed by a superhuman strength. He pulled Saras to him, embraced his body, and penetrated him, groaning and moaning. Saras cried in pain.

"You motherfucker! I am going to kill you!" Saras yelled, revulsion filling his body. The smoldering fire that had lain buried in his heart was ablaze with anger.

Malik slumped on his bed and appeared to be unconscious. Saras heard a snore escape his wide-open mouth, and hatred and revenge took hold of him. Malik's nostrils moved with each inhale and exhale. Saras stared at the red scarf loosely wrapped around his master's neck. He leaped onto Malik's back, unwrapped the scarf, and knotted it tightly around Malik's neck. He squeezed it as tight as he could, and the pressure made Malik's eyes pop open.

When Saras pulled it tighter, Malik's eyes grew wider still. Saras tightened the knot until Malik's eyes seemed to come out of their sockets. Then Saras watched him go limp and motionless. He jumped away from the bed, ran to the kitchen, opened the back door just a crack, and cautiously peeped out. No one was in sight. He slipped out quickly, and like a madman, sprinted toward the hills.

A week passed. Even as a shepherd, Saras had not seen a place as serene as where the healer had brought him. Sunlight poured through the window. Saras got up from his bed and wobbled to the door. He stood there watching the old man gardening—planting, replanting, and tending. Saplings of plants, flowers and herbs were ready for replanting. The old man squatted on the ground next to a mound of potting soil he had prepared by mixing dirt and cow dung. He filled various sizes of terracotta pots with the mixture and planted a sapling in each.

Saras put on the slippers left for him near the bed and walked to where the old man squatted. His back was toward Saras, and he wore a soiled black shirt and pajamas.

Saras stood in front of him.

"You feel good?"

Saras nodded.

"Then sit," the old man said.

"My name is Saras. I want to tell you something." He kept standing, hesitating to continue with what was on his mind.

"Saras—nice name: swan, the bird that can swim and fly." The old man looked up. "What is it you want to tell me?"

"I want to tell you that I am not the good person you think I am," Saras heard himself say.

"No one is perfect."

"But I have done something horrible!"

The old man waited for Saras to continue. But Saras was unable to utter the truth.

"No hurry. Tell me when you are ready." The old man, his gray hair and beard covered with dirt, looked up. Slowly, a grin appeared on his face. "Have your wounds healed?"

"Yes, they have."

"Would you like to help me in the garden? Become a gardener?"

"I have never worked in a garden."

"Nothing to it. You can learn," he said. "Are you a hardworking young man?"

"Yes, I am, and I feel fine."

"If you feel so fine, Saras, get to work," he said with kindness in his eyes.

Saras helped him plant the seedlings of flowers and vegetables in various-sized pots. When the work was done, they had filled three dozen or so wooden crates with potted plants. With buds sprouting yellow, orange, and purple, the plants were ready to be sold at the market.

Saras looked around and saw that he was in a valley. The old man's house was at the bottom of a hill, many hills away from the one he had tumbled down. In the distance, the people in the other huts looked like specks. The rustling leaves and chirping birds reminded him of his childhood.

As Saras got used to his new routine, he became acquainted with the women and men who lived in the valley. They welcomed him and expressed joy at the old man's "nephew" visiting him from the city. They said it was nice of Saras to come when the work was heavy and the pots had to be taken to the city to be sold. They brought food to the old man's house and told Saras he had not cooked since his wife and teenage son had died on their way back from her parents' home some years ago.

Helping the old man was a refreshing routine for Saras. Overwhelmed by his kindness, one day Saras softly said to him, "Thank you for taking care of me."

The old man nodded and gave him more chores to do: prepare the potting mix, fill more terracotta pots, add bone meal to orchids and daffodils, replant overgrown perennials that stood like a battalion into larger pots. They worked from morning until the sun rose to its zenith and descended in the western horizon. Famished and exhausted, they called it a day, bathed, and shared a meal brought by the neighbors.

They ate in silence. Saras looked around at the well-equipped kitchen that had not been used for years. He stared at the old man eating. He seemed lost in a sad thought, and Saras felt the man's pain as if it were his own.

Gurgling and swooshing sounds pulled Saras from sleep. Soothing sounds of nature salved his anxiety. From the window of his room, he gazed at the swaying branches and the flowing stream in the distance. He went outside and walked in the direction of the stream. The closer he came to the water source, the louder the gurgling and gushing became. From the nearer bank, he saw the surface of the water sparkle. The stream vanished into a pond. Closer to the pond, he noticed herbs and scented bushes with varied colored barks, some brown, some yellow, some cinnamon. He paced next to serpentine vines growing along the edges of the walk. In some places, they entwined around trees; one had wreathed itself around a statue of Rudra—the divine healer. Gorgeously magnificent with luster and richness, the variety of greens shimmered like resplendent gems.

Each day, Saras awoke excited to help the old man work in the garden, which was actually as large as a farm. Early one morning, he heard the sounds of the old man loading crates onto the back of his bullock cart. The crates were filled with the pots they had prepared the previous week.

"Where are you taking them?" Saras asked.

"To the plant warehouse in the city. I also need to buy seeds and fertilizer for the autumn crop," the old man said as he hopped onto the cart. "I'll see you in the evening." The old man grinned and rode toward the city warehouse.

Saras stood motionless as the bullock cart disappeared into the horizon. A chickadee flew above, swishing the leaf-laden branches. *He will hear of Malik's murder and know that I am a criminal. He will inform the police. They will arrest me and put me in jail. They will hang me.*

His legs shaking with fear, Saras sat on the ground. He was tired, tired of running, tired of hiding. He did not want to run away anymore. He sat there for a long time until an idea energized him. He was going to prepare the best meal of his life. He would pour the secret ingredient in all his preparations—his love and admiration for the Healer of Plants. His fear was soon replaced by the act of cooking with care and concentration.

Saras heard the bullock cart stop in front of the hut and he ran to the front door. He examined the old man's face. "Did you sell all the plants?" he asked.

"Yes, I did."

"And bought all the things you needed?" Saras kept searching the old man's face.

"Yes, I did," repeated the old man.

"Did you hear anything in the city?" Saras could not resist asking.

"Hear? Like what?"

"I don't know. You are the one who went to the city."

"Nope. Now help me carry these things to the storage shed." He pointed to the burlap sacks he had loaded in the cart. One by one, they carried sacks and bags inside until the cart was empty.

After the work was done, the old man took a bath and finally came to the kitchen. Saras was restlessly waiting for him to sit. He wasn't sure what bad things his savior had heard in the city, and he was eager for him to taste the meal.

The old man sat down. "I'm famished," he said. "And this kitchen has never smelled so good since I lost my wife and our boy."

"I cooked for you, Baba... I cooked for you."

"You did? Bless you! I can't wait to taste the food. Let's eat!"

"But I have to tell you... I must tell you... I killed a man... I killed a man and ran away as fast as..." Saras cried. "I wanted to run away from you too, but I am tired, so tired..." Saras sobbed.

The old man held Saras in a gentle embrace. Then he patted his back and head, still holding him close to his chest. "You did not kill anyone, Saras! I know you tried, but he was not dead. I inquired and got the whole story. I knew most of it the day I found you. You tried to do what many others wanted to do. Many others are thirsty for that man's blood. He was caught in the act of doing what he did to you. He was charged and is in prison. You are here safe with me, and no one knows. No one can harm you anymore. Come, let's eat, son." The old man released him from his embrace, held Saras's hand, and led him to the eating space in the kitchen.

Saras was filled with love for the old man. He loved him the way he loved Ma and Baba. He could never love anyone more than the Healer of Plants, the Healer of Men.

I Nourish the Universe
and the Universe Nourishes Me

I did not know whether I was the tree or a man. Vegetation infused my arms. My brown hair grew pale green leaves and clusters of mauve flowers. The chest hair grew into tendrils and my belly was bound in thin bark. Then my arms turned into branches and my legs twisted into trunk. My feet changed to roots penetrating the earth. Had I metamorphosed into wisteria? I lost my ability to move but gained another sort of independence. Warm sun eased my shoulders and back; rain nourished my leaves and buds. I felt comforted, relieved of the stress that I did not even realize had entwined me.

Sweating profusely, I woke in a desolate room. The dream felt so real that I touched my arms and head to see if I was still the wisteria. But I was in an infirmary, sent there at the tail end of convalescence from a nervous breakdown. The hollow feeling inside had somewhat subsided, but my loneliness was amplified in the solitary room.

Outside it was bitter cold. I took a hot shower thinking of the project I had been working on just before I'd collapsed. For twenty years I overcame deadlines, the rat race, office politics, competition, backbiting, balancing budgets, promotion, demotion and then I was fired. Past memories bombarded my mind. I combed my hair and looked at myself in the mirror. Dark circles framed my eyes and a pale complexion gawked back at me.

A breakfast tray sat on the table facing the fifth-floor window. But I was not hungry. Horribly lonely, I could not imagine my future. I threw myself face down on my pillow to choke back the sobs.

An image of me as a teenager flashed through my mind, being summoned by a pounding at the front door. My parents should've been home by then, but I had gladly left my AP homework on the desk and made my way downstairs. I opened the door. My grandmother, always impeccably dressed in mismatched clothes, burst out crying and hugged me. I was unable to fully understand what she was desperately trying to tell me. "Why did I live to see this day! Oh God, have mercy on this child! Why do I have to break his innocent heart!" She kept crying until I realized that my parents had died in a car crash. My body stung after I understood what my screaming grandmother had said. From that day on she took care of me until she passed away.

I looked out from the window to an expansive bird's eye view. From the front entrance of the building a stone pathway led away from the infirmary to vast wilderness. In the middle of dense vegetation, a black circular wall enclosed an empty space, as desolate as the hollow in my heart. That emptiness tugged at me. Like my cold insides, everything outside was covered with snow. I was a disagreeable man living a meaningless life with no future in sight. Angry and alone. I was completely unaware that my emotional condition was so desperate. I ground my teeth, cursing myself.

A stream of awful and appalling thoughts passed through my mind. *How could they fire me? What if I never recover? Will I die and be forgotten? No one will ever know who I was. That I ever lived. No one will care.* Such thoughts terrified me.

My grandmother used to pray when she was afraid. The day she died, I prayed for her. I had never done so before although she wanted me to. She wanted me to find God within myself.

I sat up and tried to pray now. My thoughts shifted inward. I found myself in a dark shadowy place. I longed for something, anything, to comfort me, but when my eyes adjusted to the darkness, my thoughts raced back to my past and obscured my view. Like cobwebs, the memories that I wanted to forget returned. I tried to let go of them. But they stuck to my body and mind. I descended into gloomy darkness, unable to penetrate the cobwebs or stay with my breath.

I turned and faced the lunch tray. The caregiver must have replaced the morning meal. But I was still not hungry. Twittering sounds of birds came from the window. There was nothing to do in the room. I donned my coat, gloves, boots and hat and walked down the stairs, out through the main entrance onto the pathway leading to the woods and the wall. I passed snow-covered trees, evergreens, climbers, bushes and empty flowerbeds.

The circular wall of black granite blocks seemed too high. Its upper edge was covered with the dried branches of vines and creepers, though the treetops behind it were visible. To find an opening, I decided to circle around. But the wall was hidden behind tall evergreen bushes. After fifteen or twenty minutes I arrived at the same place where I had started. The wall seemed to have no door. If there was one it was concealed by evergreens.

I heard a bird calling. I looked up, searching. On the largest branch of the tallest tree, I thought I saw a small phoenix-like bird displaying his magnificent iridescent plumage.

Since my childhood, I had imagined the beautifully breasted mythological bird, with its rainbow-colored train flowing majestically toward the earth, its green, blue, red and gold plumage glittering under the sunshine. Its magnificence brought a smile to my sour face. I stood gazing at the heavenly bird until it flew away. Then the sun's rays were blinding. When my vision returned, I wondered if I had really seen a little phoenix. *Did it actually stand in front of me? Will I ever see him again? I wonder where he lives.*

I returned to my room. Dinner was on the table. I knew I was supposed to eat but I was still not hungry. I lay down and closed my eyes. The image of the bird stayed in my mind's eye.

In the dead silence the only thing I could hear was my breath coming in and going out. Thoughts about work ebbed away. I had a glimpse of a maze of corridors with hundreds of closed doors.

Early next morning my memories returned. I screamed louder than my grandmother had the day my parents died. That piercing pain rushed through my body again. Tears rolled down my face.

"You must eat!" I heard the nurse say. "Otherwise, you won't get better."

"I know," I responded automatically. I looked away and wiped my eyes.

The next day, I walked to the wall hoping to find an entrance or see the fantastic little phoenix again. But I could not find either. Each morning I returned again and again. The daily routine felt like a slog. I longed to find the bird.

One day, as I was walking close to the wall, something wonderful happened. A bird darted through the air. *Was it him?* It flew toward me and alighted on a big clod of earth in front of me. It was beautiful, brilliant and red. *Was it the one I had seen on the day of the dazzling sun that had blinded me? Had I simply wished it to be a phoenix, the bird of my imagination?* I watched as the cardinal tilted his beautiful head to one side. He looked at me curiously with dewdrop eyes. We both sat there quietly.

"I'm lonely," I finally whispered to him. "May I call you Phoenix? Can we be friends?"

He seemed to nod and step closer. I wanted to pet him but was afraid he might disappear. We stood there looking at each other. Then he flew away.

When I returned to my room, I felt a bit hungry.

Next morning, I sprinted around the wall to visit my friend. I couldn't find him. I ran a second lap along the pathway, fighting the cold wind that rushed at my face and held me back. Long, bare sprays of climbers that I now recognized as wisteria covered the wall. Though leafless they swayed in the wind. Being outdoors stirred my blood. Big breaths of fresh air filled my lungs.

I ran back to my room, sweating by the time I arrived. I splashed my face with water in the bathroom and noticed a flush of red on my cheeks. My eyes looked brighter. No longer did I glance disdainfully at breakfast or push away my lunch plate. I ate whatever I was served. I never missed my walk and jog around the wall. Weeks passed.

And then, one day as I was jogging, a gleam of iridescence caught my eye. I heard a welcoming sound. It was Phoenix coming toward me! When he stood close by, I petted his soft feathery shining head. As I spoke, he seemed to understand, again tilting his head left and right. Looking intently with black jeweled eyes, he twittered and hopped between me and the wall.

"How are you?" he asked.

"I'm fine. How are you?"

"The breeze is gentle."

"Yes, it is! Let's walk together and enjoy the warm sun."

We walked together along the wall. "I missed you, Phoenix!" I said, smiling.

"Me, too."

After a while, he spread his wings and made a darting flight to the branch of a tree inside the wall. How I wished I could see what was behind that wall.

"Walks seem to be helping you regain your strength and cheer you up," the nurse said as she cleared the dinner plate.

I nodded. Physically stronger and mentally lighter now, my nights were not fretful; I slept soundly. And I was no longer so lonely. I had made a real friend.

The following week, rain poured in torrents. From the window I saw the distant landscape hidden behind the gray mist and clouds. My friend Phoenix must be waiting in the lush foliage of the tree. There was no way I could go out.

I asked my nurse for a journal. She gave me a ruled notebook. I began to jot down my recent observations about being in nature, about Phoenix and about myself. One morning's journaling led me to write freely and uninhibited. I poured out everything that had accumulated in my mind. But as soon as I woke from my sleep there was so much more to empty. Too much past debris. In the afternoon I lay on my bed reading a book about gardening borrowed from the sanitarium library. Then I felt tired and fell asleep.

Another day I dozed off, and again in my sleep I wandered into a long corridor that branched into other corridors. All doors were shut. I walked up a flight of steps which led to yet more corridors. It seemed no one except me was in the huge rambling building. I walked for a long time without thinking of turning a door handle. Finally, I tried to open one, then another and the next. They all seemed locked. At last, I was able to open one with difficulty, only to face stark darkness. The dread woke me.

For several days the weather outside remained disagreeable. I was restless and bored. Then the rainstorm suddenly ended. The gray mist and clouds were swept away by the wind. A brilliant deep blue sky revealed itself. Springtime was coming! I did not recall ever paying any attention to changing weather or getting excited about the spring season. I wondered what it was like in the innermost space where Phoenix lived. Were bulbs sprouting, green leaves and petals opening, evergreen bushes and wisteria climbers coming to life?

I ventured out again, hearing a call, and saw Phoenix pecking the earth. He looked a bit shy, pretending he just happened to be there. Gladdened, I said, "You came to greet me, didn't you?"

I saw him smile and nod.

"I missed you! Do you realize you have changed my life? You have revived my spirit, friend!"

He came closer.

I gently touched his feathery soft back. His red waistcoat was like satin. He puffed his breast out as if to show pride. Then he hopped over a pile of freshly turned earth looking for seeds and insects.

"What is behind the wall?" I asked.

Little Phoenix turned toward the wall and hopped.

A gust of strong wind rushed down. Untrimmed branches of hanging ivy and wisteria waved, their trailing sprays swaying vigorously. I stepped closer to where he had hopped. Behind the close evergreen bushes and loose trails I caught a glimpse of a shiny doorknob.

My heart thumped. Phoenix tilted his head to one side as if he too was excited. As I turned the knob my hand shook. I used both hands and was able to open the door. It creaked as I opened it slowly to slip through. I let him fly in and then shut the door behind us.

We were now inside the circle—the most magical and mysterious place I could imagine. My breath caught at the heavenly sight. The inside of the wall was covered with leafless stems of climbers so thick they matted together. Numerous long tendrils resembled swaying curtains. I could not tell if they were just waving in the breeze or alive. There were empty flowerbeds and brown grass, evergreens and leafless bushes. And a small stream, its banks still covered with snow, meandered through the dormant garden.

Everything was still; I could listen to the silence. Phoenix looked at me without stirring.

"Let's walk," I whispered. We stepped softly lest we awaken someone or something. The ground seemed barren. Not a sign of sprouting bud anywhere. *Was the ground dead? Beyond reviving?*

Then I noticed something sticking out of the black earth—a tiny, pale green point pushing through. Crocus, hyacinth, or daffodil? I carefully looked for other similar sprouts. Once I spotted one, a hundred others came into focus. I searched and found a sharp piece of wood and a razor-edged rock. I knelt down and dug and winnowed out weeds until a clear place was made around as many sprouting bulbs as I could manage. "Now they can breathe freely," I said to myself. My own breath felt calmer.

An agile brown squirrel moved restlessly and inquisitively, while several robins clung to a branch as they watched me garden. A snow-white rabbit passed by, sniffing with its quivering nose.

The earth was thawing. Life energy was emerging from somewhere.

Every morning I spent hours weeding and clearing spaces around sprouting life. The crowns of the bulbs looked like onions tops. My gardening book said bulbs lived for years even if no one helped them. They helped themselves. They spread underground and produced new bulbs. They had so much to teach. I had so much to learn.

I noticed brown lumps swell into green on thicker branches of the swaying tendrils. I touched them and felt more energetic and awake. The sun and showers had nourished vines and creepers, bushes and bare trees with the warmth, light and moisture as it had nourished me. But clouds came in and it drizzled. Then it thundered and the showers seeped through the space I had opened around the bulbs, reaching the roots and new growth.

Little Phoenix, his feathers getting redder with each day, kept me company.

It rained heavily for days. I had to stay in my room reading or writing in my journal. I often found my thoughts drifting to a dark space. This time nothing obscured my view, no cobwebs of thoughts. I walked through a corridor and without hesitation put my hand on one door handle. It turned without difficulty. This alarmed me. I waited for a few moments, took a long breath and pushed open the door. From utter darkness slowly a form emerged, a peaceful, calming image.

A few days later the sky was blue again. I jumped out of bed, ran to the window and opened it. The world looked touched by magic. All around, the sun spread gold dust that penetrated the black earth and helped life fully sprout.

Sun lit the circular space inside the wall that looked like a manicured garden. Fresh new life pushed through everywhere. Flowers and buds that had seemed dead now swelled. Purple and yellow crocuses unfurled. Amidst this joy came a delight more charming than all—my friend Phoenix was holding twigs in his beak to build a nest.

Who kept creating something out of nothing? Light from darkness? A cosmic dance from stillness?

Then one day, a new miracle was revealed. I saw six eggs in his nest. A pale brown female cardinal was keeping them warm with her feathery breast and caressing wings. The wonder and magic outside made my inside stir. I felt it in my bones. In that rapturous realization, I threw up my arms exultantly and shouted, "I will revive! I will be healthy again! I will live!"

My old lifestyle had filled my soul with blackness. The air around me had been poisoned with overwork, too much stress and gloom. Now, new beautiful thoughts pushed out the old hideous ones. A healthier life returned to me. Blood began to flow freely, and strength flooded in. Bubbling streams made me laugh. I fully comprehended the bird whom I had named Phoenix was in reality a red cardinal. It had come down to the earth for me and incarnated as my friend. Wordlessly it had helped me release something that previously kept me bound. I had forgiveness in my heart. Comforting thoughts guided me, and I was filled with gratitude. I was overcome by a singular calmness.

"You will be discharged soon," the nurse said. "Your recovery in three months was magical. We were expecting you to stay for six."

"Nothing magical!" I said. "I nourished the universe and the universe nourished me." The words flew from my mouth. "But thank you as well, nurse, for helping me get better."

The day I left, the outdoors was an untamed gold and purple and violet blue and flaming scarlet, and on every side were sheaves of tall white and ruby lilies. In the foreground stood the fabulous cardinal, accompanied by his female partner and their brood of six. Had they come to bid me farewell? The little chicks, with their chests held high, chirped.

I felt part of the cardinal's family. He had saved my life.

THE BLACKENED MIRROR

I was a portrait painter. Young and self-taught. I started by copying black-and-white images of wrinkled old people, famished children, laborers carrying loads, and farmers plowing fields—all laboring for food and shelter. I imagined their pain, their suffering.

My mother was a bricklayer, and I, a dreamer. Each of us owned two sets of clothing: one covered our body and the other hung daily in the sun to dry. Mother worked hard to provide us with two meals a day, but I was content with only one if I could buy art supplies with what remained.

From the time I was nine until I turned sixteen, my aim was to feel at one with the person I painted. I also became conscious of my mother's struggle to survive. She tried persuading me to become a bricklayer, but she did not succeed. The day she discovered what I did while she worked, she hit me hard, so hard that I bled. From then on, I hid my art. It frustrated her that I idled away my days doing unpaid work.

"It is a sin to waste a life!" she screamed one day.

"I am not wasting my life; I do what no one else can do!" Then I brought out artwork from underneath my bed and placed it before her.

One by one, she looked at each drawing until tears welled in her eyes. From that day on, she stopped pestering me. When she returned home every evening, she demanded to see my work. She looked, critiqued and encouraged me to hone my skills and transform unfortunate people's lives into beautiful art. She began showing off my work to neighbors. Some expressed amazement at my God-given talent. A few disdained me for not being man enough to take care of my mother. I paid no heed; art consumed me. I sold my first work for a pittance.

One scorching afternoon, two men brought my mother's corpse home. Sunstroke had killed her. I was devastated. For months, I neglected my art, and with it, myself. Everyone suffers, but each of us suffers in his own way. I suffered alone.

Around this time, I turned eighteen and decided to sell my art on the street. I spread a dhurrie on the busiest corner of my neighborhood. I sat there capturing the semblances of photographs—famous leaders, well-known personalities, Bollywood stars— and put them up for sale. My imitations drew people's attention. Passersby stopped for a few minutes to watch me draw and paint.

"That is so lifelike!" a man said.

"God has blessed you with such a gift, son!" an elderly lady commented.

"Can you draw my face? I'll give you twenty rupees!" a young man asked.

"Twenty rupees, sir? For all that work?" I stared hard at him.

"How much do you want?"

"Fifty?"

"Are you a conman or an artist?" he said.

I ignored him and continued to draw.

"That line he just drew is worth twenty rupees!" someone shouted. "Give him what he is asking!"

"Why don't you get your picture made?" the first man said with irritation.

"If I had the money, I would!" the shouting man replied.

"What about thirty rupees?" the man asked.

"What about thirty-five?" I said, my heart beating fast.

That was my first. Soon after I raised my price to fifty, then seventy; soon, people were paying a hundred rupees to get their faces drawn. I made hundreds of drawings—profile or full face, bust or full-length, monochromatic or full color.

A year after selling my first portrait, I installed a canvas canopy to protect me from rain and heat. I set a wooden table and comfortable chair beneath it. On another table, I displayed several portraits of famous people. Passersby took more notice.

One day, as I was absorbed in sketching a scene, I heard someone say, "*O ladke*! Hey boy, this is not the way for a fine artist to work—like a beggar!" I looked up. A well-dressed older man had picked up a portrait and was examining it.

"Not a beggar, sahib! I am a painter of portraits," I said with pride.

The man introduced himself as Ravi Verma. He said for the last thirty years he had painted billboards advertising the Bollywood movies showing in the local cinema halls. However, he no longer had the energy of a young man to paint large works by himself. He needed an assistant. He offered me my first job; I was only too happy to accept.

Ravi Verma took me to his studio, which looked more like a warehouse. I was awed at the size of the heads and torsos and hands he drew on forty-by-thirty-foot canvases. My works seemed miniscule in comparison.

Ravi Verma asked me to call him Vermaji. For the first few days, I observed him painting. He drew a grid on the white gesso surface that I helped prepare. He stood on scaffolding facing the canvas and drew ovals, circles, triangles, and rectangles until a composition came alive—a group of people whom I readily recognized as famous Bollywood stars. I watched as he transformed the two-dimensional surface into a three-dimensional scene. He brought familiar faces to life on screen-size canvases: heroines with almond eyes, luscious lips, and voluptuous busts and hips; heroes with handsome faces and dreamy eyes. His depiction of lanky or stocky villains, all with lecherous expressions, smoking cigarettes or holding glasses of whiskey amused me.

For the first few months as an apprentice, I was given the work of stretching raw canvas on wooden frames, applying gesso on the surfaces, and mixing and blending colors. In time, he let me fill in large areas with the appropriate flat paint. That did not require much skill, but it helped me gain confidence.

After a day's work, I washed brushes and bowls and cleaned the floor splashed with multi-colored paint.

Within one year under Vermaji's supervision, I had learned to shade a chignon or show a curl on a heroine's forehead. Slowly, I learned how to paint ears, hands and eyes and make them look real. Finally, I painted a face without his assistance.

The best day of my life was when he let me paint all the figures on a billboard. Upon examining the completed work, he said, "The student has become the master."

I initially thought I had misunderstood, but from then on, he filled in the large surfaces with flat paint while I painted the figures and faces. I was ready for it. My skill and passion transformed into something much more than I imagined. Full of energy, I painted with my whole body.

Relieved to see that someone would continue his legacy, one day Vermaji said, "Your work vibrates with emotions. Hear me, son. You will go places."

Eventually, I began to get bored with painting the same faces over and over again. I wanted to paint live models and make portraits with personality. I wanted to work independent of restraints and make vibrant and original portraits. I grew restless to leave, but did not want to disappoint the man who had supported me. I had developed an affection for my employer. Would he get angry? Would he be sad? When I opened my heart to him, though, Vermaji understood my frustrations and my desires. He said he too was thinking of closing the business, of retiring. I thanked him for being my mentor, and we bid each other a sad but friendly goodbye.

Like the Bollywood stars I had painted for five years, I dreamed about becoming rich and famous. I did not want to work in a warehouse; I wanted to work in a studio, have my own atelier. I did not want to live in an ordinary flat; I desired my own house. No, a mansion. I wanted to possess a motorbike. No, a car. I imagined a life of opulence and luxury.

Vermaji had given me the names and addresses of potential clients who were wealthy, and I introduced myself and showed my portfolio. I looked covetously at their mansions and vehicles, and told myself, *All in good time, all in good time!*

Within days, I found my first patron, a director-producer with an unattractive face and manners but a very attractive purse. He was pleased with what I had done. No sooner had I finished that commission and my name spread wildly by word of mouth. I received so many jobs that I was kept occupied for a year. The more portraits I made, the more recognition I received. Although I exhibited my work in group shows, I had painted enough portraits for a solo exhibition. Patrons were glad to oblige me when I asked to borrow their portraits, especially when they learned they would be displayed for other people to admire.

I first gained recognition at the local and state level, but then reviews of my shows began to appear in national newspapers. By the time I faced my late thirties, my deep driving desires had become reality. Art connoisseurs knew my name, and art admirers recognized my work. When the Ministry of Culture and Arts constructed an extension to their building, they asked me to paint four murals: Mahatma Gandhi, Rabindranath Tagore, Jawaharlal Nehru, and Indira Gandhi.

I painted the semblances of those great personalities, and I painted life-size images of city and suburban folks—suited and booted businessmen and local personalities looking smug as they posed; women decked in ornaments studded with gems modeled in their silk and chiffon saris; and children dressed in fashionable clothes sat restlessly to have their faces painted so as not to disappoint eager parents.

The more paintings I made, the more famous I became. All the families in society's upper echelon wanted my portraits to adorn the drawing rooms of their mansions. I received more commissions than I could handle. My bank account ballooned like a man who overeats. Was this the life I had wished for?

I met Shanti at the opening of one of my art shows. A writer and lover of painting, she had accompanied her father, a real estate magnate. Before they left, he asked if I would paint a portrait of him and his daughter, and I agreed.

I arrived at their home with my painting paraphernalia. They had selected a room, a chair, and a pose in which to have their image made—the father in a Nehru jacket and churidaar pajama, seated in an elaborately carved walnut seat, and the daughter standing next to him in a silk and brocade sari, decked in her late mother's gem-studded gold ornaments. I couldn't take my eyes off her. They posed for hours, the father's expression lost in thoughts and the daughter smiling intently at me with dark almond-shaped eyes. Her presence inspired me to make one of my best works. The day I signed my name to their portrait, I asked her if she would marry me. She consented.

We honeymooned in the valley of Kashmir, and for the first several years returned there to holiday and celebrate our love. But gradually, our holiday time—I should say my holiday time—dwindled, and soon we stopped vacationing altogether. Why? Because I could not say no to new commissions. My work consumed me.

For several years, Shanti did not complain. She would spend a few weeks with her best friend Shakila, instead. More years flew by. By the fifth, she begged me to take a break from my work, something she would have never done earlier. She suggested we take a few days away from my so-called "creating." I did not stop to think what she meant nor pay heed that she wanted my attention. I was obsessed, more with myself than my art. Unable to see from Shanti's perspective, I did not see myself. Money was pouring in, and I saw no reason to block its flow.

Fortunately, though, I did not ignore the cues and clues my body began to give me. My back ached a bit, and, at times my joints felt swollen, legs more tired at the end of the day than previously. Yet, at times, I pushed these signals aside, still more concerned with how to delineate my clients' appearances with elegance and power than with paying attention to the message of an inner voice.

One fine spring evening, my wife and I were invited for dinner at the house of one of my old patrons, a businessman turned friend, Manoj Pathak. I had painted him, his wife and their four children. The portraits hung in their living room and hallway. By now, painting silky black hair, black almond eyes and beautiful skin had become second nature to me. I could paint a picture with my eyes closed—their creative significance and their uniqueness superficial, confined to their surfaces, only as deep as the pigment.

After enjoying a sumptuous dinner, we sat on their back porch to have hot masala tea.

"Life seems to be going quite well for you, young man!" The elderly businessman patted my back. "You have everything a man dreams of. Could you imagine all this when you painted the billboards?"

"I couldn't. I'm fortunate!" I said. "Yet life seems to be flying by, don't you think?" I don't know why I said this to Manoj.

"Indeed! But we can't hold on to life, can we?" he said thoughtfully. "Anyway, I have something to tell you that should please you."

"Good news is always welcome!" I was eager to hear what he had to say.

"Recently, I had a chance to meet the Maharaja of Saurashtra. He was searching for a portrait painter. I told him about you and your extraordinary skill.

He wants to get his and the maharani's portrait made."

"Oh!" I should have been thrilled. But I was not. "Thanks for your recommendation, but Ashok Patel, a young artist, is as good," I muttered.

"Of course! But this commission is for you, my dear friend. This is the opportunity of a lifetime!" He sounded more enthusiastic than me. "And the honorarium will be something you could only dream of." He moved, crossing his legs.

To my own surprise, I did not want to travel. I asked, "Is the maharaja planning a long stay and a trip to New Delhi? It would take me several weeks to paint a double portrait."

"Oh no! No, no! He is not planning to travel. Too much responsibility in his state, you know!" he said, giggling with pleasure.

"How does he expect me to paint his picture?"

"You have to go to Saurashtra." He narrowed his eyes.

At that moment, our wives joined us. Our host repeated to Shanti the maharaja's desire to have a double portrait painted. She said something about her own portrait with her father, then added, "At least this patron will take him away from his studio."

While driving home, I asked Shanti if she thought I had traded my creative freedom for popularity and wealth. At first she did not respond. When I repeated my question, she said my asking that question meant I partly believed it.

"I don't know, but something from within is bubbling up, putting a doubt in my mind about my art," I blurted.

"I have been begging you to take a break, to get away from it for a while. Perhaps this trip will do you good; you'll return refreshed and renewed. Perhaps you'll make something original."

"You think we should accept the maharaja's offer, then?" I looked expectantly at her.

"I don't know about the maharaja's offer, but going to Manipur Village in Saurashtra sounds like a good idea."

"How do you know about this village?" I was glad to hear her excitement about visiting this place.

"Shakila has a cabin there. She talks about it all the time. It sounds like the most picturesque and mysterious town," she said. "There is magic in the air, Shakila says. Your mind will clear, your heart open, and your anxieties dissipate. Trust me, I feel it." Shanti placed her hand on her heart. "Perhaps we can spend some days in Shakila's cabin before you see the maharaja!"

"In some godforsaken village? In a cabin? Why don't we stay in a hotel?"

"You'll love this place. So inspiring!"

Having ignored my dear wife's wishes for so long, I couldn't say no to her.

It had been a month since the evening at the businessman's house. We left my atelier and our mansion behind. We traveled by train to the unfamiliar and unknown village that Shakila found magical and that had mesmerized my wife.

From Ahmadabad, we took a bus toward Manipur. We drove on unpaved paths through cornfields where stalks were ready for harvesting. Enclosed in husks, ripe yellow corn lay hidden behind silky golden hair. We crossed chili fields lush with the long pointed green leaves of red hot pepper plants. Our bus made one stop for passengers to use the latrines and step down to a historic well. Reaching into the water, we cupped our hands to drink and cool our parched throats, quench our thirst and wash our faces.

Women in intricately embroidered backless cholis, blouses and brightly colored heavily pleated long skirts sold glass bangles and handmade trinkets. Their profiles were blurred behind muslin veils. In an open-air market, turbaned men, majestic in their white kurtas and pajamas, sold vegetables and fruit in circular baskets.

The bus dropped us at the edge of a vast field, and the only way to reach our destination was by bullock cart. We hired one, hopped in, and held our suitcases between our legs as the bullocks trotted off. The cart scurried along a rough path flanked by red pepper fields. Water-filled potholes splashed us, and the blue sky above blessed us.

At the edge of the pepper fields, the driver cried, "Ruk! Ruk!" and the bullocks halted. The driver asked us to jump out and stood to help us.

I descended as he helped my wife down. With only a loincloth around his waist, I could see his ribs and shoulder blades. Exposed to the sun, the hue of his dark skin had intensified. I was reminded of my childhood when my mother and I had little to eat, just struggling to keep our body and soul together. He was the kind of man I used to paint. I tipped him more than his week's salary. He said if I liked he would wait for me as long as I wanted. He would drive us whenever and wherever we wanted to go. I thanked him but gently refused his offer.

A boy stood watching as the driver left, then walked closer to us.

"Do you know a caretaker by the name of Jaidev?" I asked. He nodded.

"Where is he?" Jaidev was to give us the key to Shakila's cabin.

The boy nodded again and asked us to follow him. He led us away from the flaming expanse of pepper fields to a narrow lane before stopping in front of a mud hut. Then he disappeared as abruptly as he had appeared.

Shanti and I beheld the dramatic view of a solitary hut silhouetted under a large banyan tree. The rays of the setting sun haloed the dwelling. In the background, iridescent orange colored the western sky into a heavenly space. From where we stood, details were blurred, but a swing hanging on the front porch became visible. A circular window behind it mesmerized me, invited me in. I felt an urge to enter the hut. We ascended the five porch steps. The swing creaked in the mild breeze.

Shanti, tired from the day's journey, settled on the swing to rest. I peered through the circular window and saw the interior of an unfurnished room, which I entered through the door. No smell.

No color. Inside, on the front wall, I saw a blackened mirror hanging on a nail beneath an alcove. I picked it up. There was no reflection. Its black surface stared back at me. Then something uncanny happened. I felt uneasy, alone. I do not know why. I felt as if I had lost something. No, I had an urge to search for something, but did not know what I was supposed to find. Suddenly I felt as though I would amount to nothing until I found this nameless object.

I wanted to walk outside and sit next to my wife. When I turned to leave, I saw an old man sitting in the corner of the room, behind the open door. Seated on a mat, his legs were crossed. His hair was matted, his eyes half-closed, with a beige shawl wrapped around his upper body. His left hand lay over his left knee, thumb touching index finger. With his right hand, he turned a rosary. Who was he? Jaidev's father?

"Namaskar, Babaji!" I greeted him. My voice croaked. I cleared my throat. Sitting still, he continued to turn the string of beads.

Feeling like an intruder, I did not want to disturb him more than I already had.

The bitter smell of burnt rice drew me toward the kitchen. A pot of rice on the mud hearth had boiled over; it was dried and charred. The coal had turned to ash, and smoke seemed to escape through the window above the hearth. It left a lingering odor. The sunlight reflected upon the still life, and I paused. Making a viewfinder by crossing two fingers of my two hands and looking through it, I slowly pivoted on my heels with my knees gently bent.

I stopped at different positions when my finger-frame focused on an appealing view. Compositions of white, black, gray and orange-gold surfaced in my consciousness. The evening light glistened on the pots and pans as it brushed their surfaces; the sheen of highlights contrasted with dark kitchen nooks. My creative instincts gushed. How I wished I had my canvas and paints. But the burnt odor drew me back to the present.

I stepped from the kitchen to the porch. In the silence I heard water dripping from a faucet opposite where Shanti rested. Seeing her eyes closed, I tiptoed toward the drip. The water had filled a tin bucket that now overflowed. I tightened the faucet and returned to sit on the swing at the small space left near my wife's feet. The swing creaked and woke her up.

"Did you get the keys?" she asked.

"Not yet." I could not let go the image of the blackened mirror from my mind.

"Didn't you find the caretaker?" She raised her head, eyes half-closed.

"I will. Shanti, I feel something in this house... something I cannot describe... something..."

"What are you talking about?" She sat up.

"I found a blackened mirror that I can't get out of my mind. A man is meditating in that room. Something in there is calling me back. Stay here until I return."

I walked back inside. The old man's eyes were still closed. I again walked to the alcove and picked up the mirror. I needed to see my face, but it wasn't there. What could this be? Black paint? Soot? I pulled my monogrammed white handkerchief from my pocket and used spit to rub the mirror's surface, first mildly, then frantically. Slowly, the gunk and grime came off. I walked to the water faucet, wet the soiled handkerchief, and again rubbed its surface until it glistened. In the process of cleaning the mirror, the handkerchief turned into a dirty rag.

I walked back to the room with the mirror in hand. From the window I saw Shanti pacing outside. I looked at my reflection. It looked back at me, pierced me with its gaze. *"Who are you?"* A soundless voice alarmed me. It was as if I was looking at myself for the first time. At that moment, someone's presence startled me.

"It scared you, didn't it?" Babaji stood in front of me.

"What did?" I asked, aghast.

"The dark mirror!" Babaji smiled. "I too was unable to see my true reflection—inward. I must have been your age then... it was years ago... when I saw my Self."

"Why is it that since I found this mirror I have felt confused, disintegrated?" I was desperate to know, and Babaji asked me to sit down. We sat cross-legged on the floor facing each other. He asked me about myself, and I gave him the highlights while he listened attentively.

"As a child, dear son, you were your authentic Self. But as you grew older, your desire for power, possessions and position increased. You showed only your masked face to the world, even to your Self. So much so that you began to see your Self only as others saw you—with a mask. Your authentic Self, thus neglected, went dormant."

"I don't remember losing touch with my Self. When did I put on the mask?" I asked.

"When you became disconnected from your heart. When you started to paint unauthentic semblances of people. When instead of expressing your deep-seated urge to paint the human condition, you started to decorate surfaces. You got disconnected from your heart, your soul. This is your story, my story, the story of everyone, whether you are professionally successful or unsuccessful, rich or poor. Ultimately, each of us at some point must face the emptiness of our masked Selves and search for our authentic Self."

Babaji continued: "Many years ago, I tried to look at my own reflection. Hidden behind it, I saw someone else. Who was it whose heart beat in unison with mine? Was someone else beside me living within, equally engaged in my daily affairs? But I did not pay attention. Who was it that wore the clothes I wore, lived in my house, witnessed my thoughts, actions, words, watched over me, and when I was at a crossroads, nudged me in the right direction? But I paid no heed; worldly affairs devoured me. I was enticed by pretense while my divine Self loved me from within."

At that moment, I felt charged with the same flow that used to pass through me when I was inspired. Long ago, it had directed me, taken pleasure in my work, and been my constant companion. Now I was controlled by outer circumstances. I was told what to do and when to do it. The quicksand of success had made me forget who I really was. I had let the dazzle of fame eclipse the light of my inspiration, the light of my life.

From the window, I saw Shanti attentively listening to a man. Before hanging the mirror back on the wall, I turned to thank Babaji, but he was gone. I was alone in the room. His sudden disappearance jolted me. But I grounded myself and hung the mirror where I had found it. I walked back slowly to where my wife was.

"This is Jaidev, the caretaker," she said.

"Sorry for the inconvenience, sir! Someone directed you to an abandoned house. Please follow me to my office. I'll hand you the keys to your cabin."

"Abandoned?"

"Yes, sir. Nobody has lived here in years. Some even believe it is haunted. Please come."

I held Shanti's warm hand and squeezed it gently. She smiled back at me. We quietly followed Jaidev. As I stopped momentarily to take another look at the house, my earlier life reeled through my mind.

Silence Heard

Madhuri wanted to befriend silence, desired to surround herself with the quiet of noiselessness. She was the ninth child and had lived with her boisterous siblings and devoted lovable parents for sixteen years. Until she got married and went away to the United States, she had never experienced quiet, only heard about it from her father who in his youth had left home for one year to live in the wilderness. He would narrate little tales of listening to the silence and natural sounds.

From the minute she woke to the moment she went to sleep, Madhuri yearned for a few moments of solitude. Four brothers (two of whom were married), four sisters, and one or two uninvited cousins (who came to the capital city from small towns to attend college) filled the four-bedroom house full to bursting. Siblings shared bedrooms on the second floor and a barsati on the third.

In the wee morning hours, through the open window of the bedroom she shared with her two sisters, she was awakened by the howling of the vegetable and fruit vendors. They saved mothers time by bringing produce to their doorsteps. A little later, the sound of gushing water into the bucket and the scent of *shikakai* shampoo wafted in through the open bedroom door. Simultaneously, the smell of ghee and the sound of her mother's expert palms patting dough balls into flat parathas in the kitchen floated in.

At the sound of a toilet flushing, Madhuri would jump and rush to the WC before someone else could occupy it. She wished for a house with two WCs or even three. *I can dream, can't I?*

Only after she had done her business would she hear news from the radio followed by classical music from her parents' bedroom. Simultaneously the pans and pots would clang as her mother instructed the help to set the breakfast table.

Usually when Madhuri arrived at the dining table dressed in her school uniform, her siblings had already started breakfast. Cups of hot milk tea were lined up on the table as mother fried paratha after paratha on the iron pan. But on mornings when her oldest sister braided her hair, she was the first to sit by herself at the table and enjoy some solitude.

Later at school, while writing or solving math problems or working on a chemistry experiment, Madhuri's ears had a respite. But then again recess was noisy and chaotic.

One day when her oldest brother helped her with homework, she complained how loud noises bothered her. "I wish I could spend a whole day in silence."

He thought for a moment and then gently pushing a lock of hair behind her ear said, "Like me, you are a contemplative person, little sister. We belong to a family that may be rowdy, but it sure is animated and we love each other. We can't avoid noises and sounds but we can make them part of our lives, enjoy them for what they are."

"Get used to them" was what she tried to do. On Sundays and holidays, after the morning bathroom and breakfast rush, the cleaning lady came to sweep, mop and dust the windowsills and furniture. Siesta would have been wonderful if her sisters were not chatty, giggly and gossipy. Madhuri tried to ignore all that.

The evenings were filled with the din of familiar voices, Bollywood songs, siblings' laughter and talking with friends. These tones were normal, not the hubbub of recess. Her brothers and their friends followed a cricket match on the radio, grunting with the losses and cheering, jumping, laughing with the wins.

Her oldest sister took music lessons and the third sister learned sitar. Their Gurujis came to the house to teach them in the afternoon. In the evening, Madhuri left for her art class and walked fifteen minutes to reach school. Art class was comparatively quiet. The teacher talked only when he gave instructions.

After she returned from class, dinner was served in two sittings because the dining table could fit only eight. The first included Madhuri (being the youngest), her father, brothers and the sister closest to her age. At the second seating her mother, three older sisters, two sisters-in-law and any visiting cousins dined. The servants were the last to eat.

For a little while the atmosphere quieted. Then in floated the sounds of washing dishes, cleaning of the kitchen, conversations behind the walls. Finally, just before everyone was ready to go to sleep, when she was changing into her night clothes, when the house had a chance to settle down for the night, she heard the stray dogs on the street barking and howling.

No sooner did she climb into her bed ready to relish some quiet than it was broken by the rumbles of snoring in various pitches and styles until Madhuri fell asleep herself.

Was there a place in the world where silence and solitude were permanent residents?

At sixteen, in art college, the homey sounds were replaced by the comings and goings of roommates and dormmates. Madhuri's days were spent in the classroom, at the library, at art shows, movies and musical recitals. Meeting other students, getting to know them, chatting, laughing, conversing, complaining about the day's events was fun. Then it was time for homework.

After dinner, quiet time was strictly observed in all dorms—a silent interlude in which she could mentally compose paintings while writing her art history essays, the imagined compositions that were yet to be painted. More silence followed during hours the students spent studying the human figure from live models, painting landscapes and portraits. This was followed by daily practice of outdoor sketching.

Yet while the students worked silently in the studio, frequently she could hear songs blaring through loudspeakers from the neighboring village. Some days Bollywood melodies were replaced by wedding songs and other days a political leader convincing the village people to vote for him.

At nights, too tired to sleep, Madhuri imagined the familiar sounds of her home—even noises she had not liked. Her eyes would well up.

While painting, there was no time to reminisce about the past. Making art drew the senses inward. No sensory input disturbed her, not even noise. In her psychology class she learned that in complete absorption all the five senses and thought became one. Everything that surrounded her receded to the background. Her complete attention and awareness were absorbed into the work she was focused on.

The year Madhuri graduated from college she married a man named Manohar. The marriage was arranged by her parents. He came from the United States to meet her. They met several times, liked one another and gave their consent and got engaged. Six months later, they were married. Together they took a flight back to a foreign city that was distant and different in every way.

Stepping out from the cab, Madhuri looked up at the ten-story building with its windows shut. It was midday. Not a soul was in sight. With her husband she rode an elevator, stopped at the seventh floor and walked through a hushed corridor. No noise came from any neighbors living on the same floor. He stopped, unlocked the door to his apartment and welcomed her to a sunny place that was to be her new home. The windows of the living room faced the university campus where Manohar was studying for his doctorate.

She found herself caressed by a quiet that she had become aware of as soon as she entered the building. Her desire had been fulfilled. A smile bubbled up from within and spread wholeheartedly on her lips. She was going to luxuriate in this blessed soundlessness.

Every morning after her husband left for work, inside as well as outside of their apartment was nothing but silence. She could breathe in that quiet, dive in it, swim in it, fly in it. Finally, the abstraction she wanted to befriend was here to stay.

Inside the apartment it was warm and silent. By now, the familiarity of her new home felt comforting. She glanced at the sofa, the central table, the four-chair dining table, the bookcase. She couldn't remember a time before that moment when she had an opportunity to sit in silence and do nothing. Just herself enveloped in it.

She thought of her mother, her father and her siblings living in the home filled with never-ending voices, noises, sounds and felt rather bad for them. For a moment she wanted all of them to join her and enjoy the silence. The next moment she realized the foolishness of her love.

When the daily routine was set, Madhuri enjoyed breakfasting with Manohar, kissing him goodbye and then sitting on the sofa to read or sketch. The apartment was so quiet that she could hear her own heartbeat. Such peace and quiet triggered tears that trickled down her face.

The apartment was located in a lonely neighborhood in a big alien city. Day by day she was getting used to the grocery store, parks, pharmacy and homes of a few of Manohar's colleagues. The excitement of spring and summer months began to wear off, first to autumn season and then to early winter. The apartment building began to feel like an island surrounded by distances difficult to traverse. What she observed, what she heard, what she smelled all was foreign, alien. Unaccustomed to the ways of the new people she met and unfamiliar with cultural norms, Madhuri turned inward.

As the year rolled by, the pleasure of solitude turned into desolation without her even realizing it. There were mornings when she wished Manohar didn't have to leave. Slowly but surely, day after day the silence she had cherished began to change its color. The complete quiet she had desired to befriend had transmuted into loneliness. How could this happen? IIow could an abundance of something she craved for turn sour?

In the silence of her living room she tried to recall the sounds of her childhood that she used to abhor with vehemence. The sound of water trickling from a faucet into a plastic bucket, Bollywood songs, cricket match commentary, hawkers selling their wares, honking cars, laughter and the constant chatter of her siblings refused to return with the vividness she now craved.

Instead, the deafening silence buzzed in her ears. She locked her apartment, walked to the end of the corridor, rode down the elevator, walked around the building and its environs and returned home. With grownups gone to work and the children to school, the building felt ghostly. In that, the sound of her heartbeat echoed.

Madhuri found herself restless. She thought of painting again. After graduating she had neither the opportunity nor the desire to paint. The art material she had brought with her had remained packed. She had her sketchbook, drawing pad and pencils and collapsible easel. She sat at the dining table with her sketchbook and began to scribble. No image came to mind. She drew random lines, filled in some dark shapes, textured a few forms. How does one paint sounds? Hubbub? Perhaps color would inspire something that black lines could not.

She purchased a pack of stretched canvasses, then placed one on the easel ready to paint. She squeezed a bit of burnt sienna on the palette, dipped her drawing brush in linseed oil and mixed it with the paint. Perhaps a touch of cerulean blue here, a Prussian green there and vermillion in between would laugh, chat, sing. She walked back a few steps, squinted at what she had done. What she saw didn't cheer her up or calm her down. The canvas looked flat. Torpid. Passive. She wanted her painting to neutralize or equalize how she was feeling. But it didn't work. Silence returned. She placed the palette and brush on the side table and flopped on the sofa.

She heard herself inhale and exhale. Pangs of separation surfaced. She tried to recall the sounds of her childhood. This time the silence receded. The ghosts of the old noises and sounds came forward stirring more memories. Quiet, calm, peace, tranquility; how she had longed for it. And now when it was overflowing, it overwhelmed her. Her wish was finally granted. And she didn't like it at all.

She couldn't sleep that night. But at some point she must have fallen asleep because she woke up terrified. The feeling the nightmare had stirred refused to leave. The whole next day the terrifying feeling stirred in her mind and swirled in her heart. Like a zombie she did the daily chores and when they were done, she glanced at the canvas she was working on. It didn't inspire her to continue. She paced restlessly. The more she paced the less her anxiety became. Then an insight. *What about painting the horrible nightmare?*

She drew sketches of the images she remembered from her nightmare. Next she sketched to paint it on a fresh canvas. For days she worked on that painting. Finally, the painting was complete. It depicted Madhuri hanging from the edge of a pitch-dark well. Her grip was slipping. She might fall any moment into the bottomless pit below. She was clutching the slimy wall for her life, screaming for help. But no one was around to hear her. The element of sound didn't exist. The thought of falling into the soundless oblivion terrified her.

It felt as if she had not simply painted but pinned down the horror. No more of a minute feeling like an hour. No more restlessness. It was as if the sadness and pangs of separation were arrested on the surface of the canvas. Did the process of painting heal her? Was the self-doubt sucked via paint into the dry canvas?

In the evening, when Manohar returned from the university Madhuri showed him the painting.

"You seem to be feeling better, darling. Is it the painting? You have not been yourself for weeks."

"The silence is getting on my nerves. It terrifies me even in my dreams. But painting seems to help."

"Come, sit near me."

She sat next to him. He kissed her and warmly squeezed her. "I suggest you get out of the house more often, go shopping, visit the museum, go for a long walk."

"It is freezing outdoors. How can you even suggest a walk? I hate this weather." Her whole life she had lived in tropical places.

He laughed gently, kissed her again this time on her lips and pointed to the bookcase. "Add reading to your painting schedule. We have a decent collection of books."

The next morning after sending him off she scanned through the books, picked one and sat on the leather armchair next to the bookcase to read. On the side table were bundles of selected letters from her parents and siblings she had saved through the years. She set the book aside and got lost in rereading the excerpts. The old letters stirred a medley of warm feelings that made her sad.

A new canvas at the easel stared at her. Painting her nightmare had been healing, so she thought, *Why not make another?* She rose, touched her forehead. It was damp. She walked to the bathroom to wash her face. In the mirror her reflection stared at her. It seemed to say, *"Paint me!"*

Madhuri whispered, "Paint you?" Then she abruptly walked back to the easel and stared at the half-painted canvas that she had left there. She replaced the canvas with a sketchbook.

She dragged a full-length mirror that stood on a stand in the bedroom. She positioned it to the left of her easel so that she could look at herself. She began to sketch to warm up her fingers. She observed the details of her facial features and copied, first sketching rough lines and eventually finer lines—hairline and forehead, brows with eyes, nose and lips, chin and neck with the dip of the throat—until a visage emerged. She stepped back to make sure what she drew standing close to the surface had the appearance of what she wanted it to look like.

Having sketched satisfactorily she replaced the sketchpad with a drawing book to make more formal and better representations of herself. For many days she practiced her drawing skills until she found some merit to what she had drawn. When she was pictorially comfortable with what she had achieved and felt ready to paint, she fetched a brand new canvas from her bedroom closet and placed it on the easel.

She began to make herself. With a thin brush dipped in the color burnt umber she drew an outline of her head, neck and torso. Each day she worked on her portrait at the same place, same time. With all her senses drawn within and her focus on her physical details, the silence receded although she was immersed in it. It was as if studying the details of her face, neck, torso and hands made her familiar with herself. A semblance emerged. A sad smile. A tired smile. Her family seven oceans away. What was she doing here?

A short distance away the resemblance was stark, no veils, no mask, no pretense. The sad smile with the penetrating gaze was asking her, *"What do you really want?"* The portrait and her reflection were two different selves. The reflection, just like her, only reversed but the portrait reflected how she felt within.

On one snowy morning, taking a break from her painting routine, she curled up on the leather armchair with a book. Through the windowpane she looked at the world outside, blanketed in snow, still and beautiful. The only sounds she could hear were the occasional tick, hiss and crackling of the radiator and the ice maker. She closed her eyes and realized that a big part of her heart was still back in her childhood home. But when she opened her eyes the familiar surroundings in which she had lived for years with Manohar felt foreign. She yearned for her childhood home.

Canvas by canvas she transferred the feelings and thoughts about the upheaval of leaving her family behind, coming to the new world and eventually getting to know her new husband. She depicted her craving for silence, finding what she craved yet no longer craving it. In fact, she now longed for those childhood sounds. Her questions and queries slowly transformed into images. Even some murkiness within that was not letting her be at ease with herself washed away when she painted.

She realized no one overcame sorrow and grief of separation in a season or two. It took years. Balance slowly returned to her life. Her foggy mind became clearer. She painted another dreamlike depiction. The rectangular canvas was divided into two sections. On the left, a woman with a striking resemblance to Madhuri removed blobs of slimy-muddy-amoeba-like creatures from a bucket of water. The creatures had turned the water dirty. On the right, the same woman diligently discarded all the dirty creatures, thus turning the water crystal clear, so transparent that the fish floating at the bottom were visible.

Having finished the painting, Madhuri felt unburdened of the petty thoughts floating through her mind. Her mind was clear like the bucket of water.

She had been painting daily. As she sketched, drew and painted she felt an inner connection between herself and a presence within. This link spread a wave of delight like a drop of red water-color on wet Japanese handmade paper. She felt that same presence awakening within but this time it was stronger. She had felt it when she completed her self-portrait, a glowing spark in her heart.

Several weeks passed. By the time she began to doubt if a new idea would ever arise and inspire her to paint, another image floated in. It was so vivid that she had to paint it.

A woman with a serene expression caught a whiff of an exquisite bonsai tree laden with miniature oranges with lush green leaves. With her eyes gently closed, the woman inhaled the scent of the citrus fruit as if mesmerized. Madhuri captured the woman's face so well that she felt happy within.

Even after Madhuri finished the painting she kept mulling over the composition's meaning. Upon careful examination she noticed that she did not make the tree look natural. It seemed manmade. Why didn't she paint the bonsai tree to look natural? Did it reflect that something in her was not authentic, that she needed to work at making her true to herself? Did she have to understand and unknot the clash between solitude and isolation within her?

The silence had found its place inside, a trustworthy and wise companion to consult whenever she needed to make a decision. There was a richness in that silence. It was not loneliness at all but a sort of calm, tranquility even. Each time the thought, *How I wish my mother, father, sisters and brothers lived close by,* passed through her mind and sourness churned in her belly, she turned her attention from whatever was making her feel uneasy and focused on the sacred place of inner silence and solitude. The silence she once so desired had transmuted into loneliness, restlessness and desperation. But her creativity had settled the sediments of her mind to the bottom, clearing the water, nourishing a plant—albeit artificial— finally bringing about an inner calm.

That spring Madhuri and her husband visited her family in New Delhi. As soon as the taxi dropped them off outside Madhuri's home the thrill of seeing her parents and siblings sent a current of delight through her whole body. The volume of her heartbeat rose. "The music of sounds in this house is screaming for me to hurry in," she jokingly said to Manohar.

In the outer verandah that faced the kitchen, her parents sat cross-legged on a wooden settee. They attempted to get up to greet the guests but Madhuri insisted they remain seated. She hugged her mother tight and stayed a few moments longer in the warm embrace of that bosom. Oh, how she had missed her mother's touch, her smell, and most importantly the sound of her voice. Madhuri did the same with her father only to realize how frail both of them had grown through the last five years. She watched Manohar hug them. Their movements were slower, their backs a bit bowed. She sat next to her mother and her husband on a chair facing them.

"Where is everyone, Ma?"

"Your sisters are at their own homes. They will certainly visit you at some point."

"It has been a long, long time, our sweet daughter," her father remarked. "Your oldest brother moved to Mumbai for better opportunities. The one younger to him was transferred to Jammu. The wife of the youngest did not want to stay in a joint family, so they moved to an apartment but not too far from here."

"Why didn't your letters make any mention of all these changes, Ma? And where is the third brother?"

"He is the only one who lives here. They have gone to work, and the children are at school."

After drinking tea, Madhuri walked through the house. The kitchen, the bathroom, the bedrooms all were quiet. Just like her apartment in America she could hear the silence. To her own amazement she did not like it. How she wished she could dive into the hubbub of those sounds. The din, the ruckus, the brouhaha had their own ambiance; how she wished she had immersed herself in them when they were alive. Now they were gone. *"Each time of life must be appreciated for what it is. Make these part of our lives, enjoy them for what they are,"* her brother had once advised. Everything changes.

"I miss the old times, Ma," she said when she returned and sat back on the settee.

"Countless lives are unlived because of craving, if not for this then for that." Her mother patted her back. "Like a coin, all worldly things have obverse and reverse," she went on. "The reverse of sound is silence—you always wanted silence, dreamed about it. When you finally got it in America you felt lonely."

"Yes, Ma. After a few years the silence that I craved for turned into isolation, and solitude into loneliness, recently to desperation."

"Reading your letters was painful for me. I could feel your sadness and sorrow in your words." Ma put Madhuri's hands between her palms and massaged them. "How do you feel now?"

"Painting and writing letters to you and reading your replies saved me. I painted every day and made several self-portraits."

"How did these help?"

"The isolation and loneliness transmuted into an inner quiet that keeps nourishing me," Madhuri said and looked at her mother's face. She saw her mother's eyes light up.

Fear of Death

THE SOUND OF FALLING LEAVES

I am in the winter of life. Unknown darkness approaches. From my bed through the window, I watch leaves floating downward. One, two, three. One here, one there. Yellow, orange, bronze moments of my past fall like the pitter-patter of rain, only to decay on the green grass, while raindrops needle the murky puddles, disappearing like the days of my life.

I close my eyes. Today too will be forgotten in the cauldron of memories. Who will remember that there ever was a tree with lush green leaves which in the autumn lost its grip, firmness and vitality, that the leaves let go of its branch which had nourished them through the year? For a tree there is anticipation that after a dormant winter it will return to life. But for me there is no coming back. *Will the leaf and I go to the same place when I let go?*

My wife Theresa died young. I miss her. Out of my eight siblings I'm the only one left. Being the youngest, I watched them pass one by one. I have good childhood friends and college mates who are still alive. I wonder how they are doing. I think I should write letters, at least to my best high school buddy in Mexico.

I open my eyes to pick up the notepad from my bedside table drawer and start to compose a letter. My hands are too cold to write. I change my mind. I better call. But he does not have a phone. I will call our common friend who has one.

I sit up and turn my legs slowly. My feet do not reach the floor. I jerk my cold hands out of my vest pockets and somehow manage to stand. Once comfortably seated on my wheelchair I trundle toward the telephone on a corner table.

My fingers tremble when I dial the number. I watch the door though not expecting anyone at this time of the late morning. Children knock before entering. Grandchildren burst in if they reach the door ahead of their parents. My senses are failing. I am no longer fortunate to fully take in their sweet glimpses or hear their gentle words.

Many years ago, or was it decades, when I heard the babies babble, young feet running upstairs through every room of our home... Eve, Zoe, Adam! One by one they left for college. One by one they got married. One by one they had children. They frequently visited. But after Theresa passed away, I visited them two or three times a year and spent weeks, even a month with their families.

I live alone in my apartment now. A day nurse helps me do things that I can't do myself. I am not allowed too many "visitors" or to go out until I get better. What does that mean? Who gives such orders? Don't they understand that touching, hugging, laughing heal an ailing heart? Why do I need to sit alone with my tired pale weak heart in my chest? Why would the people who are supposed to love me even listen to such orders?

I dial our common friend's number. The bell rings. But no one seems to be home to pick up the receiver. Each and every one I call must be occupied with their immediate world. I hang up and ten minutes pass. I try the number again, a number in a distant place, thousands of miles away, in a high-rise building, in an apartment. I imagine the sound of footsteps walking to the phone or a wheelchair trundling close. I grip the receiver in anticipation with my wrinkled hand and clutch it closer to my ear.

"Hello! May I know who it is?" my friend's wife says.

"Hello, Meena. This is Tom Perry. How are you? How is Ashok?"

"Good to hear from you! Ashok is not good. He is on a respirator."

"Oh!" A tremor passes through me. "I am sorry to hear. I was thinking of him. When will we be able to talk?" A few moments of silence follow on the other end.

"Hello? Meena?" Then I hear her crying.

"He doesn't have many days left, Tom. I'll tell him you called. Thank you for thinking of us."

"I'm at a loss for words... and you know I'm never at a loss for words."

"I know." She utters a sad goodbye and gently hangs up.

For minutes I sit motionless. My feet hang from the edge of the wheelchair.

I had imagined talking to Ashok about the old times. Talk about nothing. Talk about the smells pulling up from the windows of his apartment complex. Or hearing the noises of our neighborhood on a hot yellow noon through the open window. The hooting of metal horns, the squeaking of brakes, the calls of vendors selling bright bananas and plump mangoes.

I squeeze my eyes tight and imagine sniffing the odor of stone alleys wet with morning rain. I feel the sun warm my shoulders and cheeks. I am twenty-nine years old again, walking, smiling, happy to be alive, alert, drinking in colors and odors.

I shake off my thoughts. I can't spend the rest of my day thinking of Ashok. I call another common friend. After ten or twelve rings he picks up the phone. We exchange greetings. My enthusiastic tone gets diluted by his feeble voice.

"What's wrong, man? Are you okay?" I enquire.

"Okay? No, not okay. With nobody else around, nowhere to go, how do you suppose I'm okay? No, I'm not okay." I hear a rasp in his voice.

"I'll call you again. We'll talk," I say to him.

The shock of a loud tap on the door jolts me. My mind rushes back to the present.

It is my nurse dressed in white. She smiles but her gaze shifts from the bed across the room to the phone.

"Why do you do this to yourself? You promised you wouldn't. You will hurt yourself." She repeats what she has said to me umpteen times.

"Why do you want me to die before my time? Chatting with friends may cheer me up and heal my heart."

"Temporarily calls have to go, whether I am here or not here. You can't get out of bed by yourself."

"It is my phone and my home. Don't forget who pays your salary."

"You pay me to help you get well, not to get you excited. As soon as you feel better you can call as many people as you want."

She wheels my chair across the room. "Back to bed now, young man!"

She helps me back into my bed.

"I'm going to the store for a short time. Please, no hanky-panky," she says and leaves, shutting the front door behind her.

I want to do normal things. I can do everything, albeit slowly, very slowly. I haven't gone anywhere in months, I say to myself, my chest not so thick with pain as it was last week.

I lay comfortably though a bit cold. I hear people under a different sky, different sunlight doing different things. I hear faint, tinkling music of drums and harmonica grinding—oh, a lovely, dancing tune. I put up my hands as if to click pictures of an ancient temple amidst banyan trees, my middle-aged body yet muscular with flesh feeling the hot pavement underneath my soles.

I imagine people in that faraway land preparing for a siesta, the shops closing, the women slowing, vendors quieting their shouts to sell their wares. Was I once among them or was it a chimera? Now the place has turned into my fantasy, dubious, distant. Mexico City, Jaipur, Kyoto... just as this here is a dream in my bedroom of a suburban home at the edge of a quiet park.

Again, I close my eyes. At last, the clearest, most improbable sound of all—the sound of a green trolley car going around a corner—a trolley burdened with beautiful people and the sound of others calling out with triumph as they leap up and swing aboard and vanish around a corner on the shrieking rails. In my late sixties I can no longer leap up or swing but I enjoy the sun-blazed land. I have had a good life, a satisfying life. I have good children, loving grandchildren.

I hear light footsteps. The front door opens slowly. "Hello, Dad..."

My daughter, Eve, walks in followed by my adorable grandson, Tom Perry Jr. At first hesitant, then he runs to my bed.

"Papa!" Eve says softly and kisses my forehead and cheeks. "Your hands are cold," she says and begins massaging them. "Zoe couldn't come today. She will next week. And Adam said he will visit you over the weekend."

"Grandpa!" Tom Jr. says excitedly. "Can I read you a story?"

He lays down beside me. Having warmed up my hands, Eve slips an extra pillow under my head so that Tom can read to me. Then she covers us both with the woolen blanket.

Ahhhh!

She leaves to set lunch for us in the dining room. Tom puts his soft cheek against mine and warms me the way the sun had warmed my back many years ago, thousands of miles away.

The nurse joins us for a savory lunch of fresh tomato and cheese sandwiches on fresh baked bread that she must have brought with her.

A few hours later they leave me with my hands and heart warm, my body fed and my mind soothed and at peace. Once again, I see through the window. I hear the sound of falling leaves as they waltz to their destination earth. One, two, three. One, two, three. One, two, three. Yellow, orange, bronze twinkles of glee, good memories of the past and happy moments of today slowly turning into memories.

Everything is perfect the way it is. The autumn-colored leaves, beautiful as they are, the green grass as it is, even the murky water puddles. I have lived a blessed life and still have many years to cherish. I don't know how many. And if my mind starts to argue I will firmly say, *The only day that is alive is this day, this moment, this now*. I'll call my lonely friend tomorrow and cheer him up. The peace lulls me to sleep.

Oh Wow!

Ravi held Priya's limp hand in his grip and turned to the doctor. "Do we know how much time we have?"

His concern didn't go unnoticed by the doctor. The man glanced first at Priya then at her husband. "Maybe a month, perhaps less. I'm sorry, Priya. Sorry, Mr. Dalal."

The doctor's report incited terror in Priya. Her body stiffened. Her senses shut down. She couldn't hear the words that were being exchanged. A tear dropped on her face. She didn't care to wipe it. The doctor handed her a napkin.

Ravi took it and wiped her cheeks. Then he gave it to her. His grip tightened. His legs shook. "Are you sure, doctor?"

"I wish I could say no. I'm so sorry."

The couple remained seated as if delaying the departure from the office would somehow make Priya's terminal cancer go away. The silence that the white walls enclosed couldn't push out the fear that had floated in. Instead, they pronounced it. The two framed medical certificates hanging on the wall behind the doctor, photos of his smiling wife and children at some vacation spot on the side table, books held in perfect order by a pair of bookends, froze for a moment. If only that moment could last forever.

The doctor cleared his throat. "Can I do anything else for you, Mrs. and Mr. Dalal?"

They both got up. They thanked the doctor and shook his hand. He had been kind, caring and professional throughout her ordeal, as were the nurses and the rest of the staff. Ravi helped Priya walk to the door.

A month! A shudder passed through her.

Holding hands, they exited the office. The doctor's verdict was a fact. She must accept it for what it was. They walked down a long corridor until it branched into two. They were unsure of where to turn to reach the parking lot. They could either go straight or turn left or right. They decided to use the restroom before asking someone. Hesitatingly she let go of Ravi's hand.

Priya exited the ladies' room before Ravi was out. She could not stand still. She turned left, passing rooms occupied by single patients with a family member or a friend present... or no one. She could see a patient through the open door in one of the rooms. The monitoring machine suddenly started to make strange sounds. She slowed her pace and stood at the threshold. No visitors were in the room. She scanned the corridor to see if anyone was coming to look at the machine. No one. So she shuffled closer to the patient.

The sounds turned louder. Lights on the machine were blinking. A male patient with his head comfortable on a soft white pillow, resting peacefully, had his eyes closed with a subtle smile playing on his lips. Those lips were moving. *Was he trying to say something*? She stepped closer to his bed and put her ear down to his lips. She heard him whisper, "Oh, wow! Oh, wow! Oh, wow!" He repeated the words until his voice got softer and softer and softer and then there was silence.

"Move! Out of the way! Move!" Doctors and nurses came rushing in, all bustling at once inside the room, adjusting the monitor, feeling the pulse, consulting with one another. "He is passed," the doctor declared.

The medical personnel's voices jolted Priya. She remembered to return to her husband.

Ravi was waiting for her outside the restrooms. "Where did you go? You scared me!"

"Sorry, I was just pacing the corridor."

"I asked someone, and it seems we have to turn right to go to the parking lot."

On the way to their car Priya wondered why the patient had uttered, "Oh, wow!" right before he was declared dead. What was he wowing? Was he having happy dreams before he died? She remembered reading somewhere that when a dying person lets go of all they hold dear in their life—their power, possession, position, and most significantly the tenderness and affection for their loved ones—they feel a release that is liberating. There is a sense of freedom, a feeling of lustrous joy in letting go. The minutes she had spent with the patient watching him experience this before his senses failed had, in a strange way, somewhat alleviated Priya's fear of dying. The emotions the experience had stimulated in her were complex, not easy to put into words. What she was feeling was unfamiliar. And she felt it at a deep level. She did not have the right vocabulary to clearly explain to her husband what she had felt only momentarily. She decided to keep what she had witnessed to herself.

It had been a week since her doctor's appointment at the hospital. Her daily routine had not changed much but her movements had slowed. It was taking longer to make a cup of cardamom tea. The aroma of the leaves mixed with cardamom still soothed her. She was feeling no pain. She carried a steaming cup to the family room and made herself comfortable on her favorite chair. She turned on the television. The meteorologist was excitedly discussing the tsunami that had engulfed an island about a hundred miles from the main island where they lived.

Little island, *Kaput!* Millions of years sunk in the ocean. Forever. First the enormous wind. Then fire. Then everything submerged. Not a single man, woman or child was told that this natural disaster was going to suck the life out of them. Twenty-four hours of gloom and doom for an exotic holiday island, not very different from their main island. The disaster was being reeled on the news channel over and over again, as if it was not a historic catastrophe but a reality show.

Priya had nowhere to go; nothing new to do. She continued to do what she did every evening after supper. She tilted her rocking chair that seemed to grumble, then picked up a drawing pad and a pencil. Near a window under a standing lamp, she put final touches to a colored sketch she had been working on for days. She had almost completed a scene that Ravi liked so much that he wanted to get it framed. It depicted a bamboo gate on a path through a canopy of trees toward some unknown distant destination. She gazed at it thinking what it would be like once she died and her spirit found itself in the unknown. The thought used to terrify her but after the "Oh wow!" incident that feeling had somewhat subsided.

The sharp point of her pencil was used up and blunted. She sharpened and then sharpened it several times more before she was done. The night got darker. Through the window she saw lightning bugs glistening over the darkened grassy ground and against the silhouette of the hills, the trees and the rooftops in the inky night. So serene. Such beauty! What would she look at when she could no longer see?

She felt Ravi's kiss on the back of her head. Then his warm strong hands massaged her shoulders. "Enough of news! What would you like for dinner?"

"Surprise me! I like everything you make."

He switched off the television and put on a recording of Ravi Shankar, his namesake, playing raga Jog on sitar. Allah Rakkha accompanied on tabla. Sweet waves of music soothed Priya's mind. She loved listening to her husband practicing on sitar although he was not as good as Ravi Shankar... yet. At one point the pencil rose and pressed in rhythm with the movement of the sitar strings and the tabla beats. The sound, the composition and Priya became one.

Her sketch was almost complete. Her hands felt tired. She closed the drawing pad, placed it on her lap and placed her right hand over the other to rest a while. As soon as she closed her eyes thoughts floated in. *How can I tell Ravi the way I feel? How do I put in words and gently convey to him how the tsunami that swallowed the neighboring island is reverberating with the inner tsunami about to swallow me?* But simultaneously a contrasting thought floated in. *What if the transition to the unknown is not as terrifying as I think?*

Priya opened her eyes and looked at her resting hands. She turned both of them, observing first the backs and then the palms. She examined them as if they belonged to someone else, as if she had just discovered them. What flexibility, dexterity and power! What beautiful artworks they had assisted her to conjure on paper! She gazed at her hands with new respect, as if they had been given to her as an anonymous gift. She had never really paid any attention to them before, never admired them the way she was appreciating them now.

She thought of her hands washing her, styling her hair, opening and shutting doors and windows for her. How many meals had they prepared, how many dishes had they washed, how many vegetables peeled, flowers picked, clothing stitched? Her hands had helped her create her surrounding reality. Whatever else had happened was just a dream.

She brought her attention back to the drawing she was making. She gazed at it for a while. She had applied each line deftly, making an outline here, shading with quick strokes there, and conjuring up innumerable paths with the sharp pencil tip. Now her gaze focused on each line—each passing cloud, flying bird, open gate, path leading toward the unmapped, the undiscovered. The scene had developed under her hand, an enticing and mysterious landscape perfect in each stroke. The finest... and her last.

For fifty-eight years she had used her hands for everything she did. In a way, her life depended on her hands, and on her feet and legs and head and—oh God, she had never given attention to any part of her body! She had neglected it when healthy. Now when it was failing, suddenly she had woken to its usefulness and almost sacral beauty. Had her body tried to communicate with her all these years the way it was communicating now? Perhaps. But she had never paid heed.

She was not going to blame herself at this time. It was what it was. And all this was going to end soon. No meals to cook, no doors to open or close, no flowers to pick, no art to be made, no music to hear. Priya began to sob. The sob turned to cries. Salty tears rolled down her face and fell on the hands resting on the sketchpad in her lap. Her fingers twitched. She wiped the wetness under her eyes. Crying was not going to cure her fate.

She took another look at the drawing. There was something wrong. To fix it she would have to erase the bamboo gate. What a shame! She stared intently at the beautiful depiction. The flaw glared at her. Why had she not noticed it before? She inhaled slowly and exhaled heavily.

"What are you thinking?" Ravi asked. He leaned toward her chair and saw her erasing the gate, then he walked to the window and opened it. "Calm before the storm."

"Can a tsunami devastate our island the way it sank the small one?"

"Who knows! We're not out of it yet."

"What do you think will happen when it comes?" she asked.

"No one knows for sure what happened to the little island, or what it will do to this one if it reaches here."

"Why couldn't we stop it before it got this far and this big?"

"Nobody knows how devastation comes, when it comes, whom it affects, who suffers from it."

Through the window, a cool breeze brought the smell of jasmine and roses and cut grass into the room. She sighed. The thought, that her illness wasn't very different from the tsunami that had gulped down the little island, stayed in her mind.

Priya continued to erase what she had earlier drawn with force and confidence. Her spectacles flashed in the darkness of summer night. Through the silence she heard crickets and mosquitoes. She cocked her neck to listen.

What would she hear when she could no longer listen? They say sound keeps this world and the next world connected. Perhaps all the wisdom of the world was written or spoken to make us feel less fearful in the face of death, to give us courage and hope. Was it possible that tomorrow the doctor would call and say it was all a big mix-up? *I'll get over it in a few months. I'll be loving my husband, opening doors, stirring curries, peeling oranges, and arranging flowers. Perhaps the diagnosis was wrong. They could call and say Priya was going to be all right. "How foolish," I'll say—all that worry. I will laugh and run to my husband and give him the news. Together we'll chuckle and say, "What were we so terrified of?"*

Wishful thinking! "Foolish," she said to herself, bending her head to look at the motion of her pencil, then busied herself with the drawing.

Ravi came from the kitchen to see how she had changed the drawing. She looked up and they smiled at each other.

Two clashing stones in water had replaced the bamboo gate. The erased lines were still visible, a palimpsest of her floating thoughts, the passing clouds one over the other. She could hear her own breathing. Long and deep inhales and exhales relaxed her.

From that very moment she was not going to think why it happened. The thought of dying was not going to terrify her. She was going to imagine the unknown as a wowing dimension. And she would pray that the tsunami would never ever come to the island which they loved so much and where Ravi was going to live the rest of his life.

What followed the next day happened in slow motion. Priya lay on the bed she shared with Ravi while he sat next to her at its edge.

Gateways and pathways surfaced and sank in Priya's drawing. Clouds floated in, birds appeared and disappeared behind the clouds. The gourd head of Ravi's sitar cracked. Its wires broke, the ones that once made sweet sounds. Darkness engulfed the drawn landscape. Beautiful handiwork, so painstakingly done, dissolved, going back to where it came from. Priya was in that dimension. Ravi sat next to her in another. How she wished he could be with her where she was, feel whatever was happening to her.

"Come, my husband. Come closer. Sit beside me. Hold my hand, hold me, kiss me."

He did what she wanted. He kissed her once, then again and again—on her cheeks and on her lips. Priya looked into his eyes, her gaze lingering at his familiar face, each slope and turn and wrinkle.

"I have always loved you but never as much as I love you at this moment," she said. "Yet my time here has ended. I selfishly wish I did not have to leave you alone. Believe me, if this parting—this separation—was under my control, I would stay, wait for you. If we had children, I would be content leaving you in their nourishing, protective hands, but you have friends and some family. Take good care of yourself."

Tears dripped down Priya's temples. Ravi's eyes had not welled up because even now he was not ready to accept her death the way she had.

She had used up all the breath left in her deteriorating body. Now her breathing changed. It became deliberate, purposeful, severe. She pushed herself further than ever before. She worked at achieving, reaching, completing.

Then she closed her eyes. A smile played on her lips. And she mouthed, "Oh, wow!" Her last breath came as she saw herself walking through the landscape she had created. She passed through the clashing stones toward the unknown she had begun to map. And she murmured, "Oh, wow!"

Acknowledgments

My deep homage to the short story writers who motivated and inspired me, and on whose shoulders I stand today: R. K. Narayan, Mulk Raj Anand, Mary E. Wilkins Freeman, Flannery O'Conner, Virginia Woolf, Joyce Carol Oates, Ray Bradbury, Anita Desai, Jhumpa Lahiri and many others.

My heartfelt tribute to my adoring parents, Prem Nath Bazaz and Badri Bazaz, who made me aware of the finer things in life, both creative and spiritual. Thank you for pointing me to the joyous path of aesthetic delight, kindness and wisdom. And instilling in me a love of reading.

My deep gratitude to my husband, Manoj, for reading and critiquing everything I write. Thank you for being my most exacting critic, and for your boundless support and inspiration. Our weekend walks have always been a fertile ground for discussing art, spirituality and life. That is when so many ideas seed and eventually sprout as stories.

Most grateful to my multi-talented editor Demi Stevens (Year of the Book Press) for her insights, suggestions and thorough editing. Fortunate to have met you, Demi! Special gratitude to Jenny

Quinlan, my cover designer, who has created stunning book covers for all my fiction.

Thank you so much, Timons Esaias, for copyediting the manuscript, for your support and friendship. You have helped me more than you know.

My heartfelt thanks to Wende Dikec, Hilary Hauck and Meredith Meleti for their love, constant support, and helping me select their favorite stories from my precious story collection, *The Chance Meeting*. These four stories, now slightly revised are Cadmium and Crimson, Secret Healer, A Chance Meeting and The Blackened Mirror.

I wrote many of these stories at the Mindful Writers Retreats and Mindful Writers Group, Water Works. Many of the early drafts were critiqued by members of Pennwriters Critique Group North. My endless gratitude to you all, especially Kathie Shoop who has helped me fertilize my literary garden from when the saplings had just begun to sprout.

To my daughters and their husbands for blessing us with grandchildren Kian, Ariana and Ayaan who brighten my days like nothing else does.

Finally, to my readers, thank you for reading these stories and completing my fictional world in your imagination. Your thoughts about this book matter to me. Please share them by posting a review on Amazon, Goodreads, Barnes and Noble, or any other book site.

About the Author

Founder of the Mindful Writers Groups and Retreats (OMWG), MADHU BAZAZ WANGU'S skillful Writing Meditation Practice (WMP) combines meditation, journaling, walking, and reading. Dr. Wangu is a multi-award-winning author whose works have won *Writer's Digest*, Readers Favorite, Indie Excellence, Next Generation Indie Book, and TAZ awards. She is also the Pennwriters 2020 Meritorious Award winner.

Currently she is working on a guidebook for writers, *Unclog Your Creative Flow, Enrich Your Daily Life*, and her tenth book, *Meaning of My Life*, a novel.

She serves as a board member for Books Bridge Hope that promotes reading, writing, and literacy to the community living in shelters and on streets. She is a frequent workshop presenter at Pennwriters Annual Conferences and was a featured author for Beaver County Book Fest in 2017.

Her inspiring CDs "Meditations for Mindful Writers I, II & III" help cultivate focus, increase flow and productivity.

Visit her website: https://cutt.ly/YjcDM8T
Read her daily posts at Online Mindful Writers
Group: https://cutt.ly/ejcDWXs